THE ENDGAME

ENDGAME
BOOK 1

CLEARY JAMES

Balally Books

THE ENDGAME
CLEARY JAMES

ISBN: 9781915369109

Published by Balally Books

Cover design by Angela Haddon

1

FRESH FROM THE SHOWER, Lisa stood in front of the full-length bedroom mirror wrapped only in a towel, looking at her reflection as she brushed out her newly-dried hair.

'I've laid out your clothes for you,' Mark said, emerging from the adjoining dressing room, wearing a beautifully tailored pair of charcoal trousers and crisp, snowy white shirt.

'Thanks,' Lisa said, her eyes focusing on the reflection of the bed in the mirror and the clothes draped on it, trying to ignore the nervous fluttering in her stomach.

'Put these in for me?' Mark asked, handing her a pair of silver cufflinks and holding out his wrists.

Lisa bent her head to the task, her fingers shaking slightly as she fastened the cufflinks.

'What's the matter?' Mark frowned. 'You're not nervous about tonight, are you?'

'A little,' Lisa admitted, her eyes straying once more to the flimsy red dress and lace thong that lay on the bed. She fastened the second stud and released Mark's hand.

'There's nothing to be nervous about.' Mark smiled down at her indulgently. 'You'll look stunning.'

Right, and that's all I could possibly be nervous about, she thought. *Because how I look is all that matters.*

He held her shoulders and turned her around so they were both facing the mirror. Lisa looked at their reflection as Mark wrapped his arms around her waist, resting his chin on her bare shoulder. If looks were truly all that mattered, she had the perfect boyfriend. Tall and powerfully built, with a broad chest and strong muscular arms, Mark's toned, taut body was a testament to his discipline and self-control. He ran every morning and worked out regularly at the gym, almost obsessive about staying in shape. His face was classically handsome, with regular features, a strong jaw and full, sensual lips. But it was his warm brown eyes and thick, wavy black hair that had most attracted her to him in the beginning.

'It's just been a while since we've … socialised,' she said, meeting his gaze in the mirror. 'And you know I'm not great at meeting new people.'

Mark sighed and dropped a kiss on her shoulder. 'Well, we'll have to knock that shyness out of you, won't we?'

She gave him a shaky smile. 'I know it's silly. I do try.'

'I know you do.' He straightened behind her, his hand going to the front of the towel where she had tucked it at her chest. 'Let me look at you,' he said as he loosened it so it fell to her feet. His eyes darkened as they raked over the reflection of her naked body.

'Look how beautiful you are,' he said as his hand moved over her bare skin, cupping her breasts, stroking across her stomach and down to her thighs. 'How could you possibly be nervous when you know you're this beautiful?'

Lisa didn't see beauty. She just saw how small and

fragile she looked against him – her arms and legs so thin, her stomach almost concave. 'Too skinny' her grandmother would say. She would probably be shocked to see her now, Lisa thought, feeling a pang almost of shame.

'How can you be unconfident when you know what it does to me just looking at you?' He pulled her back against him so she could feel his erection pressing into her back. 'Feel what power you have over me.'

Lisa breathed deeply, feeling suddenly suffocated by Mark's iron-like grip across her stomach, his erection at her back and the sharp, citrusy scent of his aftershave enveloping her. She struggled to overcome a sudden surge of panic, fighting the urge to push him away.

'And I love this,' he said, his eyes hungry as his hand slipped between her legs. At his insistence, she had got herself waxed completely bare for tonight.

'Let's keep it like this. It's so sexy.' She shivered as his fingers stroked lightly along her sensitive skin. She bit her lip, hating the way her body responded to his touch.

'If I don't stop, we'll never get out tonight.' He withdrew his hand abruptly and pulled away. 'Wear your hair up,' he said, grabbing handfuls of her long, brunette hair and piling it on top of her head, looking at the effect in the mirror. 'It's more sophisticated.'

'Okay.' She nodded at him and he released her hair so it tumbled around her shoulders in soft waves.

She turned to the bed then and picked up her clothes, while Mark returned to the dressing room. She stepped into the lacy thong and pulled on the sheer slip dress, the cool silk sending a little shiver across her skin as it slid over her bare breasts. The needle-thin spaghetti straps tied behind her neck and the dress was cut low at the back, scooping down almost to the base of her spine, so that wearing a bra was out of the question. But it was one of the advantages of having 'no tits' as Mark put it that she didn't need the support and could wear a dress like this. He liked to take her out in public with as much of her body on show as possible, and she knew it would turn him on to know she was practically naked beneath the thin slip of material.

The dress had been Mark's choice, of course. She was used to him dressing her up like his doll, and as soon as he told her of tonight's dinner invitation, he had started planning what she would wear, quickly vetoing everything in her wardrobe and insisting on buying her something specially for the occasion. Her protests that she didn't need another dress had been met with anger and accusations of ingratitude. She knew how distasteful he found her careful attitude to money and she should have known better than to risk enraging him, but sometimes she couldn't help herself. She already had a wardrobe full of chic, expensive clothes, many of which she had worn only once, and she couldn't bear the wastefulness.

Predictably, Mark had flown into a rage at her tentative suggestion that she wear something she already owned. He had accused her of disrespecting his friends and not caring enough about him to make an effort. Didn't she want to look her best? Wouldn't she like him to feel proud of her?

'You'll have to let go of your niggardly attitude to money,' he had told her. 'It's unattractive and vulgar. I understand that you didn't have much when you were growing up, but your circumstances have changed. You're with me now, and this preoccupation with what things cost is tasteless and unnecessary. Your penny-pinching days are over. For God's sake, stop quibbling and just enjoy it!'

He had launched into a full-on tirade. He was a very wealthy man, he reminded her, and he was happy to lavish his money on her. Most women would be grateful for such generosity instead of throwing it back in his face. She would just have to get used to him buying her nice things, and become accustomed to the finer things in life, because he intended to give them to her. The least she could do was accept graciously. He didn't think it was too much to ask.

Lisa had succumbed to keep the peace, as she always did, but she didn't think she would ever get used to the extravagance. Mark had taken her to a high-end boutique and picked out the dresses he wanted her to try on. Then he had made her parade in front of him in them while he scrutinised her. All the dresses he had chosen were more revealing than anything she would have picked out for herself, and she had felt self-conscious as she modelled them for him. When he had finally decided on the dress she was now wearing, he had bought and paid for it without even consulting her as to whether she liked it. It had been outrageously expensive, especially when you considered how little material there was in it, she thought wryly. It was extremely short, barely covering her crotch, and the silk was as soft and thin as tissue. She had meekly suggested that it was too flimsy for a chilly March evening, and way over the top for dinner at a friend's home. But Mark had dismissed all her 'complaints', again accusing her of ingratitude, and Lisa didn't have the will or the strength to oppose him any further.

She surveyed herself in the mirror now, wishing she could wear something less revealing. She wasn't comfortable baring so much flesh, especially for people she had never met before. She felt exposed, and it only added to her nervousness about this evening. She didn't know why she felt so jittery. *It's just dinner*, she told herself for the umpteenth time in an effort to calm and reassure herself. It was true she was quite introverted and she didn't relish meeting new people. But it wasn't just that. There was something odd about Mark's demeanour tonight that was putting her on edge. She couldn't quite put her finger on it, but he seemed oddly excited … almost nervous. His whole attitude towards this dinner party had been strange ever since he'd first mentioned it a couple of weeks ago. It didn't make sense – his baffling air of eager anticipation, the meticulous planning of her outfit … None of it added up, and she couldn't help feeling that it *wasn't* just dinner. Why would he be so keyed up about sharing a meal with another couple?

She didn't know much about their hosts, only what Mark had told her. They lived in Hampstead, a wealthy North London suburb, not far from Mark's home in Highgate. Isabel was a sculptor and gallery owner, who Mark knew through his work as an art dealer. It was obvious from the way he spoke about her that he admired her greatly, both professionally and personally. He had never met her partner, Grayson Fielding, but he knew him by reputation as an acclaimed architect, responsible for some of the most outstanding and ambitious public buildings in the city as well as spectacular private homes for his super-rich clients. From everything Mark had said about them, Lisa understood that they were a wealthy, glamorous couple – clever, talented and successful. It was obvious that this evening was important to Mark and he wanted to make a good impression. Lisa got the feeling they were on a mission to woo the other couple. Maybe Mark wanted to do business with one or both of them.

But that didn't explain why he had insisted she get waxed completely bare. Perhaps he was anticipating a big night when they got home, she thought with a shiver as she arranged her hair in an artfully messy up-do. Her heart sank as Mark emerged from the dressing room with a pair of nude Louboutin stilettos. She hated wearing high heels and they were her highest, spikiest pair.

'I thought I might wear the Manolo pumps,' she said as he handed them to her.

Mark simply shook his head, and Lisa dropped the shoes to the floor, taking his hand to balance herself as she stepped into them.

'Your legs look fantastic in the heels,' he said, smiling at her in the mirror.

At least they would be sitting down most of the time, she thought wearily, already longing for the evening to be over.

'Relax, baby,' he said, obviously sensing her tension. 'You look stunning. You'll be a big hit.'

She forced a smile as he wrapped his arms around her and dropped a kiss on her shoulder.

'It'll be fun, you'll see,' he said, releasing her. He put on his tie as she leaned into the mirror to put in her earrings. 'And whatever happens tonight, just go along with it, okay?'

Lisa turned to him. 'What do you mean?'

'Nothing,' he shrugged, giving her an enigmatic smile. 'Just don't act like a hick and show me up. These are sophisticated, worldly people, Lisa.'

She could only suppose he was worried about her holding up her end of the conversation in the company of his smart friends. 'I'll try to keep up.'

'Good girl,' he said, shrugging on his jacket. 'Just relax and join in, whatever happens. Enjoy yourself. Or at least pretend to. Okay?'

She nodded uncertainly, trying to appear unfazed, but his enigmatic words did nothing to put her mind at rest.

He frowned, clearly sensing her hesitation. 'Promise? This means a lot to me, Lisa.'

'I just wish you'd tell me—'

He put a finger to her lips to silence her. 'Don't be so uptight. I want it to be a surprise,' he said with a crooked smile. 'Just trust me.'

She swallowed hard and nodded.

'Promise,' he insisted, giving her a hard look. 'Whatever happens.'

'I promise,' she whispered.

2

Lisa wished she knew exactly what she'd promised to go along with as they stepped out into the cool evening air. She pulled her coat tighter around her, knowing it wasn't just the chill breeze that caused her to shiver. Mark's car was waiting in front of the house, his driver, Andrew, standing beside it.

'Hi Andrew,' Lisa smiled at him as he held her door open.

'Good evening, Miss Matthews,' he replied, but his eyes didn't meet hers. She had given up telling him to call her by her first name. No matter how often she said it, he stubbornly insisted on addressing her formally as 'Miss Matthews', and he never made eye contact with her. She suspected that was Mark's doing.

'Thanks,' she said as Andrew closed her door and Mark slid in beside her from the other side.

Andrew obviously already had instructions as to where they were going, because he drove off without another word.

'That dress is stunning on you, Lisa,' Mark said,

smiling across at her as he sat back against the plush leather upholstery. He reached across and slid a hand up her bare thigh. 'You look so good in clothes – though not as good as you look out of them, obviously,' he added with a wolfish smile.

Lisa blushed and glanced at Andrew, but he was staring ahead, concentrating on the road, discreetly affecting deafness.

'I'm glad I can take you out again and show you off,' Mark continued, squeezing her thigh possessively.

Lisa swallowed her bile and gave him a smooth, unruffled smile. 'Me too,' she said softly, looking lovingly at him from under her lashes. She covered his hand with hers.

'You should be proud of yourself,' he said, his eyes raking over her body. 'I know it's been hard work sometimes, but it's paid off. You look amazing.'

'I only did it for you,' she said. That at least was true. She had starved and sweated herself down to a rakishly thin size zero for Mark's sake. She had never been unhappy with her body before she met him. Though she hadn't been as slight as she was now, she had always been slim. But Mark demanded perfection in all things, and his girl-friend was no exception – and to him a supermodel size zero was the ideal female figure.

So that was what she had aspired to. She had been so in love, so desperate to please him, and she had been willing to do whatever it took. When they first got together, he had eyes only for her, and he constantly told her how beautiful and sexy she was. But after a while, the jibes started to creep in – little casual remarks about her appearance that undermined her confidence; admiring comments about other women that left her feeling inadequate and undesirable by comparison. When she put on a few pounds after quitting work at his gallery, his criticism had become harsh and unrelenting. Though she was still by no means fat, he began badgering her about her weight constantly, accusing her of letting herself go now that she was sure of him. He no longer told her she looked attractive when she got dressed up for a night out, and the desire she used to see in his eyes faded. Eventually, they had stopped going out altogether, and she knew it was because he was ashamed of her.

He told her she was fat so often that she had started to believe it. She felt overweight and unattractive, dissatisfied with what she saw in the mirror. Consumed by fear that Mark would stop loving her, she had become anxious and insecure. She felt him withdrawing from her, and she was terrified of losing him. Desperate to win back his approval and turn herself into his ideal woman, she had embarked on a punishing diet and exercise regime.

Mark had helped her then. Pleased that she was making an effort, he had bought her a membership at an exclusive gym, hired a personal trainer for her, and made sure she stuck to her strict low-carb diet by monitoring what she ate.

And she had done it. She had become Mark's image of perfection. But it had been a hollow victory. Because she had quickly realised that she would never be secure in a love that was so conditional, so easily withheld. Now, instead of being proud, she felt ashamed that she had let him manipulate her so thoroughly, and in the process had become a person she didn't respect very much.

'I just wanted what's best for you – even if it does mean I'll have to fight off other men for you now,' he added with a wry smile. 'Because they're all going to want you, Lisa.'

'It doesn't matter. I don't want anyone else – only you.'

He took her chin in his hand and turned her to face

him, gazing adoringly into her eyes. 'I love you so much, baby. You're everything to me – you know that, don't you?'

'I know,' she said, forcing herself not to flinch from the force of his words. A year ago they would have meant everything to her. Now they filled her with dread.

'I can't live without you.'

'You don't have to,' she said, leaning in to kiss him because she couldn't bear the intensity in his eyes any longer.

He eventually pulled away with a reluctant sigh. 'I want nothing more than to fuck you right now, here in the car, but we don't want to mess up your dress.'

She affected a regretful smile as she smoothed her hair.

'But later …' he said.

Lisa turned away and stared unseeingly out the window. It was going to be a long night.

After a short journey, Andrew pulled up in front of a large, hacienda-style house, with a white render facade, metal grillwork at the windows and a red-tiled mission-style roof. It was a striking building, and Lisa presumed Grayson Fielding had designed it himself. As they walked up the short drive, she immediately felt intimidated by the imposing surroundings, the stylish sophistication of the house doing nothing to dispel her nerves. She fought the urge to turn and run as they stood on the doorstep and Mark rang the bell.

She felt more out of her depth than ever when the door was opened by a very chic and stunningly beautiful woman. Tall and slender with caramel-coloured skin and a thick mane of glossy black hair that ran in a silky river halfway down her back, she looked like she had stepped straight out of the pages of a fashion magazine. This must be Isabel, Lisa decided – she could see why Mark would admire her so much. Her make-up was perfect, her skin flawless, and her silver sequinned dress was understated and elegant. Lisa immediately felt dowdy in comparison. No amount of grooming and pampering could make her a match for this goddess.

'Hello, Mark. And you must be Lisa.' She spoke with a slight accent that Lisa guessed was Spanish or Latin American. 'Come in.'

Lisa was instantly reassured by the genuine warmth of Isabel's smile as she ushered them inside, and she felt herself relax a little as they stepped into a tiled, double height entrance hall.

'It's lovely to see you, Mark.' Isabel kissed him on both cheeks, and he gave her the flowers they'd brought.

'Thank you – they're beautiful,' she said, taking them from him. 'And you've brought dessert,' she murmured, glancing at Lisa. 'I approve.'

Lisa was puzzled by the remark. They had only brought the flowers.

Isabel turned to her then. 'Welcome,' she said, holding out her hand. 'I'm Isabel. I'm very glad you've come.'

'Thank you. It's lovely to meet you.' Lisa took her hand and Isabel leaned in to kiss her cheek in a cloud of subtle perfume. She even smelled amazing.

Then she held Lisa at arm's length, frankly looking her up and down. 'Grayson will be pleased,' she said to Mark, and he gave her a knowing smirk that Lisa found very disconcerting. 'He's very excited to meet you,' she said to Lisa with a friendly smile.

Lisa presumed she was just being polite. She couldn't imagine why Grayson Fielding would be remotely excited about meeting *her*. As if summoned by his name, a tall man appeared at the other end of the hall. Lisa's breath caught in her throat as she watched him walk towards them. He was quite simply the most beautiful man she had ever seen.

Tall and lean, he had a strong, square jaw, wide intensely blue eyes framed by impossibly long lashes, a thick mop of messy, copper-coloured hair and a full sensuous mouth that immediately made Lisa think of kissing. He was wearing a pair of black suit trousers and a crisp white shirt open at the collar, the sleeves rolled back to reveal strong, tanned forearms. As he joined them, his lips curved in a smile.

Isabel made the introductions, and Grayson and Mark shook hands. Lisa felt overwhelmed when Grayson turned his attention to her.

'It's lovely to meet you, Lisa,' he said as he leaned in to kiss her cheek. He smelled gorgeous, of sandalwood and spice, and she felt off balance at the touch of his soft, warm lips and the rasp of his stubble against her skin, shocked by the strength of her reaction to someone she had just met. She closed her eyes, fighting the ridiculous urge to rub against him like a cat.

'Let me take your coat,' he said as he pulled back, his eyes intent on her face.

'Thanks.' She unbuttoned her coat self-consciously, aware of his gaze on her the whole time. He turned her around to help her out of it, peeling it off slowly as if he were unwrapping a gift. She stifled a shiver as his hands slid down her bare arms. When he had hung the coat on a stand in the hall, he turned to her again, his eyes openly assessing as they swept over her body, checking her out as blatantly as Isabel had done.

'You're very beautiful,' he said, his voice thick and husky.

Lisa blushed under his heated gaze. 'Thank you.' Her voice came out as barely a whisper, so unnerved was she by this beautiful man and his strange manner.

'I'm very much looking forward to … getting to know you better,' he said with a crooked smile.

'Glad you decided to do this now, aren't you?' Isabel said to him with a teasing look.

'Very,' Grayson told her, his gaze flicking to her briefly.

'I think we're going to have a lot of fun tonight,' Isabel said, her eyes glittering excitedly as she looked at each of them in turn. 'Let's go through and get the party started.' She linked Mark's arm and led the way down the hall.

Grayson followed behind with Lisa, his warm hand on the bare skin of her back, right at the base of her spine, feeling incongruously intimate. Once more Lisa wished she was wearing something less revealing. They were ushered into a spacious dining room in the same Spanish colonial style as the entrance, with wooden ceiling beams and a terracotta-tiled floor, the arched windows decorated with ornate ironwork that was echoed in the dramatic wrought iron chandelier that hung over the table. It was a beautiful room – unmistakeably masculine, but still with a warm, homely feel that immediately made Lisa feel comfortable, in contrast to the starkly modern minimalism of Mark's house, where she still never felt truly at home. A long dining table was set for four, a row of flickering candles in the centre casting a warm, golden glow over the polished wood and glinting off the silverware and crystal.

'What a beautiful room,' she exclaimed. 'You have a lovely home.'

'Thank you,' Grayson smiled as he pulled out a chair for her.

Isabel served the food, while Grayson poured wine. Then he sat beside her, with Mark and Isabel opposite. The starter was a crab and asparagus salad, wonderfully light and delicate, and the white wine was crisp and cold.

'This is delicious,' Lisa told Isabel.

'Thank you, but I can't take all the credit,' she said, with a smile at Grayson. 'We did it all together.'

'Oh.' It must be nice, she thought with a pang, to have a boyfriend who cooked with you. She remembered when she used to cook with her grandmother, how they had chatted and laughed as they worked. It made the simple domestic tasks fun when you had someone to share them with. She missed having that kind of companionship.

'Isabel is solely responsible for making everything look so beautiful, though,' Grayson said. 'She has an artist's touch.'

'What sort of art do you do?' Lisa asked her.

'Mostly sculpture. But I've been doing a little painting recently too.'

Lisa had noticed a couple of very striking pieces when they entered the room. 'Are these yours?' she asked Isabel, nodding at them.

'Yes,' Isabel smiled. 'Grayson is my biggest fan.'

'And what do you do, Lisa?' Grayson asked her, looking at her again with that intense focus.

'Oh, I'm—' It was on the tip of her tongue to say that she was an artist too, but she pulled herself up. Mark didn't like her to talk about her art and he would mock her if she ever referred to herself as an artist now. The idea that she might still think of herself that way was laughable to him. 'I don't work at the moment,' she said instead.

'Oh?' Isabel seemed surprised. Lisa was used to that reaction – it was unusual for a woman of her age with no children not to work.

'Lisa has a full-time job looking after me and the house,' Mark said, smiling at her indulgently. 'She doesn't need to work. I keep her in the luxury to which she's accustomed.'

Lisa blushed, feeling foolish. He made her sound like a kept woman, just a decorative adjunct to his life with no purpose of her own. But then, she reflected, it was true – that was what she had let herself become.

'What did you do before?' Grayson asked.

'I worked in Mark's gallery for a while – just admin stuff,' she shrugged.

'Ah, so that's where you two met?' Isabel asked, glancing between her and Mark.

'No, we met when I was at college.'

'What were you studying?' Grayson asked.

'Art.' She glanced at Mark and she could see he was mad that this had come up. It was subtle and she knew she was the only one who would notice the flintiness in his eyes, the slight tightening of his jaw.

'Oh?'

Isabel and Grayson both perked up at this, looking at her expectantly.

'I was in my second year, but I—I dropped out shortly after meeting Mark.' She realised how pathetic that sounded. 'I didn't finish my degree.'

'That's a shame,' Isabel said.

'She didn't have the talent,' Mark said bluntly. 'It would have been pointless to continue.'

Something like annoyance flickered in Isabel's face.

'It's true,' Lisa said. She got the feeling Isabel was about to challenge Mark and she wanted to avoid any confrontation. She would only pay for it later. 'I realised I'd never make it as an artist. I was wasting my time.'

'There's merit in knowing your limitations,' Mark said, smiling at her.

Keen to change the subject, Lisa turned to Grayson. 'This is a beautiful house,' she said. 'Did you design it yourself?'

'Thank you. Yes, I did.'

'You have some interesting art,' Mark said, glancing around at the walls.

Grayson nodded. 'It's my biggest indulgence.'

Lisa was relieved as the conversation moved away from her to a more general discussion about art, a subject which they all had in common to some degree. Grayson was very knowledgeable about the contemporary London art scene. He was an enthusiastic collector and admired many of the same artists she did. She longed to join in more with the conversation, but she knew it would anger Mark if she drew too much attention to herself and risked exposing her ignorance or inexperience. So she said as little as possible.

Grayson, however, seemed intent on drawing her out. He made a point of asking her opinion about whatever was being discussed, and listened attentively to her answers. She felt his eyes on her constantly, and the intensity of his gaze made her a little uncomfortable. She wasn't used to having a man other than Mark so completely focused on her.

His whole attitude to her felt odd and inappropriate. If she hadn't known better, she would have thought he was flirting with her. But that was silly. He was clearly a courteous, considerate person, and she didn't think he would do something as offensive as flirting with her right in front of their respective partners. She didn't really know him, of course, but she couldn't imagine him behaving so crassly. Probably he had simply sensed that she was shy and nervous, and was being a kind and attentive host, trying to put her at her ease. Besides, Isabel and Mark obviously didn't feel there was anything amiss. They were perfectly relaxed and didn't seem at all put out by Grayson's behaviour towards her. She told herself she was imagining it and tried to relax. She just wasn't used to mixing with such sophisticated people. That was all. She didn't know the etiquette. Maybe that was what Mark had been trying to warn her about.

A different wine was served with the main course of beef fillet, the pale, crisp white replaced by a rich, earthy red. Lisa felt Grayson's eyes on her as she tasted it.

'What do you think?' he asked.

She cast around for something clever to say, but could think of nothing. 'It's very nice,' she said simply, smiling to show her appreciation in an attempt to make up for her lack of knowledge.

'*Nice!*' Mark scoffed. 'It's a *Château Margaux*, Lisa.' He turned to Grayson. 'You'll have to forgive Lisa. She's a bit provincial.'

She felt her face flame, mortified that Mark was apologising for her. How could he humiliate her like that? If he didn't want her to show him up, why was he pointing out her inadequacies?

'Sorry,' she said to Grayson, her voice barely above a whisper. 'It really is lovely, but I'm afraid I don't know much about wine.'

Grayson glanced at Mark with a frown before turning to her. 'It's very kind of you to say so, Lisa,' he said, smiling at her. 'I'm glad you're enjoying it.'

The warmth of his gaze immediately put her at ease, and she started to relax as they ate, and the conversation flowed easily around her. She liked Grayson and Isabel. They were knowledgeable and interesting, and she enjoyed listening to them. She didn't say much, feeling a little like a child at the grown-ups' table as the conversation turned to travel, and Isabel, Mark and Grayson chatted animatedly about cities she had never been to, restaurants she had never eaten in and experiences she had only dreamed of. She was happy enough not to take part, but more acutely aware than ever of the gulf between her and these people.

They belonged to the world, while she had only skirted around its edges.

Isabel and Mark were discussing places they had both visited in Tuscany, when Grayson turned to her.

'Have you been to Tuscany, Lisa?' he asked.

'No,' she smiled sadly. 'I've never been to Italy.'

'That's a shame,' Grayson said. 'I think you'd love it. There's so much to see – particularly if you're interested in art.'

'I'd love to go there,' she said wistfully. 'I haven't travelled much.'

'That's an understatement,' Mark said. 'Lisa didn't even own a passport when I met her. Like I said – provincial.'

'My grandparents weren't well off, so we never had holidays abroad when I was growing up,' she said.

'Your grandparents?' Isabel queried.

'They raised me after my parents died,' she explained.

'Oh, I'm sorry.'

'Poor Lisa had never been further than Scotland when we met,' Mark said.

'It was fine,' Lisa said, feeling defensive. Her grandparents had always made such an effort to take her on holiday and to make it special for her, and she had nothing but happy memories of their summer trips. 'We went all around Britain, visiting different places, and we had some really lovely times.'

'You didn't travel when you were a student?' Grayson asked.

'I never had the money,' Lisa shrugged. 'And besides, my grandparents were elderly and incapacitated, so they needed me at home—' She stopped abruptly, realising Mark was scowling at her. Her sorry tale obviously wasn't in keeping with the glamorous, successful image he wanted to present. 'Sorry,' she said, biting her lip. 'Boring story.'

'Not at all,' Grayson said, frowning. 'But it's a pity you didn't get the opportunity to travel.'

'I've been to Paris,' she said.

'Paris is my absolute favourite city in the world,' Isabel said. 'Did you like it?'

'Yes, I loved it.'

Mark had taken her to Paris the year they met, just after she'd dropped out of college – a reward, she now realised, and an inducement to bend to his will in the future. It had been first class all the way, and Lisa couldn't deny she had been seduced by the luxury – the five-star hotels, the chauffeurs, the expensive restaurants and ritzy shops. Mark had swept her off her feet. She had been so excited to be in love and abroad for the first time. Everything was new and wonderful, and she could hardly believe her luck that such a wealthy, charming and urbane man had chosen someone as ordinary as her. Mark's luxurious lifestyle was just the icing on the cake. It was bliss not worrying about money for a change, and she had enjoyed letting him spoil her. The contrast with her old life was so dramatic, she had felt like she was in a fairytale.

Maybe she had been, she thought now bitterly – except her fairytale had worked the opposite way to most. Her handsome prince had turned out to be a monster in disguise.

'Anyway, that's the only time I've been abroad so far.'

'But we're going to make up for that now, aren't we?' Mark said, smiling across at her. 'I'm going to show her the world – starting with Mauritius next month.'

'Yes,' she said animatedly, trying to sound excited about the trip. The truth was, the thought of two weeks alone with Mark, without even a few hours' respite while he was at work, filled her with dread. She would be at his mercy twenty-four hours a day for two whole weeks. She took a sip of wine, trying to dispel her gloomy thoughts.

'Where are you from, Isabel?' she asked, anxious to divert attention away from herself again. They had all finished eating, and without the food to focus on, she started to feel self-conscious. She was aware of Grayson's eyes on her and fought the urge to fidget, wishing she had something to do with her hands.

'I'm from Costa Rica,' Isabel answered.

'That sounds so exotic. I've seen pictures – it looks really beautiful,' Lisa said wistfully.

'It is, incredibly beautiful,' Isabel said.

'Like the women who come from there,' Mark said, turning to Isabel, his eyes glowing with admiration.

Lisa's stomach lurched as he lightly brushed a finger down Isabel's bare arm. The gesture was unmistakeably intimate and sexual, and Lisa didn't know where to look, shocked that Mark would be so inappropriate. It wasn't like him. However brutish he could be towards her, he never behaved boorishly in company. Had he had too much wine? She didn't think so. He didn't like to lose control, and she had never seen him drunk.

'Don't you think Isabel is beautiful, Lisa?' he asked.

'Y—yes,' she whispered, looking at him. His fingers were moving up Isabel's neck now into her hair. Lisa waited for Isabel to push him away, but to her amazement, she seemed to be enjoying Mark's attention, smiling calmly at Lisa as their eyes met across the table. Why were they acting like this, she wondered, her mind racing. Why didn't Grayson do something? Were they having an affair? Did Grayson know?

She had been avoiding looking at Grayson, but she turned to him now, desperate to cover her embarrassment and confusion. 'Have you been to Costa Rica?' she asked, her voice sounding shaky and panicked.

'Yes,' he said, glancing at her briefly. 'It's an amazing place.' As he turned back to Isabel and Mark, Lisa followed his gaze, and was horrified to see Mark pulling down the straps of Isabel's dress and dropping kisses on her bare shoulder. Isabel let her head fall to the side to give him more access as his lips moved to her neck, while his hands slid to her breasts.

Silence fell over the table, the atmosphere suddenly charged. All Lisa could hear was the hammering of her heart and the rush of blood in her veins. She felt hot and clammy, wanting to run but finding herself frozen, glued to her seat. She was unable to tear her eyes away as Mark nuzzled Isabel's neck and slowly unzipped her dress. The top fell away to reveal a sexy black lace bra. Mark kissed her on the mouth as he unhooked it, slid it off and tossed it onto the table. He lifted his head then, a challenging gleam in his eyes as he eyeballed Lisa while he caressed Isabel's bare breasts.

'So beautiful,' he murmured. Isabel lifted her arms above her head and arched into his hands as he stroked and pinched her nipples until they were hard.

Lisa was struck dumb, her face on fire. She was shocked to discover that she found the sight erotic. She wanted to get up from the table and run away, but at the same time she felt paralysed. She was aware of Grayson beside her, but she couldn't look at him. She waited for him to react, but when she finally risked a sideways glance at him, she was amazed to find that he wasn't angry at all, and seemed completely unfazed by what was happening. In fact, he appeared to be enjoying the performance. There was the hint of a crooked smile on his lips, and his eyes glittered with excitement as he watched Mark and Isabel kissing and caressing.

As if sensing her watching him, Grayson turned to her then. Lisa looked away, unable to meet his eyes. She leapt when she felt a warm hand on her leg, gasping involuntarily as it slid up her thigh under her dress. Her head spun back to Grayson in shock, and she instinctively moved to slap his hand away. But then she caught Mark's eye. He gave her a warning look, and she stopped herself. Suddenly she realised with a jolt that he wanted this to happen. He wanted Grayson to touch her in front of him the way he was touching Isabel. He wanted to watch. Her head spun and she felt dizzy as she realised the full meaning of his words earlier – *whatever happens*. This was what they had come here for – and she had promised to go along with it.

3

SHE BIT HER LIP, stifling a gasp as Grayson's hand slid between her legs, coaxing them apart. She fought the urge to clamp them together and push him away. Instead she forced her body to relax and open up to him as he stroked the soft flesh of her inner thigh. But inside she was screaming, her mind in a whirl trying to process the fact that Mark had brought her here to have sex with another man, not caring whether she wanted it or not. He was pimping her out like a whore, and he had deliberately kept her in the dark and trapped her into going along with it. It was unbelievably cruel, even for him.

She looked across at him, desperately hoping for some shred of sympathy or understanding. But he wasn't even looking at her, completely oblivious to her distress as he kissed and caressed Isabel. Her attention was drawn back to Grayson with a start as his fingers slipped inside her thong. Her eyes automatically flew to his before she dropped her head in embarrassment, trying to quell the heat that was building inside her as he touched her naked flesh. Grayson took her chin in his hand and lifted her face to his, his eyes glittering with excitement as his fingers stroked her gently. He leaned in to nuzzle her face, his mouth almost touching her, but not quite.

'You're so wet,' he murmured into her ear, his breath hot as it whispered along her skin.

She shivered.

'Are you cold?' he asked, pulling back and withdrawing his hand. Without waiting for an answer he lifted her from her seat and pulled her into his lap. He wrapped his arms tightly around her, pulling her into the heat of his body, and she felt the hardness of his erection against her back.

'Better?' he asked.

She nodded, unable to speak. She had never felt so bewildered in her life, completely overwhelmed by the strange mixture of emotions she was experiencing. She was shocked, a little frightened, and more turned on than she cared to admit. It was very confusing. But it was oddly comforting being held by Grayson.

He dropped his head to her shoulder and nuzzled her bare skin. 'May I?' he asked, his hands going to the tie of her dress at the nape of her neck.

'Oh!' Her hands flew up instinctively to stop him, but then she caught Mark's eye across the table and he threw her another warning look. 'Yes,' she said in a choked whisper, resting her hands in her lap.

He quickly undid the shoelace ties and Lisa felt everyone's eyes on her as the thin strip of silk fell to her waist. She instinctively covered her breasts with her hands before she could stop herself.

Grayson dropped a wet kiss on her shoulder. 'Please don't,' he said, his hands resting over hers. 'Let me look at you.'

'Don't be such a little prude, Lisa,' Mark said impatiently.

'She's shy,' Isabel said. 'I think it's sweet.' She smiled encouragingly at Lisa.

'Not everyone is such a natural exhibitionist as Isabel,' Grayson said, and Lisa felt an unexpected pang at the fondness in his voice.

'If you've got it, flaunt it, right?' Isabel said with a toss of her head. Lisa envied her confidence.

'Well, Lisa doesn't have a lot to flaunt. Not like you,' Mark said, his eyes dropping to Isabel's breasts. 'But she makes up for it with her mouth,' he told Grayson. 'Get her on her knees and I guarantee you'll think you've died and gone to heaven.'

Lisa cringed at his crudeness. There was no warmth in his tone, none of the affection with which Grayson spoke of Isabel. She might have been a hooker he had hired for the night for all the care he showed her.

She was grateful that Grayson ignored him. He turned her slightly in his lap so she was facing him and gave her an earnest, pleading look, his eyebrows raised. Slowly she let her hands fall and Grayson looked at her, his gaze was so intense that Lisa had to force herself not to cover her breasts again.

'You're beautiful,' he breathed, his hands cupping her breasts. 'You have amazing skin,' he murmured, his gaze on his hands as he gently caressed her breasts, his thumbs brushing lightly over her nipples. He smiled as they hardened to his touch, and Lisa felt herself blush furiously.

She was aware of Mark watching her and tried to swallow down her panic and shock. Just go along with whatever happens, she reminded herself. There would be hell to pay later if she did anything to spoil Mark's plans for the evening or to 'show him up' in front of his sophisticated friends.

'Well,' Isabel said, pulling away from Mark, 'you guys

don't want to spoil your appetite for dessert. I have something very special planned.' She pulled her dress back on and zipped it up. 'Lisa,' she said with a smile, 'will you come and help me prepare it?'

'Yes, of course,' Lisa said, relieved for the excuse to escape. She wasn't naive enough to think she was off the hook completely, but at least it would give her a breathing space to regroup and prepare herself for whatever came next. Grayson released her and she retied her dress, glad of the chance to cover up again. She felt Grayson's eyes burning into her as she followed Isabel to the kitchen. It was another large airy room, a more contemporary interpretation of the classic Spanish style of the entranceway and dining room. Hexagonal terracotta tiles covered the floor and the white ceiling was crossed with dark wooden beams. A table and chairs of dark wood stood in the centre of the room, surrounded by painted white cabinets and stainless steel appliances.

'So, what's for dessert?' Lisa asked as Isabel opened an enormous fridge.

'Strawberries, cream, chocolate sauce,' Isabel said as she removed containers and placed them on the worktop. 'And you, of course.'

Thankfully she was too focused on what she was doing to notice Lisa's shock.

'Maybe some ice cream too. How do you feel about that?' she asked, turning to Lisa, her perfect eyebrows raised in query.

'About ice cream? I—I like it,' Lisa said hesitantly.

'Mmm,' Isabel gave her a conspiratorial smile. 'The cold can be rather delicious, can't it?'

'Um … what would you like me to do?' Lisa asked, trying to ignore her misgivings as Isabel busied herself assembling the ingredients.

'You could get undressed.'

'Oh.' Lisa felt her skin burning. What the hell was going on here? 'Yes, of course,' she said, trying to sound as if this was what she had been expecting all along. 'Should I … take everything off?' *Please say no*, she begged silently.

Isabel turned to her, looking her up and down thoughtfully. 'I think you should leave the shoes on,' she said, nodding to Lisa's feet. 'They're very sexy.'

Lisa nodded, grateful when Isabel turned away again and began preparing strawberries. Her hands shook as she untied her dress, and she tried to quash the curling fear in her stomach as she let it fall from her shoulders to pool on the floor at her feet. This night wouldn't go on forever, she told herself. No matter what happened, whatever she had to endure, in a few hours she would be home again, safe. She just had to get through it.

Nevertheless, she struggled not to cry as she slid her thong down her legs and stepped out of it, feeling utterly miserable. As she straightened up again, she found Isabel watching her. She felt so exposed, and more than a little ridiculous standing in the middle of the kitchen in nothing but her high heels. She fought the urge to cover herself with her hands as Isabel looked her up and down.

'Very nice.' Isabel gave her a warm smile of approval. 'You have a fantastic body, Lisa. Lie on the table,' she said, nodding to it.

Lisa clambered onto the table and lay down on the cold, hard surface. She closed her eyes and concentrated on taking slow, deep breaths, trying to calm herself. She felt Isabel's hand in her hair and opened her eyes to find her standing beside her with a small pillow.

'Lift,' she said softly. When Lisa did so, she slid the pillow under her head. 'We don't want you hurting yourself when things get … intense. Comfortable?' she asked, smoothing Lisa's hair behind her.

Lisa nodded, her throat too tight to speak.

'So, do you play much with other couples?' Isabel asked conversationally as she took a tub of cream and a spoon from the worktop.

Lisa wasn't sure how to answer. She didn't know what Mark had told Isabel. Would he want her to pretend they did this sort of thing all the time? Or was it okay to admit she was new to all this as long as she joined in?

She gulped as Isabel came to stand beside her and spooned two dollops of cream onto her breasts.

'No,' she said finally, deciding honesty was the best course. It was probably obvious what a clueless newbie she was anyway. She licked her dry lips as Isabel swirled the cream around in concentric circles until only her nipples were left exposed. 'This is our first time. At least, it's my first time.' She suddenly realised she had no idea if Mark had done this sort of thing before with other girls.

'Well, we're honoured,' Isabel smiled as she moved downwards, spreading more cream across Lisa's stomach and into her belly button. 'I thought you seemed a little nervous. But I hope you're enjoying yourself.'

'Yes. It —it's fun,' Lisa said, hastening to assure Isabel that she was having a good time.

'Good. I'm glad. Maybe we can do it again sometime.' She got a carton from the counter and placed a strawberry over each of Lisa's nipples and another in her belly button, looking appreciatively down at her handiwork. 'I'm sure Grayson would like to see you again. He's very attracted to you.'

'Oh, I'm sure he's not,' Lisa gasped, horrified that Isabel would think that. 'It's obvious he really loves you.'

But Isabel just smiled. 'That's sweet of you,' she said

with a light laugh, 'but you really don't have to worry on my account. I'm not jealous. Grayson and I don't have that kind of relationship. But I've known him a long time, and he likes you a lot – I can tell.'

Lisa smiled weakly, not knowing how to respond to this. She shivered as Isabel smeared cream along her thighs.

'It's good that you're bare here,' she said, nodding to Lisa's newly waxed pussy. 'Bend your knees and put your feet flat on the table.'

Mortified, Lisa did as instructed, her ass lifted into the air as she planted the spiky heels on the polished wood. Isabel nudged her legs apart, then grabbed a small, heart-shaped mould from the worktop and placed it over Lisa's crotch.

'Now for the pièce de résistance,' she said with a smile. She filled the centre of the mould with cream, then arranged strawberries artfully on top. 'There,' she said, taking away the mould and pulling back to survey the effect. 'You look good enough to eat. I'm not going to bother with ice-cream – too messy. So we just need some chocolate sauce, and we're done.'

She took a bottle from the worktop and drizzled sauce over Lisa's body in a random abstract pattern of squiggles and splashes. Lisa shivered as the cold, thick liquid trickled onto her bare skin.

'Try to stay still,' Isabel said. 'You don't want to ruin my handiwork.'

'Sorry,' Lisa said with a blush.

'There,' Isabel said, standing back and brushing her hands. 'You're quite a work of art, if I do say so myself.'

Lisa forced a smile, feeling completely ridiculous.

'Just one last finishing touch,' Isabel said, plucking the last strawberry from the carton. 'Open your mouth.'

Lisa obeyed, and Isabel placed the strawberry between her parted lips.

'Keep it there,' she said. 'Don't bite.'

Lisa did as instructed, holding the fruit lightly between her lips.

'I'll go and tell the guys dessert is ready,' Isabel said, moving to the door. 'I hope Mark likes strawberries. They're Grayson's favourite.'

When she left the room, Lisa closed her eyes and tried to calm herself, but all she could hear was the pounding of her heart. She willed herself to lie still, though every instinct was telling her to make a run for it. She wanted to jump off the table, wipe all this food off her skin, get dressed and beg Mark to take her home. Her every nerve was on edge, and she felt sick with tension, her stomach churning in anticipation when she heard the door open with a soft click.

There was the sound of footsteps crossing the tiled floor, and when she opened her eyes again, Grayson and Mark were standing either side of the table, gazing down at her.

'Wow, you look gorgeous,' Grayson said, his eyes dark with desire.

'You've done an amazing job,' Mark called to Isabel, who was hovering by the door.

'Thank you,' she said, crossing the room to join them. 'But I had fabulous ingredients to work with.' She smiled down at Lisa.

'The best,' Grayson said admiringly, his eyes devouring her as they swept over her body.

'Well, enjoy,' Isabel said, spreading her arms as she backed away.

'Aren't you going to join us?' Mark asked her.

'No, I don't have a sweet tooth. And besides, we don't

want to overwhelm the poor girl. I'll go and get the hot tub ready while you guys have your dessert.' She winked at Lisa. 'Have fun,' she said to her, then turned and left the room.

Lisa swallowed hard as the door clicked shut behind Isabel and she was alone with the two men. For a moment time seemed to stand still, the atmosphere charged, electric. Then Mark trailed a finger through the cream at her breast, and put it in his mouth, his eyes closing briefly as he sucked. 'Delicious,' he murmured, breaking the silence.

Grayson bent to her and gently sucked the strawberry from between her lips, his breath hot in her mouth. He pulled back slightly as he chewed and swallowed, and then he kissed her again, opening her lips with his. She tasted strawberry juice on his thrusting tongue as it tangled erotically with hers.

'Mmm,' he groaned as he pulled away. 'Strawberry and you – sensational.'

Then Mark's mouth was on hers, hard and demanding, while Grayson's lips trailed down to her breasts. She closed her eyes, gasping as Grayson drew hard on her left nipple, sucking off the strawberry. Mark kissed his way down her neck, and then they were both licking, nibbling and suckling at her breasts. When she felt teeth graze her nipple, she knew it was Mark even with her eyes closed. His lips closed around the sensitive nub, tugging hard until she whimpered in pain, the violence of his touch contrasting with the sensual tenderness of Grayson's on her other side.

She became lost in the physical sensation, forgetting to feel embarrassed or ashamed, oblivious to everything but the burning need that was building up inside her. Too mindless with arousal to be self-conscious, she abandoned herself completely to the world of her senses – the touch of their mouths and hands on her everywhere, the rasp of their stubble against her bare skin, the sounds of their jagged breathing and throaty groans all feeding the growing tension inside her, stoking the throbbing between her legs.

Their tongues trailed down her body, leaving her wet skin raw and super-sensitive. She felt warm breath against her skin as lips closed around the strawberry at her navel.

'Taste,' Grayson's voice was husky, and she opened her eyes to see him holding the strawberry in his fingers. As she watched, he placed it lightly between his lips and bent to her. Lisa lifted her head to take it. Her teeth grazed his skin, the sweet juice bursting on her tongue as she bit into the fruit. He opened his lips against hers, dropping the strawberry into her mouth, and pulled back as she ate, smiling indulgently at her.

'Good?' he asked, his eyes hot as he watched.

Lisa nodded wordlessly as she swallowed, too dazed to speak as Mark trailed kisses across her abdomen. It felt so wrong to be like this with two men at once, one of whom she had met only a couple of hours ago. Yet she couldn't deny the excitement surging through her body, or the desperate need for them to finish what they'd started.

Grayson bent and kissed her again, his hands fondling her aching breasts as his tongue tangled with hers. He tore himself away to kiss his way down her body towards the strawberry heart, and then both men were licking and sucking, so close to where all that burning need was focused.

'Mmm,' Grayson groaned appreciatively against her belly. 'Sweet, strawberry flavoured girl.'

When they were almost done, Mark lifted his head from her and picked up one of the last remaining straw-berries, smearing it in cream and chocolate sauce. 'Here,' he said, holding it out to her, 'for being such a good girl.'

He watched as Lisa ate it from his fingers, his eyes darkening as she licked her lips.

Lisa shivered as Grayson licked the remaining cream and sauce from her belly and she felt his mouth move lower, kissing her thighs.

'I think I'll give our host the pleasure of finishing you off,' Mark said with a smile in his voice as he glanced at Grayson.

'Thank you,' Grayson murmured. Then he buried his head between her legs, while Mark moved to stand at the other end of the table behind Lisa's head.

She gasped as she felt Grayson's tongue licking along the soft folds of her flesh, her body jerking and bucking off the table. She was grateful for the pillow Isabel had given her, her head thrashing involuntarily against the wood as Grayson nibbled and sucked the aching flesh between her legs, gently flicking over her clit. Then Mark leaned over her and kissed her with passionate ferocity, while his hands caressed her breasts. She was pinned down by his mouth and hands, so there was no escape from the almost unbearable pleasure.

She groaned deep in her throat, an almost animalistic sound of need as she felt the heat build inside her while the two men stroked, licked and caressed until she thought she might pass out from the sensory overload. She whimpered against Mark's lips as Grayson thrust two fingers inside her, while he nibbled and sucked on her clit.

'Ssh,' Grayson breathed against her skin, putting a hand on her stomach and holding her down when her body would have bowed off the table, so she was held in place and there was no respite from the fire building inside her as he pleasured her relentlessly. It only intensified the explosive burst of ecstasy as she came, wrapping her arms around Mark's neck and screaming helplessly into his mouth as huge, shuddering waves of sensation racked her body, more intense than she'd ever have thought possible. She felt she might break apart from the force of it, but still neither of them let up, mercilessly stimulating her already fevered body until she felt herself once more pulsating against Grayson's tongue as another orgasm took hold.

As her legs started to shake, Mark lifted his head and unwound her arms from around his neck. Stretching them out to the sides, he pinned them to the table so she was helpless, completely at his and Grayson's mercy. His eyes glittered with excitement as he watched her come.

'Good girl,' he whispered in her ear as he bent to kiss her again. She squirmed and writhed uselessly against their restraining hands and mouths as her whole body shook, seeking any release it could find from the blissful torment. Finally Grayson's fingers stilled, his kisses becoming lighter, gentler, soothing her sensitive flesh. Her body started to relax, sinking down into the wood of the table as little aftershocks of pleasure rippled through her. Mark lifted his head a fraction.

'More?' he murmured.

'No,' she said in a panicked whisper. 'Please. I can't—'

He gave a throaty chuckle. 'Relax, baby.' He stroked her sides soothingly. 'I'm only teasing.'

She sagged in relief. She didn't think she could take any more.

Grayson lifted his head from her, wiping his mouth with the sleeve of his shirt. 'You were amazing,' he said, his voice throaty. 'So beautiful.' He pressed a soft kiss to her stomach. Then he straightened up, and gave her a smile, his eyes dazzling with something akin to awe.

'You did great,' Mark said as he released her hands.

She was relieved that he seemed to be pleased with her, but now that the fog of desire was starting to lift, self-consciousness began to creep back in and she felt horribly aware that she was spread out on the table completely naked while Grayson and Mark were fully dressed.

She felt boneless as she struggled to sit up, her weak limbs uncooperative.

'Here, let me help you,' Grayson said, taking her hand and pulling her up to a sitting position. Lisa let her shoes fall to the floor as her legs dangled over the edge of the table. She dropped her eyes shyly, unable to look at Grayson, embarrassment flooding through her as the reality of her present situation sank in. She was completely naked, her skin sticky with fruit juice and saliva, and she had just let this beautiful stranger eat her out on his kitchen table.

'Are you okay?' Grayson asked softly as she bent her head, letting her hair fall in front of her face to hide it.

She nodded, blushing furiously.

Grayson cupped her face, tilting her chin up so she was forced to look him in the eye. 'If it's too much—'

'No,' Lisa said hastily, aware of Mark's watchful eyes on her. 'It's not. That was ... amazing.'

'Are you sure?' Grayson frowned down at her, his thumb gently stroking her jaw in a soothing motion. 'It's okay if you want to stop. We won't do anything you don't want to do.'

He seemed so kind, genuinely concerned for her well-being, and Lisa wished she could tell him how she really felt and bring this weird evening to an end. She could tell by the strain in his features how turned on he was, and she was in no doubt that he wanted to continue. Yet she also trusted that he meant what he said, and he wouldn't take things any further if she just said the word. But there would be hell to pay with Mark if she chickened out now. She had no choice but to go through with it. 'I'm sure,' she said, meeting his gaze, anxious to convince him. 'I think it's pretty obvious I enjoyed myself.'

'Good,' Grayson smiled, brushing the hair back from her face. 'Because I want you very badly.'

Lisa smiled back shakily, trying to hide her nerves. She was grateful when the door opened and Isabel came into the room, causing a diversion. 'How was dessert?'

'It was delicious,' Grayson murmured as he stroked a finger down Lisa's arm. She shivered as it grazed the side of her breast.

'Compliments to the chef,' Mark said, grinning as he wrapped his arms around Isabel from behind, pulling her into his body.

'Mmm, I can feel how much you enjoyed it,' she said, wriggling against him.

'I'm ready for seconds,' he said, bending to kiss her shoulder.

'Well, the hot tub's all set. And Lisa's making me feel rather over-dressed.'

'I can help you with that,' Mark said, brushing her hair aside as his fingers went to the fastening of her dress. Isabel dropped her head to the side, closing her eyes as Mark nuzzled her neck while he slowly slid down the zip.

Grayson took Lisa's hand and helped her off the table. 'What about you?' he asked, a smile in his voice as he wrapped his arms around her from behind, pulling her against him, so she felt his rock-hard erection at her back. 'Are you ready for seconds?'

'Yes,' she whispered shakily as he gently bit her earlobe.

'Good,' Grayson said, his breath hot in her ear. 'Because I can't wait to be inside you.'

Lisa bit her lip, stifling a gasp. Her heart hammered in her ribs, and she hoped that if Grayson could feel it he would put it down to excitement rather than the shock and fear his words caused. Her eyes darted in panic to Mark and Isabel, but they both had their eyes closed, Mark's head buried in Isabel's shoulder as he peeled off her dress. Lisa was thankful that at least no one was looking at her now because she didn't think she could hide how desperate she felt in this moment. She had never felt so trapped and hopeless. She was going to have to let Grayson fuck her – and no matter how beautiful or kind he was, no matter how much pleasure he would give her, she didn't want it. She didn't want any of this.

She tried to tamp down the rising panic in her chest as she realised she was perilously close to tears. This was what she had come to, she thought miserably – fucking strangers for a quiet life. She had sunk as low as she could possibly go. Her boyfriend had brought her here to pimp her out to another man, and she was going to go along with it, as she always did, just to keep the peace. Was there no limit to how much she would debase herself to avoid antagonising Mark?

She struggled to calm herself, sucking in a deep breath as Grayson kissed her neck and shoulder. She had to be in control when she faced him again. But then Isabel's eyes flew open and suddenly they were looking right at each other. Isabel's eyes widened in alarm, and Lisa knew that all her panic and distress must be etched on her features. Shit! She tried to force a calm smile onto her face, but she knew it was too late. Isabel had seen.

4

PLEASE DON'T SAY ANYTHING, she begged silently, scarcely daring to breathe.

'Why don't we continue this outside,' Isabel said smoothly, and Lisa allowed herself to relax a little. Perhaps she had been mistaken, and Isabel hadn't noticed anything after all.

Grayson lifted his head, and Lisa saw Isabel catch his eye. She gave a barely perceptible shake of her head, a slight frown furrowing her brow. Grayson's arms dropped away, and Lisa whipped around to see him frowning back at Isabel with a questioning expression. They seemed to be having some sort of silent exchange with their eyes, and as she watched, Isabel mouthed one word at him. Lisa couldn't tell what it was, but it had an immediate effect on him. He seemed startled, and she caught his horrified expression before he quickly averted his eyes and stepped away from her, putting distance between them.

'Come on,' Isabel said, turning to Mark. 'I can't wait to get you in that hot tub.' She took his hand and led him to the door. 'Grayson, maybe you could show Lisa where the bathroom is. I'm sure she'd like to clean up.'

'Aren't you joining us?' Mark asked, already unbuttoning his shirt in the doorway.

'I think I'd rather have Lisa all to myself,' Grayson said.

'Be my guest,' Mark said with a shrug. 'But remember what I said – make sure you get her on her knees,' he added before following Isabel from the room.

Lisa cringed at the way he talked about her as if she were his property, a gift that he could bestow on whomever he chose.

There was an awkward silence as the door closed behind them. She was aware of Grayson, standing very still beside her. Sneaking a look at him, she caught the dazed expression on his face before he turned away abruptly. Suddenly galvanised into action, he moved to the end of the table and picked up Lisa's dress and thong from the chair where she had left them.

'Um … take your clothes,' he said, holding them out to her, but not meeting her eyes. Lisa took them from him, clutching the dress to her.

'Come on, I'll show you where you can take a shower.' Grayson reached out a hand as if to guide her, but quickly withdrew it, throwing her an apologetic look.

Lisa wasn't sure what had changed, but something was very different in Grayson's attitude. Suddenly he seemed hesitant and unsure of himself. He was silent and subdued as he led her to the bathroom, and whereas earlier he couldn't keep his hands off her, now he seemed to be going out of his way to avoid touching her. He kept a respectful distance between them as they walked side by side down the hall. Lisa felt unnerved, thrown off balance once again by the sudden change in his behaviour, and she moved stiffly, her body rigid with tension as she wondered what was going to happen next.

He led her to a small shower room. Lisa stepped inside and turned to him, still clutching her clothes to her body to cover herself. Grayson remained on the threshold, his arms folded. 'There are clean towels there,' he said, nodding to a cabinet against the wall. He seemed to be avoiding even looking at her now, his eyes darting around as he spoke, looking anywhere but at her. 'You should find everything else you need in the shower.'

'Thanks.'

'Come back to the kitchen when you're done.'

He pulled the door closed, and Lisa immediately darted across and turned the key in the lock, grateful to have some privacy. She had thought maybe Grayson intended to fuck her in the shower, and she was relieved that he didn't. At least it gave her some time alone to compose herself and get psyched up for whatever came next.

But had he changed his mind about fucking her at all, she wondered. It seemed strange that he had given her her clothes. There wasn't much point in getting dressed again if he was going to have sex with her as soon as she was ready. She wished she knew what Isabel had communicated to him in that silent exchange. Had she somehow let him know that Lisa was out of her depth? If so, maybe he was planning to go easy on her. Mark had talked up her oral skills. Perhaps Grayson would just get her to give him a blowjob, and he would let her keep her dress on while she was doing it. On the other hand, maybe he just didn't find her that attractive naked. She didn't have a lush, sexy body like Isabel. She looked in the mirror, cupping her small, shapely breasts in her hands.

But there was no time for brooding. Whatever he

wanted, she shouldn't keep Grayson waiting too long. She quickly stepped into the shower, washing away the stickiness of strawberry juice and saliva from her skin and trying not to dwell on how it had got there. She kept her head out of the spray as much as possible to avoid getting her hair wet. The warm water was soothing and relaxing, and she fought the temptation to linger. She couldn't hide in here forever, she thought, shutting off the water and stepping out of the shower. She dried herself quickly and put her clothes back on, grateful to be covered up again. The dress that had seemed indecent just hours earlier now felt comfortingly modest. Everything was relative, she thought, smiling wryly at herself in the mirror as she smoothed her hair. She took a deep breath, steeling herself, and went to rejoin Grayson in the kitchen.

She padded barefoot down the hall and hovered uncertainly in the doorway before going in. Grayson was leaning against the worktop and looked up as she entered.

'Everything okay?' he asked with a gentle smile. He was making eye contact with her again, she noted.

She nodded stiffly, her tension returning. 'Yes, thanks.'

'Would you like something to drink? Tea? Coffee? Something stronger?'

She could probably use something stronger to steady her nerves, but tea sounded comforting. She was surprised he was offering it, though – it didn't really seem in keeping with the spirit of the evening.

'Tea would be lovely.'

He opened a cupboard. 'Earl Gray, Ceylon, jasmine?'

'Jasmine, please.' It was her favourite – she found it so calming and soothing. It might help her relax.

He nodded. 'Um … have a seat,' he waved vaguely in the direction of the table.

Lisa sat, watching in silence as he switched on the

kettle and busied himself with making tea. His attitude had changed so quickly and dramatically, it was hard to believe that only a short time ago he had gone down on her in this very room. Her eyes drifted to the table, and she blushed at the memory of his mouth on her. Everything had been cleared away now. He had obviously spent the time she was in the shower cleaning up in here.

'Here we go.' He set a tray on the table, jolting her out of her thoughts. Then he sat beside her and poured tea from a Chinese-style pot into little bowl-like cups. He handed her one, and she cupped her hands around it, breathing in the soothing flowery aroma.

'I brought you some chocolate cake,' he said, setting a plate in front of her with a big slice of dark, fudgy cake. 'You haven't had any dessert.'

'Thank you, but I don't really eat sugar.' She pushed the plate away.

'I think you should have something sweet. I get the feeling you may have had a shock.' He smiled ruefully to himself, shaking his head. Lisa got the feeling he was laughing at himself rather than her, but she didn't understand why.

She took a sip of her tea. 'What makes you think that?' she asked.

He looked at her carefully. 'You haven't done anything like this before, have you?'

'No,' she admitted, feeling very gauche. 'Did Mark tell you that?'

'No,' he said, his tone scathing, a contemptuous curl to his lip. 'He didn't.'

She blushed. He clearly found her lack of experience distasteful. Was that why he'd stopped – because he was disappointed? He'd obviously expected someone much more experienced and sassy – someone like Isabel. 'I'm sorry.'

He frowned. 'Christ, don't apologise! It was too much for your first time. It's perfectly understandable.' He shrugged. 'But why didn't you say something if you were uncomfortable?'

She shrugged. 'I didn't want to … spoil it for everyone.' She couldn't tell him the real reason – that she was afraid of Mark.

'Jesus!' He rolled his eyes. 'So you'd have let me—' He broke off, raking a hand through his hair in a gesture of frustration, his expression pained. 'I told you we'd stop anytime you wanted to. Didn't you believe me?'

'Yes, of course. But I thought I could … go through with it.'

He sighed. 'If Isabel hadn't come in when she did—'

'She said something to you.' Lisa frowned, still curious about their silent conversation. 'What was it?'

'Red.'

'Red? Just that?'

'It's a safe word she uses sometimes when we're, um, playing … certain games. It's a signal that she's not enjoying what we're doing and she wants to stop.'

'That's why you suddenly changed your mind,' she said. 'About having sex with me.'

'Yes. She saw that you were … overwhelmed. I'm sorry I didn't see it myself. I should have been paying more attention.'

'It's not your fault.' Lisa took a sip of her tea.

'You haven't touched your cake,' Grayson said, nodding to it.

She pulled the plate to her and picked up the fork on its side. Maybe she could eat it, just this once. She wasn't going to pile on the pounds after one slice of chocolate cake. And if Mark should find out, she could say that Grayson had insisted she eat it. Mark could hardly argue with that – not when he'd made her promise to go along with whatever happened tonight. If that included eating cake, then so be it.

She took a tentative bite of the cake, savouring the feel of the thick, glossy icing in her mouth. It was delicious – dense, moist and rich.

'I'm sorry if I've spoiled your fun. 'I mean I'm sure this wasn't how you expected the evening to pan out,' she said wryly. 'Drinking tea with me in the kitchen.'

'Don't be ridiculous. It's only fun when everyone's enjoying themselves. Anyway, Isabel is more into this sort of thing than I am, to be honest. I just go along with it for her sake – to make up the numbers, as it were,' he said with a crooked smile. 'I mean, it's no hardship, obviously. But it's not something I particularly crave.'

At least Grayson didn't appear angry that she had upset his plans for the evening. In fact, he seemed almost as embarrassed as she was. But she couldn't let it end like this. What if Mark discovered they hadn't had sex? He'd be so mad if she didn't keep her promise.

'It's not that I wasn't enjoying myself,' she said. 'It was just a bit of a shock when I realised what tonight was about, and it knocked me off balance. I felt a bit out of my depth because you all knew what was going on and I didn't. If I'd been prepared—'

Grayson went very still. 'What do you mean?' he asked, his voice laden with dread. 'What did you think was going to happen tonight?'

'I … I just thought we were going to have dinner.' She blushed at how stupid that sounded now. She felt such an idiot, realising she had been the only one out of the loop.

'Oh, Christ!' Grayson put his head in his hands. 'And then I practically assaulted you—'

'You didn't assault me. You couldn't have known—'

'I should have realised.'

'How could you?'

'Well, let's just say you're very different to the type of woman Isabel usually ropes in for her games.' He rolled his eyes expressively.

'But I wasn't unwilling – I never said no. I would have let you do whatever you wanted.'

'*Why*?'

'Because—' She looked down at her hands, wringing her fingers. 'I promised Mark I'd go along with whatever happened tonight.'

Grayson raised his eyebrows. 'But he didn't tell you what it would be?'

'No. He—he wanted it to be a surprise.'

'Jesus! I'm so sorry. Please believe I would never have touched you if I thought for a second it wasn't what you wanted.'

'It's okay,' she said, blushing. She just didn't want to talk about it. It was too mortifying.

'It's not okay,' he said angrily. 'Mark should have told you. He had no right to bring you into a situation like this unknowingly, like you're his toy to share. And I don't appreciate him making me party to it.'

Lisa flinched at the anger in Grayson's tone. He was furious about what Mark had done. What if he confronted him about it?

Grayson drained his cup and sighed heavily. 'Finish your cake,' he said, 'and then if you'd like to go home, I'll get you a car.'

'Oh.' Her heart started to pound. Obviously Grayson

meant to be kind, but he would just get her into trouble. But if he wanted to get rid of her, what could she do?

'Lisa?' He frowned at her. 'What's wrong?'

'Nothing. I just—' Maybe she could seduce him, she thought. It shouldn't be that difficult. He had been all set to have sex with her earlier. She put down her cup determinedly. 'Look, I was a bit overwhelmed earlier because I didn't know what to expect. I was taken aback, that's all. But I'm fine now. So, if you'd like to finish what we started earlier,' she said with a suggestive smile. She reached a hand out and touched his leg tentatively.

'Stop,' he said softly, putting a hand over hers.

Feeling rejected and humiliated, Lisa fought the urge to recoil. Instead she reminded herself how hot he'd been for her earlier. At least thanks to Mark she had plenty of experience appeasing men with sex. 'Like Mark said, I'm very good with my mouth.' She looked up at him seductively through her eyelashes. 'Why don't I show you?'

'Lisa, stop it,' he said gently, pushing her hand away, his expression almost pitying. 'Please.' He raked a hand through his hair. She could tell he was affected by her, but he was determined to resist her.

She swallowed hard. She couldn't let him send her home. If she couldn't seduce him, she was just going to have to throw herself on his mercy and hope for the best. 'Um … I'd like to wait for Mark, if that's okay. Would you mind if I stayed here until he's … ready to leave?'

'No, of course not.'

'Thank you,' she said, relieved.

'You're really enjoying that cake,' Grayson said with an indulgent smile as she forked up the last bite.

'It's delicious. I haven't had cake in a long time.' Maybe he was right and she'd needed the sugar, because she felt more relaxed now. Perhaps that was why she suddenly felt brave enough to be open with Grayson about what she wanted.

'Grayson, can I ask you a favour? Would you mind if we, um ...' Maybe she wasn't feeling so emboldened after all.

'What?'

She took a deep breath. 'I promised Mark I'd go along with whatever happened tonight, and ... well, I don't want to let him down.' She bit her lip. 'Would you pretend that we—that I—?'

'You want him to think we've had sex?'

'Um ... yes.'

'Sure, no problem – if that's what you want.'

'Thank you,' Lisa breathed a sigh of relief, finally able to properly relax. As the tension left her body, she suddenly felt overwhelmed by all the tension and emotional turmoil of the evening, and she found herself blinking back tears. She was aware of Grayson's eyes on her face, scrutinising her.

'Lisa,' he began tentatively. 'I don't really know you, and I'm sorry if this is out of line, but ... is Mark abusive? Are you afraid of him?'

'Oh no,' she said, striving to keep her tone light. 'He doesn't hit me, if that's what you mean.'

It was true, strictly speaking. She had used the present tense, and he didn't hit her anymore. But that was more down to the fact that she had learned to walk on eggshells and manage his moods than to any restraint on his part. He still hurt her physically in other ways. He was often rough with her during sex – biting and scratching, digging his fingers into her skin so hard he left bruises, fucking her violently until she could barely stand afterwards.

'There are other forms of abuse,' Grayson said. She

looked up to find him watching her face intently, and she hoped her dark thoughts hadn't shown on her features.

She gave him a reassuring smile. 'He just … gets frustrated with me.' She chose her words carefully. 'Like he said, he finds me very provincial and naive. He gets annoyed when I can't keep up. I'm trying to be more sophisticated, but …' She trailed off.

'You're lovely as you are.' Grayson lifted a hand as if to stroke her cheek, but then checked himself and dropped it.

'He finds me quite ignorant, I'm afraid,' Lisa said with a shaky smile. 'And he's right. There's so much I don't know about. I didn't finish college. I don't know about wine – I can't say clever things about it. I haven't travelled. There wasn't any money …' She trailed off. She shouldn't be telling him this. He was just being kind. He wasn't interested in her shitty life story.

'Those things aren't important,' he said, his eyes intent on hers. 'People don't care about that stuff – not people who are worth knowing anyway. What matters is what kind of person you are. You seem kind and decent, and anyone can see that you're intelligent. You don't need money or a degree to validate you. You shouldn't allow anyone to make you feel small because you haven't had the opportunities or advantages in life that they've had. That doesn't make them better or cleverer than you – just luckier.'

Lisa looked down at her hands. She felt tears stinging the backs of her eyes. He was being so kind, it was going to make her cry.

Suddenly the spell was broken by the sounds of shouts and high-pitched shrieking drifting in from the garden. Lisa blushed as her eyes flew to the glass doors leading to the terrace that wrapped around the side of the house, relieved that the hot tub was out of sight. Her eyes darted to Grayson, and he looked as uncomfortable as she felt.

'Well, you're probably going to be waiting a while,' he said. 'Why don't we go into the library? It's … quieter.'

'That would be good,' Lisa said gratefully. She could do without the humiliation of sitting here listening to Mark getting his rocks off with another woman. Not that she was jealous – Isabel was more than welcome to him. But it still made her feel pathetic and humiliated.

'Follow me,' Grayson said, standing.

5

Grayson led her back through the entrance hall to a room on the other side of the house. He opened the door and waved Lisa in ahead of him. The walls were lined with floor to ceiling bookcases, and little reading nooks were built into the alcoves. There was a sofa at one end under the window, and two big squashy armchairs in front of an oversized fireplace.

'What a beautiful room,' she said, smiling at Grayson as she stepped inside.

'Thank you. I like it. Have a seat. Would you like a brandy?'

'Yes, please.'

He nodded. 'Make yourself comfortable. I'll be back in a moment.'

When he was gone, Lisa explored the library. It was her idea of bliss. All the chairs looked so inviting, she couldn't decide where to sit. She could see herself spending hours curled up in one of the reading nooks, lost in a book, or in the depths of one of those armchairs in front of a roaring fire. Then her eyes lit on a chess board set up between the two armchairs, and she gravitated towards it. As she drew closer, she saw that there was an unfinished game in progress, and she couldn't resist checking it out. Sitting down in one of the chairs, she leaned over the board, examining the state of play. There were only a few pieces remaining, and she played the endgame in her head, her fingers dancing over the pieces as she worked out the moves each player would make. She didn't know whose turn it was, but she saw how Black could checkmate in one move. Her fingers hovered over the bishop as she tested the strategy from every angle. But there was no question about it, she decided. It was unbeatable. Her fingers were automatically reaching for the piece when the door opened, and she jumped back guiltily as Grayson came into the room carrying two globe glasses filled with an amber liquid.

'Sorry,' she said. 'I was just testing something. I would have put it back.'

'Be my guest,' he said as he placed the glasses on a low coffee table in front of the fireplace. 'You play chess?'

'Yes, I love it! My grandparents taught me – they were great aficionados of the game. I used to play a lot, but it's been a while.'

He sat in the chair opposite her. 'So, show me the move you were going to make,' he said, nodding to the board.

She hesitated a moment before picking up the bishop and moving it into position. 'Checkmate.'

His eyes scanned the board briefly, but she could tell he already knew it was game over. 'I win,' he said with a smirk, sitting back in his chair.

'You're Black?'

'Yes.' He picked up his brandy glass and lifted it to her in salute.

'Oh, that's not fair! I would never have left my king

exposed like that in the first place. I'd have seen that move coming a mile off.'

He grinned. 'Yeah, Isabel's not very good.'

'Oh, will she mind that I've finished her game?'

'No, she'll be delighted. She's not that fond of chess. She just plays occasionally to humour me.'

Like he plays her games, Lisa thought. 'Can we play?' she asked eagerly. The words were out of her mouth before she thought about it.

'Why not? I imagine we have plenty of time. But I warn you – I'm very good.'

She raised an eyebrow in challenge. 'So am I.'

'That's fighting talk.' He grinned at her. 'Okay, you're on.'

Grayson set up the board, and as they began to play, all Lisa's tension gradually seeped away. The brandy warmed and relaxed her, and she started to unwind and enjoy herself, forgetting the awkwardness of the situation as she became absorbed in the game. Grayson wasn't kidding when he said he was good, and it required all her focus and concentration to plan her strategy and try to anticipate his next move, leaving no room for self-consciousness. Besides, chess had such happy associations for her, just handling the familiar wooden pieces, following the time-honoured pattern of play took her to a better place. The familiar rhythm of the game was comforting. She could tell Grayson was enjoying himself too – she saw his eyes light up as he realised she was a worthwhile opponent.

'Your grandparents taught you well,' he said as he waited for her to make her next move.

'They did. We played all the time when I was a kid.' She couldn't help the automatic smile that came at the memory.

'You're close to your grandparents?' Grayson asked. 'You said they brought you up.'

'Yes, we were very close. But they're dead now.'

'I'm sorry.'

Lisa nodded in acknowledgement. 'They were both obsessed with chess,' she said, smiling fondly. 'They were fiercely competitive with each other. They kept up this epic ongoing rivalry all through their lives together, right up to the end. The scores were into the hundreds, but they always kept track.'

Grayson smiled. 'Who was ahead in the end?'

'My grandmother. My grandfather said she died when she did to spite him – because she was determined to quit while she was ahead.'

'They sound great.'

'They were. They were still full of life, even though they were old. They were such fun to be around. I miss them so much.'

'I'm sorry. If it's painful to talk about them—'

'No, it's nice. They're happy memories.'

She realised as she said it how much she had missed talking about her grandparents. Mark never wanted to hear about her life before him. He resented the idea of anyone else having a claim on her affection – even her family. He had subtly discouraged her from reminiscing about them, or anyone she had known before she met him. In the beginning he had said it was for her sake, to help her get over her loss. He didn't want her to upset herself by dwelling on the past. But now she saw that his motives had been purely selfish, and it hadn't helped at all – it had just made her sadder, and her grief more acute. Her grandparents had been a big part of her life, and she had nothing but happy memories of them. Suppressing those memories was like losing them all over again. It felt good to talk about them now, to acknowledge their place in her life, and it gave her a warm glow remembering how much love there had been in their home.

'So how did you meet Mark?' Grayson asked her.

She knew what he must be thinking. She and Mark looked like a very mismatched couple. He was ten years older than her, and it was obvious they came from very different worlds. 'He came to my college,' she said. 'It was our second year show.'

'What kind of art did you do?' he asked, his eyes alive with interest.

'Painting. Mark paid a lot of attention to me. He was very complimentary about my work. He sort of became my mentor.' She smiled wryly at the memory. 'He swept me off my feet.' She had been so flattered by such a distinguished and important art dealer as Mark taking notice of her, so pathetically grateful for any scrap of his attention. She'd been dazzled by him, impressed by his success, wealth and position in the art world. She'd been so proud he'd chosen her when he was surrounded by much more glamorous, sophisticated women. But she realised now he didn't want an equal, a woman like Isabel who would stand up to him and hold her own. He wanted someone as in awe of him as she had been.

'And yet you quit.' Grayson frowned.

'I moved in with Mark over the summer, and he suggested I defer my degree and take a year out. I'd been slogging to pay my way through college, working as a waitress every shift I could get, on top of looking after my grandparents. Then they died. I was exhausted and stressed out. He offered to support me so I could take time out to just paint. So,' she shrugged, 'I didn't go back to college in the autumn.'

'And you never went back? Why not?'

'It turned out I just wasn't very good.'

'Mark obviously thought you were talented. An endorsement from him really means something.'

'He soon changed his mind,' she said with a bitter laugh. 'I guess I didn't live up to my early promise. It happens. Even Mark makes mistakes. Taking that year out woke me up to how talented I really was in the grand scheme of things. I realised I'd never make it as an artist. I'd just have been wasting my time and money returning to college.'

Grayson narrowed his eyes, studying her carefully. 'That's a shame,' he said.

The truth was it was Mark who had knocked her notions of herself as an artist on the head. His initial admiration and praise of her work had quickly turned to constant criticism and scorn, until nothing she did pleased or satisfied him. His disappointment in her was obvious. He made it clear that he thought he'd been mistaken about her talent, and that he now saw her as a trite, talentless pretender unworthy of his time and attention. He had not only shattered her confidence in her work, but he had drained all the joy from it for her. Painting used to bring her such intense pleasure, but Mark's unceasing and increasingly irrational demands gradually turned it into a grinding chore; an endless, fruitless struggle to win the approval of someone who was impossible to please. His relentless derision had finally stamped out every shred of belief she had in her work and crushed her spirit to the point where she felt it was pointless to attempt anything because she already knew it wouldn't be good enough.

'Mark needed an assistant, so I started working at the gallery.' She realised now it had been part of his campaign to control every aspect of her life, so that it all revolved around him. He had gradually eroded everything she had for herself – her art, her work, her friends – until there was nothing in her life but him.

'But you don't work at the gallery now?'

'No. Mark needed someone more qualified, more in touch with the contemporary scene.' She tried to keep her voice even, not to betray how hurt she still was by that. It had broken her heart to leave the gallery. She had loved her job there. It had allowed her to keep up with the art world even if she couldn't really be part of it. She had wanted to scream at the injustice of Mark taking on a recent graduate to replace her, explaining that he needed someone better qualified and more ambitious – someone who was serious about building a career in the arts. He had actually had the gall to cite the fact that she had never finished her degree as evidence of her lack of commitment. She wanted to argue that he was the reason she had dropped out of college. He had persuaded her that she didn't need a degree and led her to believe that he would support her in her career. She had plenty of ambition and she would have been happy to build a career at the gallery alongside him. But she had said nothing, mindful not to do anything to provoke his anger. Instead she had stood mutely by while he whisked the rug from under her feet. That was when she first realised she was afraid of him.

It had been the final step in isolating her. 'I'm just a housewife now, I guess,' she said with a shrug.

'There's nothing wrong with that,' Grayson said, 'if it's what you want.' His smile was kind, but his eyes looked troubled.

'What about you?' she asked, desperate to take the focus off her. 'Did you always want to be an architect?'

'Well, not always. I did go through a phase where I wanted to be a power ranger.'

'Power ranger? Impressive.'

'Yeah, fighting crime in a spandex suit.'

'Mmm, you'd look good in spandex,' she smiled. God, was she flirting with him? It was a bit late for coyness considering the things he'd done to her in the kitchen.

'But once I realised I'd never qualify as a superhero, I guess architecture took over. Mainly I just wanted to wear a hard hat and drive a digger.' He gave her a boyish grin. 'But I always loved building stuff, and I was a whizz at Lego. So I guess it was on the cards from an early age. What about you? What did you want to be when you were a little kid?'

She grinned. 'It's a bit embarrassing.'

'Come on, I showed you mine, you have to show me yours.'

Lisa knew he didn't intend it to sound like innuendo, but she couldn't help blushing.

'It can't be more embarrassing than power ranger,' Grayson coaxed.

'Don't be so sure. At least yours was human. I wanted to be a mermaid.'

His eyes locked with hers, his gaze openly appreciative. 'Is this your way of distracting me, so I can't concentrate on my next move? Because it's working.'

Lisa blushed, remembering too late that mermaids weren't usually portrayed as modestly as the sweet and innocent Ariel from the Disney film that had fuelled her childhood fantasies. In folklore, they traditionally sat around naked on rocks, luring sailors to their doom.

''You'd make a beautiful mermaid,' Grayson said. 'But then, you'd make a beautiful anything.'

'I didn't want to just sit around combing my long hair, though.'

'I take it this ambition was inspired by the Disney version of *The Little Mermaid*?'

'Yes, Ariel was my idol. I wanted to save people who were drowning at sea.'

Grayson laughed. 'Especially if they were handsome princes?'

'It wasn't just about handsome princes. Little girls do dream about other things, you know. Though if one had come along, it would have been a nice perk of the job.' She had thought Mark was her prince, she thought, smiling at the irony of it.

'That's the drawback of being a power ranger,' Grayson said as he moved his knight. 'No time for romance.'

Lisa laughed. She couldn't believe how easy she was finding it to chat to Grayson, especially after what had happened in the kitchen. Occasionally an image of him sucking her nipples or licking her pussy would flash into her mind, and she would blush, feeling hot all over. But then he would say something and she'd become engaged in the conversation again, and forget to feel embarrassed and shy with him.

He was a skilled and clever chess player, and Lisa enjoyed playing with someone who could keep up with her. They were well matched, but Grayson won in the end.

'Checkmate,' he said, moving his final pawn into position with a little smile of triumph.

Lisa conceded defeat with a rueful smile. Then she held out her hand for the traditional handshake and he grasped it firmly.

'Thank you,' he said. 'I enjoyed that.'

'Me too. It was fun.'

'I haven't had such a challenging opponent for a long time. You really kept me on my toes.'

Lisa stifled a yawn and glanced at her watch. She was surprised to discover it was one-thirty. The time had flown.

She wished she could come over and play with Grayson again – but this wasn't the sort of 'play' he was interested in with her, she reminded herself. He wanted a fuck buddy, not a chess buddy. The poor man was probably bored out of his mind and itching for the evening to be over. He hadn't planned on spending the night playing chess and making small talk with a boring housewife.

'I guess we should go and find the others,' Grayson said, standing up.

Lisa stood, glancing nervously at the door. She took a deep breath. 'Could you not mention the chess? I promised Mark I'd join in with whatever went down tonight, and I— I don't want to disappoint him.' She twisted her hands nervously.

'You want to give him the impression I brought you in here to have my wicked way with you?' Grayson asked, with a mischievous grin.

'Yes,' she nodded.

'Sure.' Grayson said. 'Your chess-playing secret is safe with me.'

'Thank you.' She smiled at him in relief.

'Well, I guess we should look the part.' He took off his tie and unbuttoned his shirt, so it fell open, revealing a smooth, golden chest. Then he popped open the top button of his trousers and kicked off his shoes. He bent to remove his socks, then straightened and ran his hands through his hair until it was messy and dishevelled.

'How do I look?' he asked, holding his arms out to his sides.

He looked edible. Lisa nodded, swallowing hard. 'Good,' she choked.

'Now you,' he said, nodding at her.

'What?' Lisa asked dazedly.

'You don't look like you've just been ravaged.'

'Oh!' she jolted to attention. She hadn't realised she was just standing there gaping at Grayson.

'Here, let me help,' he said, stepping close to her. Gently he removed the pins from her hair, then he teased it out, running it through his fingers until it fell in a wild, tangled mess around her shoulders. His gaze dropped to her mouth and his eyes darkened as he ran a thumb across her lips, smudging her lipstick. Lisa felt her pulse quickening at the touch of his fingers against her skin.

'There. You look suitably debauched,' he said, releasing her.

'Thank you,' she said, kicking off her shoes. She picked them up, then Grayson took her hand lightly in his and led her out of the room.

They found Mark and Isabel sitting next to each other on the sofa in the living room. Lisa was relieved that they were both dressed again, though looking as mussed up and tousled as she and Grayson were.

'There you are,' Mark said, standing as they came into the room. He looked tired, Lisa noted with relief. She hoped Isabel had worn him out and they could go straight to sleep when they got home. She felt depressed suddenly, a sick knot of dread settling in her stomach at the prospect of going home with Mark. Weariness overcame her and all her earlier tension returned.

'Did you have fun?' he asked, holding out an arm to her.

She nodded as Grayson released her hand. She went to Mark and he put his arm around her, pulling her into his side and kissing the top of her head. 'Ready to go?'

'Yes.' But she wasn't. She wished she could stay here. She yearned to go back into the library with Grayson and curl up in that armchair. She had felt safe and warm there. She shivered, and Mark ran a hand up and down her arm. She dropped her shoes on the floor and stepped into them.

'Come on, let's get you home,' Mark said, curling a proprietary hand around her ass. Embarrassed, she dropped her eyes to the floor. Suddenly she looked up and her eyes met Grayson's and she gasped at the emotion she saw in his face. He looked almost … hurt. If she didn't know better, she'd have thought he was jealous. But that wasn't possible. She was being ridiculous and fanciful. So why did she feel so guilty, as if she were cheating on him? Why did it feel so wrong to let Mark touch her like this in front of him?

She shook off the feeling, but still found herself unable to look Grayson in the eye as he and Isabel saw them to the door.

Lisa was taken aback, but touched when Isabel put her arms around her and enveloped her in a hug. 'Thank you for coming,' she said. 'It was lovely to meet you.'

'Thank you. I'm sorry I was a bit—'

'You were perfect,' Isabel said, releasing her, and the warmth of her smile almost made Lisa well up. 'I hope we'll see you again sometime.'

'Thank you for a lovely evening,' Mark said as he shook Grayson's hand. 'You must come to us next time. Let's do this again soon.'

Lisa tensed. Grayson had put up with her tonight, but there was no way he'd want to spend another evening playing chess with her while Mark fucked his gorgeous girl-friend. She expected him to make some vague non-committal response, but to her surprise, he smiled smoothly at Mark and said 'I'd like that a lot,' his gaze drifting to her.

'Great! Give me a ring and we'll arrange a date,' Isabel said to Mark.

'I'll look forward to it,' Grayson said, turning to Lisa and tracing a finger lightly down her arm.

She smiled at him, grateful that he was keeping up the charade. 'Goodbye Lisa,' he said, eyeballing her as he took her hand and raised it to his lips in a sweetly chivalrous gesture. 'Until we meet again.'

6

GRAYSON AND ISABEL stood side by side in the doorway as Lisa and Mark got into the back of the waiting car and were driven away. Grayson watched wistfully as the car disappeared around the corner. He felt Isabel's arm go around his back as he closed the door.

'So, how was that for you?' she asked, shooting him a sympathetic look as they walked back to the living room together.

Grayson let out a long sigh. 'It was … interesting.' He raised an eyebrow wryly.

'Yeah,' Isabel laughed softly. 'Not exactly what I'd promised you.'

Grayson sat down on the sofa.

'Drink?' Isabel asked him, going to the cabinet.

'Yes, please.' He was tired and he'd already had more than enough to drink, but he needed time to get his head around everything that had happened tonight, and he wanted to discuss it with Isabel.

She handed him a large glass of brandy, then flopped down beside him, laying her head on his shoulder sleepily.

65

'So how did it go?' she asked him. 'What did you do with Lisa? I take it you didn't …'

'No.' Grayson turned to her. 'We played chess,' he said with a wry smile.

'Oh, God. Sorry.'

He shook his head. 'It's okay. I enjoyed it.'

'Still … it's not how you were expecting tonight to pan out.' Her fingers stroked his leg lazily. 'Let me make it up to you.'

'No, I'm fine,' he said, putting a hand over hers to still it.

'I feel responsible. And it would be no trouble.' She smiled, but her eyes were already drooping. He could see she was exhausted.

'Really, Issy, I'm fine. I had a good time. Anyway, you look worn out.' He stroked her hair affectionately as she laid her head back on his shoulder.

'I am pretty pooped.'

'Was it okay with Mark?' he asked, his fingers massaging her scalp lightly.

'Yeah, it was good. I mean he's pretty full-on. He's a takes-no-prisoners kind of guy, you know? He fucks hard and fast. But nothing I couldn't handle. I enjoyed it.'

Grayson thought of Lisa. She wasn't as strong and ballsy as Isabel. He wondered if *she* could handle it. She was so fragile and timid. He hated the thought of Mark being rough with her.

'Was he … aggressive?' He frowned.

'He didn't hurt me or anything. He was pretty rough, but you know I like that. He didn't scare me, and I wouldn't have let him push me further than I wanted. But Lisa …' She trailed off and a worried frown creased her brow.

'Yeah,' Grayson sighed. 'I think she's a bit afraid of him.'

Isabel nodded. 'Me too. That's why I didn't let him know I was calling a halt. I got the feeling she'd have gone through with the whole thing, just to please him.'

'She as good as told me she would have. Thanks for the heads-up that she wasn't into it. Christ, if you hadn't stopped me—' He broke off, horrified at the thought of what he might have done to Lisa, not knowing that she didn't want it. He shuddered.

'Thank goodness for safe words,' Isabel said, stroking his leg soothingly. 'Lisa should have had one tonight, though I suspect she wouldn't have used it even if she had. But Mark should have seen that it was too much for her. It was her first time playing with another couple – he should have looked after her, made sure she was okay.'

'It wasn't just her first time,' Grayson said. 'She didn't even know.'

'What?' Isabel frowned. 'What do you mean?'

'He hadn't told her anything about what would be happening. She thought it was just a normal dinner party.'

'Jesus!' Isabel gasped. 'That's not cool.'

'That's putting it mildly,' he said crossly. 'He got her to promise that she'd go along with whatever happened. And then he brought her here for me to fuck.'

'Oh, my God! That is seriously fucked up. What a manipulative asshole! I knew he was controlling and domineering, but that—' Isabel broke off with an indignant sigh.

'God, when I think of the way I mauled her at the table.' Grayson leaned forward on his knees and buried his face in his hands. He thought of the way Lisa had jumped when he'd touched her, filled with remorse as he realised now how shocked and frightened she must have been.

'You weren't to know,' Isabel said, rubbing his back soothingly. 'She wanted us to think she was into it. It's not your fault her boyfriend's an abusive ass.'

Grayson turned to her. 'Do you think—' He swallowed hard. 'Do you think he hurts her?'

'Maybe not physically,' Isabel said, her eyes full of concern, 'though it wouldn't surprise me. But he's certainly emotionally abusive. I hated the way he was with her at dinner – putting her down all the time.'

'I know – it was horrible to watch.' Grayson flopped back against the sofa.

'Well, we don't have to see them again,' Isabel said, taking his hand and playing with his fingers. 'When Mark calls, I'll make some excuse.'

'Actually … would you mind if we *did* go to their place?'

Isabel raised her head and looked at him in surprise. 'Really?'

'Only if you're into it, of course. If you don't want to be with Mark again—'

'No, it's fine with me. Like I said, I had a good time with him – even if he is an asshole to his girlfriend. Besides, I owe you for tonight. But what are you going to do? Play chess again?'

He shrugged. 'Maybe. I like chess.'

Isabel looked at him thoughtfully. 'You like *her*, don't you? Lisa?'

'Yeah,' he smiled. 'I did like her.'

'She seemed very sweet. But if you're going to spend another night playing chess with her, you're going to have to let me take care of you.' She slid a warm hand onto his thigh.

He shook his head. 'Really, I'm fine. And you're

exhausted.' He lifted her hand and kissed the knuckles. 'Why don't you stay in the spare room?'

'You're sure?' She stood, yawning, and swayed on her feet.

'Sure,' he said. 'You're worn out, and if you sleep in my bed you won't get any rest.'

'Okay, then. Goodnight.' She leaned over and kissed him on the forehead, and then she was gone.

Grayson sank back into the sofa and finished the rest of his brandy. He loved the easy friendly relationship he had with Isabel. She would come to bed with him now and make love if he wanted her to, and it would be good between them. They would give each other a lot of pleasure. But equally he could choose to go to bed alone without her feeling rejected or jealous, like he was blowing her off. They could discuss the fact that he liked another woman, she could tell him about being with someone else, and it didn't change anything between them. Sometimes he thought he would never have a relationship more perfect than what he had with Isabel. But tonight he just wanted be alone and think about a girl with big soft brown eyes and long hair the colour of a newly opened chestnut.

Was it his imagination, or had Lisa tensed up again as they were leaving? He had loved how open and warm she had been in the library once she had loosened up. And then he had brought her back to Mark and watched as all that relaxation drained away. It had made him sad to see her shoulders stiffen, her features becoming pinched and strained.

His fingers tightened around his glass as he thought of how her whole body had become rigid when Mark's hand curled around her ass, humiliation etched on her face. He hated watching Mark paw her in that crude, possessive way, and he had been shocked at how jealous he had felt.

He had badly wanted to punch Mark. And he could murder him for bringing her here and putting them both in such a horrendous situation. He had as good as sexually assaulted her, thanks to that fucker. What must she think of him? She was so sweet and innocent. After tonight she probably thought he was completely depraved. If only he could have met her in different circumstances, maybe …

He smiled wryly to himself. He was being ridiculous. What did it matter what she thought of him? It wasn't as if she was free anyway. She was with Mark, and whatever issues they had, they seemed to be committed to each other. The only relationship he could hope for with Lisa was as chess opponents – which was incredibly frustrating, because it was a long time since he'd met a woman who interested him as much, or who moved him the way she had.

He thought of her naked body spread out on the table earlier. She was exquisite. He would love to get past her shyness and discover her most intimate desires, to find out what pleased her, to feel her naked skin against his and watch her face when she came. He felt himself stiffen at the thought of making her come.

But it wasn't just about sex. He wanted to get to know her too. She seemed so aloof and withdrawn, but he'd seen a different side to her in the library. The way she'd played chess had taken him by surprise. He'd expected her strategy to be cautious and controlled, and instead it was reckless, abandoned and completely unpredictable. She'd made startling tactical sacrifices and constantly kept him guessing. It was risky and clever, and exhilarating to watch. She had kept him on his toes and forced him to raise his game, and she had almost defeated him.

He felt he'd caught a glimpse of who she really was when they'd been alone together. Away from the watchful presence of Mark, she'd let her guard down a bit. He smiled as he thought of the way her features had softened when she spoke about her grandparents. She had started to open up to him, and he wanted more of that. He wanted to hear about her childhood, her dreams, her ambitions; he wanted to get to know her likes and dislikes, her opinions and interests. He wanted to know everything about her. He was already looking forward to seeing her again.

He didn't think he'd ever felt so smitten by a woman before. He enjoyed sex and he liked the company of women. He'd had plenty of casual relationships in the past with women he liked and respected, but he'd never really been in love. He'd finally come to the conclusion that he just didn't have it in him, and reconciled himself to casual relationships that were friendly, fun and undemanding. He'd thought he simply wasn't capable of falling in love. Now suddenly he wasn't so sure.

7

LISA FELT nervy and on edge again on the drive home, all the comfort and ease she had felt with Grayson ebbing away and feeling more remote and out of reach the further they got from the house. She tried to gauge Mark's mood, darting surreptitious glances at him while forcing her hands to stay still in her lap. He didn't like when she fidgeted. He seemed in a good mood, she thought, a self-satisfied smile tugging at the corners of his mouth.

'Did you have fun tonight?' he asked, turning to her and placing a hand on her leg.

'Yes.' She forced a smile.

She was relieved when he smiled back, and realised she had been on tenterhooks, worried that somehow he had found out that she hadn't had sex with Grayson or that she had disappointed him in some other way. She had been poised for criticism – that she'd been too shy and inhibited, or hadn't held up her end of the conversation, or that she hadn't behaved in a sophisticated enough way … She knew from bitter experience the myriad ways she could displease him.

'I told you you'd enjoy yourself if you just let yourself go a little, didn't I?'

'Yes, you were right.'

'Your small-town prudishness is so vulgar.'

'I know. I just—I wish you'd warned me. Then I would have been prepared and I'd have known how to behave—'

He put a finger to her lips, silencing her. 'I didn't want you to get all nervous and worked up about it. You know how you fret. I thought it would be better if you didn't have time to over-think it. And I was right, wasn't I?' He smiled at her indulgently, but his eyes were steely.

'Yes,' she whispered against his finger.

'I just want what's best for you, Lisa. You know that, don't you?'

She nodded.

'I want to open your mind – and your body – to new experiences. But you know you can trust me. I would never bring you into a situation I didn't think you could handle. I always take care of my baby, don't I?' he asked, brushing her hair away from her face so she had to look him in the eye.

'Yes, you do.' She gave him a smile.

'So, you had a good time with Grayson?' he asked, pulling away and sitting back in his seat.

'Yes. I enjoyed … playing with him.' That was true at least, she thought, feeling a little glow of malicious satisfaction at having a secret from Mark.

'You like him?'

Lisa hesitated, unsure how to respond. What answer would please him most? Did he want her to like Grayson, or would he be jealous and angry if she seemed too enthusiastic? She suspected the fact that he had engineered the situation himself would be no guarantee against one of his fits of jealous rage.

'Yes, he was very nice,' she said warily.

'Nice!' he scoffed. 'Like the wine we had with dinner was *nice*? Really, Lisa, we're going to have to expand your vocabulary.'

'I'm sorry. I just meant—'

'Did he turn you on?' he asked impatiently. 'Does he fuck hard? Did he make you come?'

'You saw,' she said in a small voice, flicking a glance at Andrew in the front. The glass partition was up, giving them privacy in the back of the car. She knew he couldn't hear, but she still hated having this conversation when he was so close.

'When we went to town on you in the kitchen? Yes, I saw. That was hot. You were so sexy laid out on the table like that. But later – when you were on your own with him? Did he make you come again?'

'Yes, he— he made me come,' she stammered.

'Good.' He turned to her, taking her chin in his hand. 'Did you let him fuck your mouth?' he asked broodingly, tracing his thumb across her lips.

'Yes,' she said faintly. 'I—I sucked him off.'

'Good girl.' He leaned in and gave her a hard kiss on the lips. 'I was so proud of you tonight,' he said, pulling back a little, his breath hot on her mouth. 'Isabel is a beautiful woman, but no one turns me on like you do, Lisa.'

She sagged with relief that he wasn't displeased with her. As the car turned into the drive, she looked forward to bed, her eyes already starting to droop. It had been a very strange night, but somehow she had got through it. She had even enjoyed it in the end. She smiled as she thought of playing chess with Grayson in his beautiful library.

They got out of the car and Mark guided her up the path to the house with a hand at her back. Once the door was closed behind them, Lisa made straight for the stairs, but Mark grabbed her arm, yanking her back.

'My turn,' he said, his eyes burning into her. 'Take off your dress and get on your knees. I want your mouth.'

Lisa knew better than to protest or hesitate. She wished he could at least have waited until they were in the bedroom, where she would have had carpet to kneel on. But she did as he told her and quickly peeled off her dress, then sank to her knees in front of him on the hard tile of the hallway. His eyes were fixed on her breasts, glittering predatorily as her fingers went to the zip of his trousers.

'Open,' he instructed, tugging on her chin as she pulled down his boxers, setting his erection free. 'I'm going to fuck the taste of him out of your mouth.'

Then he grabbed her hair in both hands and rammed his full length into her mouth. Lisa's eyes watered as he thrust mercilessly, his cock bouncing off the back of her throat until she thought she would choke.

'Relax your throat, baby,' he grunted, one hand leaving her hair to stroke along her jaw line.

Lisa tried to swallow down her panic, forcing herself to relax. She stroked his balls, hoping it would make him finish more quickly. But he slapped her hand away.

'Stop that,' he snapped. 'Hands behind your back.'

She did as ordered, clasping her hands behind her and praying that it would be over soon, while he yanked her head back and forth so roughly that she felt her neck might snap. Finally, after a few more brutal thrusts, he came with a groan, his whole body shuddering as he pumped into her mouth, holding her head clamped to him so that she was forced to swallow every drop.

Don't cry, don't cry, don't cry, she chanted in her head like a mantra. She felt so weary, defeated and hopeless in that moment, she was perilously close to tears. But Mark didn't like it when she cried. It enraged him. So she got herself under control as she swallowed the last of his cum and he pulled out of her.

'You're amazing at that,' he panted, stroking her hair. 'No one gives head like you do, Lisa.' He pulled up his boxers and zipped up his trousers, then reached out a hand and helped her to her feet. 'Sorry if the floor was hard on your knees, but I couldn't wait. I just want you too damn much.'

Lisa forced a smile. She knew she was supposed to be flattered by the urgency of his desire for her. She swayed on her feet, stifling a yawn.

'Oh, baby, I've worn you out,' he said, stroking her hair tenderly. 'Sorry. It's been a tiring night for you, hasn't it?' He pressed a soft kiss to her forehead. 'Let me carry you.'

'Thank you,' she whispered as he scooped her up into his arms. She knew he would expect her to be grateful, touched by this show of tenderness. But that was all it was – a show. He was a brute with no gentleness in him. So she responded in kind, going through the motions and playing the part of his living doll. She had to grit her teeth and bear it for as long as it took, letting her end goal sustain her while she lulled him into a false sense of complacency with her submission and acquiescence. Her performance had to be seamless. He must never sense any reluctance or hesitation on her part, nothing that would give him the slightest suspicion that she was planning to leave him. Because if he knew, he would never let her go. She was playing the endgame of her life now, and she had to keep a clear head and see her strategy through. One wrong move could lose her everything.

So she wrapped her arms around his neck and curled up against him as he carried her upstairs. She smiled lovingly at him as he put her into bed. He quickly stripped off his clothes and got in beside her, pulling her into his naked body so that even in sleep there would be no escape from him. She nestled back against him and breathed a practised sigh of contentment.

His hands drifted lightly over her breasts. 'Have you made an appointment with the surgeon yet?' he whispered into her hair, as if he were speaking words of love, and she had to force herself not to recoil from him.

'No,' she whispered shakily. 'Not yet.'

She tensed, waiting for him to say more, but he fell asleep, his deep, rhythmic breathing coming as a relief.

However, her respite was short-lived. He broached the subject again the following morning over breakfast. She always got up an hour before him on weekdays to fulfil her role as dutiful housewife. This morning, she had slipped out of bed and pulled on a robe, then pressed the snooze button on the alarm for one hour while he turned over and went back to sleep and she padded downstairs to get breakfast ready. By the time he came down, handsome and fresh in a sharp suit and crisp white shirt, she had baked bread rolls and brewed coffee, and there was a jug of freshly squeezed orange juice at the prettily laid table. It was a picture-perfect scene, she thought, like something out of a magazine – the doting, devoted housewife sharing breakfast with her handsome, distinguished man.

'You should ring the cosmetic surgeon today, set up an appointment for a consultation,' he said as soon as he sat down, shattering the illusion in an instant.

Lisa bit her lip, desperately trying to think of an excuse for not doing it that wouldn't anger him.

He gave her a sympathetic look. 'Come on, baby. I know you're nervous about it—'

'You know hospitals scare me,' she said, clutching at the slightest glimmer of understanding from him. Perhaps she could play on his sympathy. 'I don't want to have an operation that I don't need.'

He reached across the table and stroked her cheek. 'You want to please me, don't you?'

'Yes, of course.' That was true. She really did want to please him, because she knew she would suffer the consequences if she didn't.

'I just want you to be the best possible version of yourself you can be,' he said.

As if he was some sort of personal development guru, she thought, swallowing down her fury.

'I know,' she said quietly.

'Everything I do is for you.'

'I just—'

'Sometimes I think you don't appreciate how lucky you are,' he said, a chill creeping into his tone that made Lisa shiver. 'I'm happy to lavish my money on you, so you can make the most of yourself, and all you can do is quibble.'

'I know how much you do for me, and I'm grateful,' she said quickly, her smile appeasing.

'Are you?' He studied her, his eyes flinty now. 'Sometimes I wonder. I work bloody hard so you don't have to. I keep you in luxury, give you the best of everything. Most women would be thrilled to have a man take care of them the way I take care of you.'

'I know how lucky I am,' she said earnestly, putting a hand over his. 'You're so generous to me, and I do appreciate it.'

'So why do you defy me when I ask you to do one little thing for me in return?'

Little thing, she thought – it's major surgery. 'It's just—don't you think maybe I should wait to get it done until winter? There'll be bruising, and I won't be able to go topless – maybe not even wear my lovely bikinis.' They were due to go on holiday to Mauritius in four weeks, and Mark had already bought Lisa a new wardrobe for the trip, mainly consisting of sexy lingerie and very skimpy bikinis.

He studied her in silence for a moment, as if weighing up her motives. 'Maybe you're right,' he said eventually. 'There'll be recovery time too. You'll probably be out of bounds for a while. That wouldn't be much fun on holiday, would it?'

'No,' Lisa smiled, relieved.

'Perhaps it would be best if you could schedule it for some time when I'm away, so you'll have done most of your recovering by the time I get back.'

'Good idea.' Inwardly her skin crawled at the way he thought of her as if she were his toy, her body just something that existed for his pleasure.

'That's settled then,' he said, smiling warmly at her. 'Next year you'll be able to hold your own with any woman on the beach.'

Lisa seethed. She wasn't ashamed of her body, and she had no intention of getting it hacked up to please Mark. She had no complex about the size of her breasts. They were smaller since she had lost weight, but she was still by no means flat-chested. She just didn't happen to live up to Mark's image of the ideal female shape. Well, there would be no more holidays with him – not this year or next. She took a slug of coffee and reached absent-mindedly towards the basket of rolls she had baked freshly this morning.

Mark's tutting stayed her hand. 'I don't think that's a good idea, do you?' he said smoothly. 'You don't want to get fat.'

'No,' she mumbled, withdrawing her hand.

'You know you can't eat bread. It bloats you.'

She nodded as he stood. 'I wasn't thinking.'

'Lucky you have me looking out for you,' he said. He

came around to her side of the table and kissed her on the forehead. 'You know I remind you of these things for your own good, don't you? I just want the best for you.'

'Yes. I know.'

'Just salad for lunch, yes?'

'Yes, of course.'

'That's my girl.' He bent and gave her a lingering kiss, his tongue parting her lips and invading her mouth, while one had slid inside her robe, grabbing her breast. He pulled away then and went down on his haunches in front of her, opening her robe. 'I can't wait until these are done,' he said, running his hands over her breasts. 'We decided on a D-cup, didn't we?'

Like he was choosing a new car, she thought disgustedly, struggling not to show her revulsion. And there was no 'we' — he had decided the whole thing. But she just nodded.

'Maybe we should go bigger,' he said, with a wicked grin. 'Treat ourselves. What do you think?'

Lisa shrugged. 'It's up to you.'

'Well, we can think about it. If you're not having the operation for a while, we have some time to decide. I wonder what size Isabel is …'

Lisa must have allowed some flicker of emotion to cross her face because Mark frowned. 'Oh, baby,' he said soothingly, 'don't look like that. You've nothing to be jealous of. You know that, don't you?'

She nodded.

'You're way sexier than Isabel just as you are, even without the boob job.' He looked up earnestly into her face. 'You know I love you, don't you, Lisa?'

'Yes, I know.' She forced a facsimile of an adoring smile. 'I love you too.'

'The operation will give you more confidence, you'll

see. You won't feel so insecure about other women once you've had it done.' He rubbed his thumbs idly over her nipples, his eyes darkening as he watched them harden.

'Now you've got me hard again, you sexy girl. You're going to have to take care of that.' He rose to his feet, unzipped his trousers and pulled them down along with his boxers. His cock was already hard and thick. He snapped his fingers and pointed to the floor in front of him.

Lisa must have let her irritation show in her face as she slid out of her seat because he said 'Come on, baby, don't be a morning grouch.' She was relieved that he smiled teasingly at her as he said it and he wasn't really angry. It was lucky he was in a good mood this morning, and she'd got away with it. But she had to be more careful about letting her feelings show – a slip-up like that could cost her dearly.

'It's all your fault for being so gorgeous,' he said.

She didn't hesitate any longer, sinking to her knees in front of him and taking him in her mouth.

'Be quick,' he said, grabbing her hair. 'I don't want to be late.'

She was more than happy to get it over with. She stroked his balls as she sucked him deep, knowing how to make him come quickly. It didn't take long until he was pumping into her mouth.

'You're amazing,' he panted, stroking her jaw as she swallowed. 'Now you've got me all messed up again and I don't have time for another shower. You're going to have to clean up after yourself.'

She did as she was told, licking him clean. Then she tucked his cock back into his boxers and zipped up his trousers.

'Thank you.' He took her hand and helped her to her

feet, then bent and kissed her tenderly on the mouth. 'I love you so much.'

'I love you too,' she said automatically, a programmed response.

'I'd be lost without you, Lisa. You're mine,' he said, his thumb stroking her mouth as he looked down at her. 'Remember that.'

'I'm yours,' she said. 'Only yours.'

He smiled, tugging a strand of her hair. 'I'm sorry I don't have time to take care of you.'

'That's okay.' *Thank God!* She cringed at the thought of him touching her now.

'You're so good to me. I don't deserve you. But I'll make it up to you tonight.'

'I'll hold you to it.' She forced her lips into a smile.

'Now I really do have to go.' He gave her one last lingering kiss on the lips, then made for the door. 'I'll see you tonight. I won't be late. And I'll call.'

'Okay.' Of course he would call. He always called. At least once a day he phoned to check up on her, to make sure she was still here. If she didn't answer there would be an inquisition later as to where she'd been.

He turned around in the doorway. 'Don't touch your-self today, okay? I know you're probably dying to get off, but save it for me tonight.'

'Okay.'

'I promise you it'll be worth it.' He gave her a lasciv-ious grin, and then he was finally gone.

8

Lisa waited for about ten minutes after Mark was gone, her emotions in turmoil, flitting between fury and despair. She didn't know if she wanted to kick something or just burst into tears. When she was sure he wouldn't be back, she got up and ran upstairs to her bedroom. Mark had been right that she was desperate to touch something, but it wasn't herself. She rummaged through the drawer in her nightstand, quickly uncovering the old jewellery box she kept buried at the bottom. Then she sat on the bed and opened it, savouring the moment as she took out the envelope that was inside and tipped its contents onto the bed. The sight of the money strewn across the counterpane soothed her, and for a while she just gazed at it, letting it work its magic. Then she picked up the notes and counted them again and again until she felt her helpless rage dissipate and a sense of calm return.

She had been squirreling money away for almost six months now. She had to keep it in cash because she couldn't risk paperwork turning up that might alert Mark to what she was doing. He controlled all the finances, and while he spent lavishly on her, he kept a very close watch on everything she spent herself. She could only save a very little at a time by shaving pennies off the grocery shopping or 'losing' receipts and lying to Mark about how much something had cost.

It gave her a feeling that she had some control over her life. Progress was agonisingly slow, and sometimes she was tempted to leave right away and take her chances. But realistically she knew that wouldn't be a good decision. If she wanted to be really free of Mark, she couldn't do it in a half-assed way. She would have to get as far away as possible and start a new life somewhere else. It would take time to find a job, and she'd need enough to live on for a few months at least. So she had to grit her teeth and play the compliant Stepford wife for a while longer. It would pay off in the end, she told herself as she gathered up the money and stuffed it back into the envelope.

She returned the jewellery box to the drawer and took out the little photo album she kept there alongside it. She smiled to herself as she turned the pages, feeling a sense of wellbeing settle over her. The images from her childhood conjured up such happy memories – her grandparents standing with their arms around each other in their garden, squinting into the sun; Lisa and her grandmother on the beach at Brighton; playing chess with her grandfather in front of a blazing fire, a Christmas tree twinkling in the background.

She looked at these pictures from time to time to remind herself of what she wanted to get back to. She had lost sight of that laughing, carefree girl a long time ago. Now she stared at the photos wonderingly, trying to remember what it had felt like to be so secure, to know she was loved unconditionally, and to have such confidence in the world and her future. Sometimes it all seemed so remote from her that it was as if the girl in the photographs was a different person. She had to remind herself that this was who she really was; not the tense, cringing creature Mark had turned her into, afraid of her own shadow.

Her grandparents would hardly recognise the person she'd become, she thought, tears stinging her eyes. They'd be so disappointed. They hadn't raised her to be so spineless. Maybe it was a good thing they couldn't see what a mess she'd made of her life. They wouldn't understand why she had tolerated Mark's abuse for so long, and it hurt to imagine how shocked and bewildered they'd be if they knew.

She wouldn't be able to explain it to them – she hardly understood it herself. It had happened so insidiously. She had been at a very low ebb when she met Mark. Looking back now, she could see how vulnerable she had been. She had had a tough couple of years since leaving school, her grandparents constantly in and out of hospital, lurching from one health crisis to the next, and she had been permanently on edge, waiting for the results of tests and the outcome of operations. At the same time she had been trying to concentrate on her art studies as well as working two jobs to pay her way through college.

Then her grandparents had died within five weeks of one another. When Mark came into her life she was lonely and exhausted, struggling to cope with her grief and the stress of her workload. He had been kind and generous, and he'd used his money to make her life easier and more comfortable. After years of being the carer, it had felt good to have someone look after her for a change – even spoil her a little.

Mark hadn't seemed controlling then, just capable and caring, intent on making her happy. He had been so charming in those early days. Thoughtful, sweet and romantic, he was the perfect boyfriend. Even now with the benefit of hindsight, she couldn't see any warning signs that should have put her on her guard. He had been possessive, but she had found that flattering. They were in love, and it was natural for it to be intense in the heady early stages.

Later, as she came out of the fog of grief and loneliness that had enveloped her since her grandparents' death, their relationship had started to feel suffocating. But it would have seemed arbitrary then to ask Mark to back off and give her some space. She had been so grateful for his attention before. Besides, she loved him and she didn't want to hurt his feelings. She thought that as their relationship grew, it would naturally evolve into something calmer and steadier.

Instead his fixation on her only grew stronger, and as she started to see things more clearly, she realised she had gradually let him take over her entire life. It had happened by degrees, almost without her noticing, a series of decisions and choices that had all seemed innocuous and rational at the time. It had made sense to move in with him to save money on rent when they were spending all their time together anyway. She understood when he didn't want to spend time with her friends, who were all so much younger than him. It had been a relief to give up her part-time jobs and let him support her so she could concentrate on her studies. When he encouraged her to take a year out from college, she had felt like the luckiest girl in the world to be given the opportunity to paint full-time for a year. It hadn't felt like free-loading. It was only until she finished college, and besides, Mark was going to sell her work through his gallery and he was confident he would soon be earning high commissions on it.

She had made so many allowances and compromises. For his sake, she had divided her life into compartments, keeping her friends separate because Mark didn't get on with them. But he wasn't happy with that either. He resented her going out without him, and accused her of sleeping with other men when he wasn't around. To appease him, she had stopped going out with her friends, and instead invited them to the house. But he had alienated them all, making no secret of his dislike for them. They had persevered for a while, but he was rude and dismissive, treating them with contempt until eventually, one by one they had drifted away. In the end, Lisa was relieved when they gave up. She couldn't endure any more nights of tension, watching him humiliating and insulting people she cared about.

It was only then, when she was in so deep there was no way out that he began to show his true colours. He became increasingly impatient with her, frustrated with her lack of education and experience, contemptuous of her work, scornful of her efforts to please him. He started to criticise everything about her – the way she dressed, how she looked, the way she spoke and the things she said – until she felt she could do nothing right. Even sexually, he found her inadequate. Still desperately in love with him, Lisa had learned to cope with his violent mood swings, trusting that if she just waited and rode out the storm, the man she had fallen in love with would return. He always did, and she lived for those times. He made her feel so special and cherished. Filled with remorse, he would plead with her not to leave him, and she would forgive him, glad to have the real Mark back.

But soon the good days were outweighed by the bad, and she started to wonder if she'd ever known the real Mark at all. He had slowly chipped away at her confidence and eroded her self-esteem until she barely felt like a person anymore, and then he had taken control. Scared of losing him, she had been an easy target for his manipulation, and she turned herself inside out trying to be what he wanted. He thought she was too fat, so she went on a diet. He liked her in high heels, so that was what she wore. She always gave in, at first because she was desperate to please him; later because she was afraid of him. Gradually her whole life became circumscribed by his rules and demands. He would lay out the clothes he wanted her to wear when they went out. He ordered for her in restaurants, and if they were eating at home, he told her what to cook. She tied herself in knots trying to please him, but it was never enough. His rages became steadily more terrifying, and she was constantly on edge, second-guessing her every move, fearful of his reaction.

The first time he had hit her, he had been so wracked with remorse, she had actually felt sorry for him. Consumed by guilt and self-loathing, he had sobbed in her arms like a child, swearing it would never happen and begging for her forgiveness. Her stomach turned over now at the thought of how she had comforted him, assuring him that she trusted him and promising that she would never leave. She saw now with sickening clarity that she had been setting a precedent – giving him permission to do it again; reassuring him that she would tolerate anything.

If only she had walked out there and then. Maybe he would have let her go. But she had been naive and trusting – and desperate to be loved, if she was honest with herself. When he told her he would change, that things would be different, she was all too eager to believe him. She'd been so besotted, one word of praise or admiring look from him meant the world, while his touch lit up her whole being. It had made her so happy knowing he loved her and wanted her.

His sweet words and affectionate gestures meant nothing to her now. In fact, she dreaded them. She knew they were meaningless and she hated the pretence. Sex had become something she merely endured. Sometimes she couldn't help her body responding to his touch, but she resented him for making her come, feeling only humiliation that he could still exert his will over her in that way.

She preferred to be numb. And mostly these days she was. She played dead, sleepwalking her way through her life on autopilot, hardly caring whether he hit her or kissed her – it was all the same in the end. She was simply surviving, breathing in and out, biding her time until she could get far, far away from him and start living again.

Sometimes she wondered if she could make it by herself. It had been a long time since she had been independent, and she had nothing of her own left – no money, no friends, no work. She hardly even knew who she was anymore. But last night she had felt a new sense of hope. She smiled as her thoughts strayed to Grayson and the time she had spent alone with him in the library. Despite all the embarrassment and humiliation she had suffered last night, ultimately it had buoyed her up and emboldened her. For the first time in a long time, she had felt like herself again. Playing chess with Grayson, talking about her grandparents, her childhood, her artistic ambitions – it had brought her back to herself. She remembered what it was like to be that person, and it had felt possible that she could be that person again.

9

Lisa felt a mixture of excitement and apprehension the following Saturday evening, as she put the finishing touches to the preparations for dinner. Mark had rung Isabel during the week, and they had arranged for her and Grayson to come over tonight. Her heels clicked on the polished tiles of the floor as she moved around the table, giving a final tweak to the artfully arranged glasses and silverware, making sure everything sparkled. She had spent the past two days planning, shopping, cooking and making both the house and herself beautiful for the occasion. When she wasn't arranging flowers and planning the menu, she was having manicures and facials, and generally getting herself primped and preened so she wouldn't look out of place in Mark's picture-perfect dinner party scene.

She smoothed the pale blue runner that ran down the centre of the table so that it lay perfectly flat, then arranged candles along it. She was placing an arrangement of white roses in the centre when Mark appeared in the doorway.

He crossed the room and pulled her into his arms. 'This looks lovely,' he said, his eyes scanning the table.

'Thank you,' she smiled.

He dropped a kiss on her shoulder. 'And you look amazing.'

He had insisted on buying her a new outfit for the evening. He had taken her shopping, and chose a short black leather skirt and sheer black chiffon top. It was very daring and sophisticated, the sort of thing an A-list star might wear on the red carpet. The top was completely see-through, and Mark had insisted that wearing anything underneath would completely spoil the effect. She tried not to look as uncomfortable and embarrassed as she felt in the gossamer-thin black blouse that clung to her like a second skin, her naked breasts clearly visible through the filmy material.

'You're so beautiful,' he said now, holding her arms out to the sides while his gaze swept over her. 'I like you wearing clothes that show off your body.' There was a hunger in his eyes that once would have set her pulses racing.

'You look very sexy yourself,' she said, smiling up at him. He was wearing a beautifully cut black suit with a grey silk shirt open at the neck.

'You're in a very good mood,' he said. 'Excited about seeing Grayson again?'

She hesitated, her smile faltering. Was it that obvious? She liked Grayson and she *was* looking forward to seeing him, even though she wished she didn't have to be half naked when she did. But what was the right answer? Did Mark *want* her to be excited about seeing another man or would it make him angry and suspicious?

'Don't worry,' he said with a teasing smile, tucking a

strand of hair behind her ear. 'I won't be jealous. This was my idea, remember?'

'I'm only doing this for you, Mark. If it was up to me, I wouldn't be with anyone but you.'

'I know. It's only because I know you feel that way that I can do this. If I felt insecure about you, the thought of you with anyone else would drive me crazy.' He smoothed her hair, looking into her eyes. 'You know it's the same for me, right? You know you have nothing to be jealous of?'

She nodded.

'This is just a bit of fun … recreation. It doesn't mean anything. You're my life, Lisa.' He bent and gave her a soft kiss on the lips. 'But I like to see you letting go of your inhibitions and having fun.'

'It *is* fun.'

'See,' he said, 'I know what's best for you.'

'Always,' she replied.

'So, what are we having for dinner?'

'There's crab salad to start, then rack of lamb with spring greens and new potatoes—'

'No potatoes for you, though,' he said with a playful tap on her nose.

'No.' She maintained her light smile with an effort. 'And for dessert, we're having poached pears with iced pear parfait.'

'Sounds excellent. Everything's under control then?'

She nodded. 'Yes.'

'Good. I have something to give you,' he said, taking her hand and pulling her from the room.

He led her upstairs to their bedroom. Sitting down on the bed, he pulled her to stand in front of him.

'You're stunning,' he said, his eyes raking over her appraisingly. 'That top is incredibly sexy. And your legs look fantastic in this skirt.' He ran a hand up one stockinged leg. 'I knew they would.'

'You have great taste,' she said, resisting the urge to tug at the hem.

'There's just one finishing touch I'd like to add,' he said, his eyes glittering wickedly. 'An accessory I want you to wear.'

'Oh?' Lisa tried to look pleased and curious about the gift.

He opened the top drawer in the nightstand, and took out a small box. Lisa caught a glimpse of something small and silver as he opened the lid and took out whatever was inside – a piece of jewellery, she assumed, but she couldn't make out what.

Mark curled a hand around her ass and pulled her closer so she was standing between his legs. Then he held the object up to show her. It was small and egg-shaped.

'I want you to wear this,' he said.

Lisa peered at it. It looked like a pendant, but there didn't appear to be a chain. 'What is it? How do I wear it?'

He smiled crookedly and pulled her closer, sliding one hand between her legs under her skirt. 'You wear it like this,' he said, pulling her knickers aside and spreading her open with his fingers. She gasped as he pushed the egg inside her and pressed it against her clit. 'How does that feel?'

'O—okay,' she said faintly, frowning at him in confusion.

He took another small object from the drawer, and to her horror she saw it was a tiny remote control. 'How does it feel now?' he asked with a smirk as he pressed a button on the remote. Lisa gasped, her eyes widening as she felt the little egg vibrate inside her. She pressed her thighs together in panic, trying to contain the feeling as the vibrator stimulated her clitoris. 'G—good,' she choked out, putting a hand on Mark's shoulder for support.

To her relief he switched it off, smiling up at her flushed face as she relaxed. 'I don't want to get you all wet before our guests come,' he said as he stood, sliding the remote control into his pocket.

'You want me to wear this ... now? At dinner?' she asked faintly, her heart pounding with dread.

'Yes, I do.'

Was he going to give Grayson the remote control – another toy for him to play with, along with her?

'I want to know you'll be thinking of me. Even when you're with him, you're mine, Lisa. Only mine.'

'I don't need this to remind me,' she protested. 'Mark, you know I only agreed to be with Grayson to please you. Please don't—'

'Ssh,' he said softly, placing a finger on her lips, but his eyes were cold and flinty with warning. 'You know I wouldn't do anything to hurt you, don't you?'

She gulped and nodded.

'You're the most precious thing in the world to me, Lisa. I just want to help you to push your boundaries, explore your sexuality. I wouldn't do anything I didn't think you could handle. You trust me, don't you?'

She nodded, blinking back tears.

'Good girl.' He placed a soft kiss on her forehead, then smiled down at her, rubbing her arms comfortingly. 'It'll be fun, you'll see. You enjoy yourself when you let go of your inhibitions. You did the last time, didn't you?'

'Yes, but—please,' she begged. 'I'm not ready for this. It'd be so humiliating—'

He frowned. 'You think I want to humiliate you?' He looked wounded.

'No,' she hastened to reassure him. 'I know that's not your intention. But that's how I'll feel.'

He sighed. 'Do you think you could try to get past those feelings? For me?'

'I am trying,' she said. 'I just need more time. Please be patient with me.'

He frowned slightly, a dangerous flicker of annoyance in his eyes. 'Haven't I been patient?'

'Yes, you have, and I'm grateful. But this isn't easy for me. I'm trying to be more sophisticated and uninhibited, I really am. But it's not easy for me. I need to take it slowly. I was really looking forward to this evening, but I won't be able to relax and enjoy it.'

'Baby steps, eh?' He smiled down at her indulgently and she relaxed a little. She could see he was relenting. 'Okay. How about a compromise?' He pulled the remote from his jacket pocket. 'I'll leave this here.' He put it back in the drawer and slid it shut, and Lisa nodded eagerly. 'But will you do something for me in return?'

'Yes, anything.'

'Leave the vibrator in? It will please me just knowing it's there, and you can get used to the idea of it without worrying about me playing with it in public. It'll be our secret.'

Lisa hesitated.

'The remote will be safely shut away in that drawer. You do trust me, don't you?'

'Yes, of course,' she answered hastily.

'So we have a deal?'

'Yes.' She nodded enthusiastically. 'Thank you.'

'No problem.' He drew her into his arms and kissed her. 'I forget sometimes how shy you are,' he said, studying her face as he stroked her hair. 'You need to get over that.'

'I'm trying, honestly,' she said with a shaky smile.

'I know you are, and it means a lot to me that you try for my sake. But we can take it as slow as you like, baby.'

'Thank you,' she whispered, sagging with relief.

'Maybe we can play with that later when we're alone,' he said, jerking his head at the drawer.

'I'd like that.'

'Come on.' He held out a hand to her. 'Let's go down. Our guests will be here soon.'

'I just need to touch up my make-up,' she said. 'I'll follow you down in a minute.'

She waited until Mark had left the room, then opened the drawer to reassure herself that the remote was still there before following him downstairs.

When they opened the door to their guests, Lisa was surprised by how happy she was to see Grayson again. He handed her a bunch of flowers as they stepped inside, kissing her on the cheek while Mark took Isabel's wrap.

'Thank you. They're beautiful,' she said as she took the flowers from him.

'Not as beautiful as you,' he said. 'You look stunning.'

'Thank you.' She blushed as his eyes dropped to her breasts before sweeping back up to her face. She felt so exposed, and longed to cover herself up.

Isabel greeted her warmly. 'You look beautiful,' she said as she embraced her.

The conversation flowed easily over dinner, and Lisa relaxed as everything went without a hitch, relieved that Mark had no cause for complaint. The food was perfect, and Grayson and Isabel showered her with compliments.

'Lisa is a very talented cook,' Mark said, beaming at her with pride.

'This is a great house,' Isabel said over dessert. 'You have some wonderful pieces.' She nodded to the artwork on the walls.

Mark turned to her and they began discussing art.

'I'd like to see some of *your* work,' Grayson said, turning his attention to Lisa. 'Do you have any here?'

'Oh, no. My stuff isn't good enough to put on show. I was just a hack. I don't do it anymore anyway.'

'Still, I'd like to see some.' He looked at her intently, like she was the most fascinating person on the planet and he was trying to figure her out. 'It's such a shame you gave up.'

'You wouldn't say that if—oh!' Lisa gasped in shock as she felt a pulsating sensation between her legs. She'd forgotten about it over the course of dinner, but the little egg was vibrating inside her. Yet how could it be? She'd checked the drawer last thing before she came downstairs to make sure the remote was still there, and it had been. She glanced across the table at Mark. He was turned away from her, seemingly engrossed in conversation with Isabel. But one of his hands was in his jacket pocket.

As another wave of sensation rippled through her, she gasped again, grasping the table.

'Lisa? What's wrong?' Grayson frowned in concern.

'Nothing,' she said shakily, pressing her thighs together and trying to control her breathing. But her whole body jerked as the vibrations intensified and she bent over, clutching her stomach, trying to absorb the sensations.

'Are you ill?' Grayson asked urgently, pulling her hair away from her face. 'What's the matter?'

She shook her head, biting hard on her lip and trying desperately to regain control as the ripples of pleasure built deep inside her.

Grayson looked anxiously across at Mark. Mark turned to him finally, a wide smile spreading across his face.

'She's fine,' he said. He pulled the little remote control from his pocket then and held it up for them all to see. 'I'm just toying with her.' His eyes glittered with cruel intent, watching Lisa as he pushed a control on the device and the pressure on her clit increased.

'Mark —please—' Lisa gasped, her eyes pleading with him, begging him not to do this. It was his way of bringing her to heel, of showing her she was his. She had been talking about her art and he hated when she talked about her art. She clutched her stomach, praying for it to end. How could he humiliate her like this? 'Please,' she whispered.

'Please – more?' he asked with a wicked grin, sliding the control on the remote.

Lisa whimpered helplessly as the vibrations intensified, stimulating her sensitive nerve endings relentlessly and pushing her over the edge. She bent her head, tears stinging her eyes as her body shook uncontrollably. All she could hear was the pounding of blood in her ears as she lost control. She kept her head down, her hair hiding her face. She couldn't look at any of them. She felt so humiliated. She was vaguely aware of Isabel's voice telling Mark to stop, and Mark joking that it would be cruel to stop now. But their voices sounded far away and muffled.

Then she felt Grayson's strong arms around her, pulling her into his lap. He wrapped his arms tightly around her, and she clutched his shirt, burying her face in his shoulder as her orgasm ripped through her.

'Ssh,' he whispered, running his hand up and down her spine, and stroking her hair soothingly as the spasms finally subsided. As her body went limp, she burst into tears. She couldn't help it – she was too overwrought. But she quickly regained control of herself, blinking away the tears and wiping her eyes before she lifted her head. She kept her eyes downcast, too embarrassed to look at anyone.

'That was hot,' Mark said. 'Would anyone else like a turn?' He waved the remote in the air.

'Don't be such a jerk!' Isabel snapped at him.

'She enjoyed it,' Mark protested. 'Didn't you, Lisa?'

She nodded dumbly. She knew better than to contradict him.

But Isabel had no such compunction. 'She didn't seem to be enjoying it to me.' Then, her tone softening, she asked 'Are you okay, Lisa?'

Lisa raised her eyes then. Isabel looked mutinous, and Lisa could tell she was ready to call Mark out on his behaviour. 'Yes, I'm fine,' she said, trying to sound as cheerful as she could. Isabel's concern was touching, but she would pay for it later if Mark was made to look bad in front of their guests.

'Are you sure?' Isabel asked uncertainly.

'Yes, really,' she insisted.

'We're working on breaking down her inhibitions, aren't we, baby?' Mark said.

'Yes. I'm trying to be more … adventurous.' She smiled shyly at Isabel.

'Maybe I pushed you too far,' Mark said to her, his tone all loving concern. He stood and came around to her side of the table. Putting his hands on her shoulders, he dropped a kiss on the top of her head. 'Sorry if I upset you, baby. You okay now?'

Lisa gulped. 'Yes,' she said, giving him a bright smile.

'I should have seen that it was too much. But you were so sexy, I got carried away. I'll pay closer attention in future, okay?'

She nodded.

'Good. Well, why don't I show you the rest of the house?' he said to Isabel, holding out a hand to her. 'There's some more artwork upstairs I'd like you to see.'

'Really?' Isabel said with a smile as she stood. 'You want to show me your etchings?'

Mark laughed. 'You two might like to play with this,' he said, handing the remote control to Grayson. Lisa saw Grayson's jaw tighten as he took the device from Mark, and she was shocked at the barely concealed hostility in his eyes. But he said nothing.

'Well, Lisa may have let you off the hook,' Isabel said to Mark as she came around the table and took his hand, 'but I still think you were an asshole. I'm going to have to teach you a lesson.'

Mark grinned. 'I'll accept whatever punishment you see fit,' he said as they left the room.

'Are you okay?' Grayson asked her softly when they were gone. He was still holding her and his hand rubbed her back soothingly.

She nodded, hanging her head as mortification flooded through her.

'I don't think we'll be needing this.' Grayson tossed the remote onto the table. 'Hey,' he said, taking her chin in his hand and lifting her face. 'Please don't be embarrassed.'

She looked at him shyly from under her lashes. But how could she not feel awkward after what had just happened? She squirmed in his lap, gasping as she suddenly felt the hardness of his erection against her leg. 'Sorry,' she mumbled, pulling away.

'Now I'm the one to be embarrassed,' he said with a rueful smile as Lisa climbed off him.

At least there was something she could do about that, she thought – something she knew she was good at. When it came to blow jobs, she was confident that she could give even Isabel a run for her money. She dropped to her knees in front of Grayson.

'Let me take care of that,' she said, reaching for his zipper.

'No.' He frowned, batting her hand away so suddenly that she reeled back.

'Sorry,' she breathed, stricken by his rejection and wishing the ground would open up and swallow her. 'You don't want …' Her eyes slid away.

'Lisa,' he said, reaching for her, 'of course I want you. God, I would have thought that was obvious,' he said with a wry smile.

She blushed.

'How could I not want you?' he continued with a pained expression. 'You're an incredibly sexy woman. You're beautiful, you have an amazing body, you're so responsive—'

'Then why—'

'But I don't want you to do that because you feel you have to.'

'I'm not. Last week was different. I didn't know what to expect. But tonight I'm prepared.'

'Lisa, I didn't come here tonight to have sex with you. I know it's not what you want.'

'Why did you come, then? If you knew …'

He smiled crookedly. 'I was hoping maybe a game of chess?'

Lisa couldn't help smiling.

'You don't have to worry about Mark – I won't tell him what we really get up to when we're alone together. So what do you say?'

Lisa grinned. 'I would like a chance to get you back for the other night.'

'Great!' He stood, taking her hand and helping her up. 'Lead the way.'

10

LISA TOOK Grayson to the little study at the back of the house. She knew there was a chess board in one of the cupboards there. Mark used to play with her occasionally when she had first moved in, but he didn't really care for chess himself and he hadn't indulged her by playing for a long time. The study was Lisa's favourite room in the house, and the only one where she didn't feel out of place. Decorated in a style reminiscent of a gentlemen's club, the deep greens and browns gave it a feeling of cosiness and warmth that was lacking in the rest of the house. It didn't have the charm and comfort of Grayson's library, but it was a lot more relaxed and homely than the stark, minimalist style that Mark usually favoured.

She quickly found the chess set, her eyes darting anxiously to the door as she set it on a little inlaid table between two armchairs upholstered in rich brown leather. What if Mark were to catch her playing chess with Grayson?

'May I?' Grayson asked, pointing to the lock.

'Yes, please,' Lisa said gratefully. It was as if he'd read her mind.

'Now we don't have to worry about being disturbed,' he said, turning the key in the lock.

Lisa smiled at him, relaxing. He was so considerate, so kind to her. If only she could have met someone like him instead of Mark, she thought wistfully – how different her life would be now. She dismissed such fanciful thoughts as she set up the board and Grayson settled into the armchair opposite her.

They were a little more familiar with each other's style of play now, and they were less tentative with each other. Grayson surprised Lisa by adopting a more risky strategy than he had last week. He kept her guessing, constantly forcing her to raise her game, and she found it exhilarating to play with someone who could challenge her. Once again, she lost her shyness as she became absorbed in the game, and they chatted easily between moves.

'Was it your grandmother who taught you to cook like that?' Grayson asked.

'She taught me the basics. She was an amazing cook, but more of the plain home cooking variety. The fancy cheffy stuff I learned myself. I took some courses.' That had been Mark's idea. The simple hearty food that she had loved as a child wasn't refined enough for his taste.

'You can't beat plain home cooked food,' Grayson said.

'Especially home baking.' Lisa thought longingly of her grandmother's scones, pies and cakes. 'My grandmother was a great baker. She'd always push the boat out on my birthday and make me a really elaborate cake, decorated according to whatever my current obsession was.'

'Did you have a Little Mermaid cake?' Grayson asked with a smile.

'Seventh birthday,' she answered.

'So it was just you? You were an only child?'

'Yeah. My parents died when I was just a baby, so …' It occurred to her that she knew nothing about his background. 'Tell me about your family. Do you have brothers and sisters?'

'Three sisters. I was completely outnumbered,' he said with a roll of his eyes, but there was an unmistakeable fondness in his voice. 'All older than me too, so I was pretty much their slave.'

'It must be nice having a big family,' she said wistfully. 'I'd love to have had a brother or sister.'

'They're all married now, so I have lots of nieces and nephews too – and brothers-in-law, so there are some more men in the family.'

'Do you see a lot of them?'

'Yeah, we're pretty close. My parents moved to Cornwall when they retired, so we don't see them as regularly, but we all get together as much as we can.'

It all sounded so normal and uncomplicated, and Lisa found herself thinking how lovely it would be to be Grayson's girlfriend, to be part of his life. But even if that were possible, she felt unworthy of someone like him now, tainted by her twisted relationship with Mark. Grayson may be infinitely more worldly than her, but he had an integrity and purity that she had lost and would never get back.

'How long have you and Isabel been together?' she asked him. He was contemplating his next move, his dark lashes lowered as he studied the board, his thumb stroking absently over his mouth.

He glanced up at her. 'We've known each other for about five years,' he said before returning his attention to the board. 'We've been lovers, on and off, for most of that time.'

Suddenly the silence was shattered by a high-pitched squeal from somewhere upstairs. Lisa blushed, but Grayson just chuckled.

'Sounds like Isabel's enjoying herself,' he said as he moved his knight.

'Don't you mind?' Lisa asked. She bit her lip, regretting the words as soon as they were spoken. She shouldn't have asked.

But Grayson just looked at her calmly. 'No,' he shrugged. 'Why should I mind?'

'Well, because … she's your lover.'

'I'm not jealous. We don't have that kind of relationship.'

She nodded, pretending to understand, but she didn't. She couldn't get her head around these cool, sophisticated people with their open relationships. How could you be so intimate with someone and yet remain so detached? She didn't think she'd ever comprehend it.

'Isabel and I are friends. We're not exclusive – never have been. We're not in love.'

'So you're friends with benefits?'

He smiled. 'I suppose you could call it that.' He moved a pawn into a vulnerable position, and Lisa bent her head to the board, considering how to respond.

'Do *you* mind?' She looked up to find Grayson watching her closely. 'Does it upset you that Mark's with another woman?'

'No,' she answered. It was true. She was actually relieved that he had turned his attention to someone else, if only for a short while. She didn't care about him being unfaithful, with or without her knowledge. But if she was committed to him as she pretended to be, if she was still as in love with him as she had been in the beginning, she would be devastated by what was happening now. She didn't understand Mark wanting her to be with Grayson when he claimed to love her so completely and exclusively.

'You don't look so sure,' Grayson said.

She gave him what she hoped was a reassuring smile. 'I would have minded … once.' She shrugged. 'I guess this is all just new to me. But I'm getting used to it.' She bent her head to the board again.

'Have you had many lovers, Lisa?' he asked quietly. She looked up to find him still watching her.

'No.' She took his pawn.

'How many?'

'Three.' Then an image of his head buried between her legs flashed into her mind. 'Four since, um … last week,' she amended, feeling herself blush.

Grayson took her meaning. 'Oh, I don't think I count,' he said with a small smile. 'Was Mark your first?'

She shook her head. 'No,' she said, her voice barely audible.

'But he's the last? There's been no one since him?'

'No. Not if you don't count.' For some reason she felt a little pang at the thought that he didn't want her to think of him as one of her lovers.

'I'm sorry,' he said with a rueful smile. 'I'm being rude and making you uncomfortable. I just want to get to know you better. You fascinate me, Lisa. I wish—'

'What?' she asked, her throat feeling suddenly dry.

He sighed. 'So many things. I wish we could have met under different circumstances.'

His words echoed her own thoughts so exactly she felt a little spooked.

'I wish we had more time,' he continued. 'I wish you were coming home with me tonight instead of staying here with him.'

She watched his fingers, mesmerised, as he picked up

his rook and moved it across the board. She felt stifled suddenly, trapped. Something was happening between them, some chemistry that made her feel hot and cold, frightened and excited all at once. She watched his fingers as they rubbed against his beautiful mouth, remembering the touch of them against her skin, the heat of his mouth on her body, the slippery wetness of his tongue …

'I wish I could kiss you again. I wish you wanted me to touch you,' he said, looking up at her through heavy-lidded eyes. 'I haven't been able to stop thinking about you since last week – how soft your skin is, how sweet you taste, how responsive you are. I wish—I wish I counted.'

Her breath caught in her throat, and her heart raced. She flicked her eyes up to his and their gazes locked, captivated.

'That's a lot of wishes,' Lisa said, trying to lighten the atmosphere. But her laugh sounded hollow and false.

'If you're dreaming, might as well dream big,' Grayson said with a smile. Then he became serious again. 'If I were Mark, I'd mind very much about you being here with me. If you were mine, I wouldn't want to share you with anyone.'

Suddenly the air seemed very still. Lisa realised she was holding her breath.

'If only he knew he has nothing to be jealous about,' Grayson said.

But that wasn't true, Lisa thought. She couldn't help feeling that what was happening between her and Grayson now was far more intimate and meaningful to her than if she'd simply fucked him.

Grayson looked away first, breaking the spell. 'Sorry,' he said, shaking his head as if waking himself up. 'I'm being inappropriate.'

Lisa gulped, not able to speak.

'Your move,' Grayson said. She had a strange feeling he wasn't talking about chess anymore.

As if in a dream, she moved her castle to seize victory. 'Check,' she said.

He looked at the board and then up at her and their eyes locked. He knew he had lost. He held out his hand to her, conceding defeat, and they shook, but he didn't let go.

'You're shaking,' he said, frowning in concern. He clasped her hand tighter, warming it. 'Are you cold?'

She shook her head dumbly, confused and unnerved by the aching need that consumed her. She wanted him. The realisation took her by surprise. It had been a long time since she had felt the thrill of sexual desire. And the beauty of it was that she could act on it. She didn't even have to feel guilty. It was what Mark wanted.

Their eyes met and held.

'Your move,' Grayson said hoarsely.

As if in a trance, Lisa leaned in and touched her lips to his tentatively. He sighed into her mouth, his eyes fluttering closed as he cupped her face and kissed her back; soft, sensual kisses, his lips clinging to hers. He drew back momentarily to push the table aside and pull Lisa into his lap. She went willingly, winding her arms around his neck as he pulled her into his body. His hand curled around the back of her head, his mouth opening over hers. His breath was hot, and he tasted of wine as his tongue met hers, softly probing and teasing, fanning the flames of desire that licked along her veins and feeding her hunger so she craved more and more. She moaned as his free hand ghosted over her breast, feeling her nipple harden under the warmth of his palm. She pushed into his hand, greedy for his touch as their kisses became more urgent, their tongues tangling erotically.

Grayson groaned deep in his throat as he tore his lips

away, kissing his way down her neck and across her collar-bone to her breasts. She arched her back, her fingers curling into the short hair at the nape of his neck as his tongue flicked across her nipple until it was hard and taut. Then his lips closed around it, sucking on it through the sheer material of her blouse, while his fingers teased and caressed the other one.

Rational thought receded, and Lisa became a purely physical, instinctual creature, driven by desire and need, solely focused on doing whatever felt good and feeding the hunger burning inside her. She felt Grayson's erection against her hip and reached for it. He groaned as she pressed her hand against his hardness, grabbing her by the waist and moving her so she was straddling him. His hands slid up her legs and cupped her bottom as she ground her hips against his.

Suddenly there was a loud crash from upstairs, followed by a shriek. Startled, Lisa and Grayson broke apart. They stared at each other in silence, breathing raggedly. Then the sounds of laughter drifted down from above them. Grayson reached for Lisa again, kissing her while his hands roamed restlessly over her body. Lisa kissed him back, but the interruption had snapped her out of her trance and brought her back to reality. She tried to get back to where she had been, to empty her mind of every-thing but Grayson, the touch of his hands, the feel of his body against hers. But it was no use. She was aware of things beyond this room, of Mark and Isabel upstairs. Unwelcome thoughts crowded in to compete with the sensation of Grayson's soft, wet mouth on hers, the smell of his skin, the heat of his body.

She still wanted him desperately. She still wanted him to take off all her clothes and kiss her. She wanted to feel his mouth on her everywhere, the touch of his hands, the feel of his bare skin against hers. She wanted his weight on top of her, the heat and hardness of him inside her. But the rational part of her knew that it would only feel good for a short time, and then it would make her sadder than ever. Because when they were done, she would stay here with Mark and he would go home with Isabel. Nothing would have changed. She would have a lovely memory. But if it was good with Grayson – and somehow she knew it would be – it would only make her want more. And she could never have more.

As if sensing her withdrawal, Grayson's kisses became lighter, more hesitant, his hands on her gentling.

'Lisa?' He pulled back, frowning at her in concern.

'Sorry.' She bit her lip.

'You want to stop.' It was a statement, not a question. He closed his eyes, as if in pain, and let out a sigh.

'I can't. I'm sorry.'

'Don't be,' he said, opening his eyes again.

His hands dropped away and she wanted to cry, yearning to throw herself back into his arms and damn the consequences. Instead she lifted herself off him.

'It's not that I don't want to,' she said as she stood up. 'I can't explain—'

'Lisa, it's fine. You don't owe me any explanation.' He leaned forward on his knees, breathing heavily, obviously struggling to regain control.

'Will I see you again?' he asked, looking up at her.

'I don't know. I guess it depends on Mark. Would you want to?'

'Of course. I like you, Lisa. Obviously I'm attracted to you too, but I enjoy spending time with you. I'd like if we could be friends.'

She frowned. 'Even without benefits?'

Grayson chuckled. 'Even then.'

'I'd like that. I like spending time with you too.' That was an understatement. It was the happiest she'd been in years. 'But I don't know if it's going to be possible. Mark —' How could she explain that Mark wouldn't mind if she fucked Grayson, but would fly into a jealous rage if he thought she was friends with him?

But Grayson just sighed and nodded understandingly. 'He's a very lucky man.'

Lisa stood, smoothing out her skirt. 'I guess I should go and find him.'

Before opening the door, she checked her appearance in the mirror. Her blouse was creased, her nipples still hard and prominent under the sheer material. She looked flushed and dishevelled, the traces of arousal still lingering in her dark pupils and swollen lips. At least she didn't have to fake it this time. She glanced at Grayson and he looked just as rumpled.

They found Isabel and Mark coming downstairs as they emerged from the study. Lisa felt a pang of jealousy as Isabel went straight to Grayson and put an arm around his waist. There was something so casually affectionate and familiar about the gesture, and the way they murmured softly to each other in low voices so that only the two of them could hear. It made her glad she hadn't let things go further with Grayson because she knew it would have hurt more to see him gravitate towards Isabel now, and to watch them leave together looking like they belonged with each other.

'We must do this again soon,' Isabel said, as they stood in the doorway.

'Yes, let's arrange something,' Mark agreed. But no firm plans were made, and Lisa wondered if they would be.

'I had such a lovely time tonight,' Grayson whispered

in her ear as he kissed her goodbye. 'I hope I'll see you again soon.' He pulled back, looking deeply into her eyes as he took her hand in both of his and kissed it.

Then he snaked his arm around Isabel's waist and they left. Lisa stood in the doorway with Mark, waving them off, and wondered if she would ever see Grayson again. And what would happen if she did?

11

Lisa felt a lot more optimistic in the days that followed than she had in a very long time, and she knew it was due to the time she had spent with Grayson. It had given her a new sense of confidence in herself, and she was no longer overwhelmed by the hopelessness of her situation. She had already been determined to escape and build a new life for herself away from Mark, but up to now she hadn't really been able to visualise that life or to fully believe in it. She'd had nothing but grim determination to keep her going. But Grayson had reminded her of who she really was and given her a glimpse of what her life could be like without Mark. When she was with him, she had actually been happy, and it shocked her when she realised how alien it had felt to laugh naturally, to speak freely and behave spontaneously, instead of constantly second-guessing herself and rehearsing her every move. Suddenly the new life she had dreamed of seemed within her grasp, and she moved towards it with a real sense of purpose, no longer simply going through the motions. It was as if she had been feeling her way in the dark all this time, and now finally there was some light ahead to guide her.

She had found herself looking forward to the weekend, buoyed up by the hope of seeing Grayson again, and she was disappointed each day when Mark made no mention of any plans. She didn't dare to bring up the subject herself and risk arousing his suspicion and jealousy. By Friday, she had resigned herself to the fact that it wouldn't be happening. So she hadn't been surprised when he told her at breakfast that he had made dinner reservations at Locale, his favourite restaurant.

'Just the two of us,' he'd said, gazing at her adoringly. 'I want you all to myself this weekend.'

She had returned his loving smile and pretended to be touched by the romantic gesture, hiding her disappointment that she wouldn't get to see Grayson. But it didn't crush her spirit, because even if she were never to see Grayson again, he had given her something that no one could take away. Memories of the time they had spent together would flash through her mind every so often, and they warmed and sustained her – their conversations, their chess games, the lovely things he had said to her … Heat came to her cheeks as she thought of other things – the softness of his mouth on her, the gentle touch of his hands, the relentlessness of his tongue and lips on her heated flesh as he pleasured her. But instead of feeling shame or disgust, those memories warmed her too.

She felt almost light-hearted now as she got ready for her day. It was the same vacuous round of shopping and salon visits as always, but she didn't care because she no longer let it define her. She leaned into the mirror as she applied a final coat of lipstick to her expertly lined lips. Then she pulled back and smiled at her reflection in the mirror, pleased that for once she didn't see a stranger looking back at her. It was the same expertly made-up doll face, but there was a glimmer in her eyes now, a spark of life in her features that hadn't been there before. There was a glimpse of the old Lisa behind the mask, and it filled her with hope. This was the person she used to be, not the pathetic shell of a human being Mark had turned her into. This was someone worth fighting for.

But for now there was shopping to do. Mark had told her to buy a new dress for tonight, leaving the choice to her.

'Surprise me,' he'd said before kissing her goodbye this morning.

She used to enjoy dressing up for Mark, she thought, with a sad smile. There was a time when she had relished the opportunity to surprise and delight him, and she would throw herself into searching for the perfect outfit, excitedly anticipating his pleasure as she chose what she thought would appeal to him most, and glowing with pride when she was rewarded by the obvious appreciation and desire in his eyes that told her she had got it right.

But slowly he had sucked the joy out of it, and now it was just a chore, another demand to be met. She turned to the open wardrobe, her eyes running over the rails of expensive, barely-worn clothes. The last thing she needed was a new dress. But there was no point in arguing. Mark would just take it as an insult and reproach her for being ungrateful. He never ceased to remind her how lucky she was, how enviable most women would consider her luxurious lifestyle. She knew he was right about that. From the outside, she seemed to have it all, and no doubt many women *would* envy her – but only because they didn't know the reality behind the glossy facade. This beautiful house was a prison; her handsome, indulgent boyfriend her jailor

– and her life of apparent ease and luxury was in truth little more than slavery.

She shook her head as if to dislodge such negative thoughts. She wasn't going to dwell on the past or wallow in regret about what she had lost. From now on she would focus on the future, keep working steadily towards that glimmer of light in the distance and trust that she would get there eventually. She just had to play Mark's game for a little while longer, she told herself determinedly as she swung her bag onto her shoulder and checked herself in the mirror one last time before leaving the house.

'Oops, sorry!' She was coming out of the Bond Street hairdressing salon, checking a text from Mark on her cell phone, when she collided with someone. 'Excuse me,' she moved to sidestep them without looking up as they apologised to each other.

'Lisa?'

She looked up then, and it took her a moment to place the tall, slim girl in front of her.

'Rose! Hi!' she said as she recognised her. Rose had been in her year at art college. They would have graduated together if Lisa had stayed on.

'How are you?' Rose asked. 'I haven't seen you in ages.'

'I'm fine, thanks. How are you?'

'Great! I've just been into Gallery Six,' she jerked her head towards the end of the road. Lisa knew the gallery. It was in Mayfair, close to Mark's, and almost as prestigious. 'I'm having my first solo exhibition there next month,' Rose beamed.

'Oh, that's really exciting! Congratulations!'

'I know! You must come to my opening.' Rose's excite-

ment was palpable, her eyes dancing with joy, and Lisa felt a twinge of envy.

'So what have you been up to?' Rose asked her. 'I'm surprised I haven't heard anything – I thought you'd be mega-famous by now, taking the world by storm. You were always the big star at college.'

'Was I?'

'Oh, come on, don't be so modest – you know you were. We were all so jealous when Mark Reader zoned in on you and made you his protégé. So what have you been doing?'

Lisa shrugged. 'Nothing much. I don't paint anymore.'

Rose frowned, appearing genuinely shocked. 'You don't? So what are you doing now? Don't tell me you've taken up sculpture? Everyone I know seems to be doing that lately.'

'Um … nothing. I gave up art altogether.'

'You're kidding! But you were so talented.'

'Not talented enough, it turned out,' Lisa said with a self-deprecating smile.

Rose frowned. 'So what do you do?' she asked. 'Weren't you working at Mark's gallery for a while?'

'Yes, but not anymore. I—I'm not working at the moment.' Lisa tried to make it sound like a temporary thing.

'Oh.' Rose's smile faded and her eyes swept over Lisa, seeming to take her in properly for the first time. Lisa felt very self-conscious, realising how she must look with her freshly styled hair, her expensive clothes, and the designer shopping bags on her arm. Rose was casually dressed in skinny jeans and pumps with an oversized sweater, the sleeves rolled up to her elbows. She looked young and arty, and she made Lisa feel stuffy and middle-aged, even though they were the same age.

'Well, you seem to be doing okay anyway,' Rose said with a little smirk. 'Are you still with Mark?'

Lisa cringed. She could tell exactly what Rose was thinking – that she had bagged a rich man and promptly given up work to become a pampered housewife. 'Yes, I am,' she answered with a defiant tilt to her chin.

'Well, good for you.' Rose looked at her with a mixture of curiosity and amusement that made Lisa uncomfortable. 'You should definitely come to my launch – and bring Mark. I'll send an invite to his gallery, shall I?'

'Yes, do. We'll try to make it.'

'Great! What are Susie and Daniel up to these days?' Rose asked, naming Lisa's two closest friends from college.

'I don't know,' Lisa shrugged. 'I … haven't seen them for a long time.'

'Oh, you don't keep in touch? That's a surprise. Hey, I'm meeting up with Anna and Nikki for drinks tonight. You should come. I'm sure they'd love to see you and catch up.' Anna and Nikki were fellow college classmates.

'Thanks, but Mark and I are going out tonight,' Lisa said, surprised that she felt genuine regret. She hadn't been particular friends with Rose, Anna or Nikki at college, but she suddenly felt it would be good to reconnect with people from that time, people her own age. She glanced at her watch. She had some time before she had to be home. 'We could go for a drink now?' she suggested on an impulse.

'Oh, I'd love to,' Rose said, 'but I've got to get back. I'm doing some temping at a little PR company on Regent Street. Dull as hell, but it pays the bills. Sorry,' she said with an apologetic grimace, 'but some of us have to work for a living.'

There was just the hint of a sneer in her smile, and the derisive way her eyes once more flicked over her body made Lisa glad she wasn't able to join her for a drink.

What had she been thinking? Rose was a bitch. She had been fiercely competitive with Lisa at art college, and there had always been an undercurrent of spite and jealousy beneath her overt friendliness. Now that her star was in the ascendant, she would no doubt love the opportunity to gloat over her former rival. It would just be depressing, and Lisa could do without that. Besides, they had nothing in common anymore. What would they even talk about? It would be awkward and uncomfortable at best.

'Some other time maybe,' Rose was saying now as she turned to go.

'Yes, definitely,' Lisa smiled. But they both knew it was a pretence. Neither of them even bothered to make a show of swapping numbers.

'I'll tell Nikki and Anna I met you.'

'Yeah, say hi to them for me,' Lisa called after her. Rose was probably dying to tell her friends about bumping into her. She could imagine them all gossiping about her tonight over cocktails, Rose laughing as she filled them in on the fact that she had abandoned her art to become a trophy girlfriend.

She stood still in the street, almost dizzy with envy as she watched Rose walk away. She looked so young and carefree, sauntering down the street in her loping stride, bubbling with happiness about her solo show. Exciting things were happening for her, and life seemed to be opening up before her, full of possibilities. Lisa knew how it felt. That had been her once.

She tried to shake off the feelings of bitterness and resentment as she turned to walk in the opposite direction. But the encounter with Rose had unsettled her, and she felt almost paralysed by regret. It preyed on her mind what Rose had said about Lisa being the star of their year, the one they all expected to have the big breakthrough. She had believed that herself once. Mark had believed it. She had been so excited about embarking on her artistic career, full of hopes and plans for the future, and sure that good things were going to happen for her. Having Mark's backing gave her good reason to be confident, but it wasn't just that. She had believed in what she was doing; believed in her own talent.

She had been walking on air in those days when she had first moved in with Mark. It had been bliss having so much time to devote to painting, and Mark talked about giving her a show when she had produced enough work. It had seemed like it was only a matter of time. But nothing she produced was ever good enough for him. He rejected piece after piece, and gradually he had stopped talking about her show. When she had nudged him about it one day, he had looked at her pityingly.

'Oh, baby, I'm sorry,' he had said. 'I didn't want to hurt your feelings, but you're just not good enough yet. I have the gallery's reputation to think of. I can't show this stuff just because you're my girlfriend. I'd be laughed out of town.'

She remembered how she had fought back tears, trying to be grown-up about it and take it on the chin.

'Maybe next year,' Mark had said consolingly. 'You just need more time to develop.'

Mark's criticism stung, but she had told herself she was lucky to have it. He knew what he was talking about, after all. He was a star-maker. She just had to do better. So she had thrown herself back into painting, working harder than ever, determined to produce work he would be proud to represent.

Her show never materialised, but finally he had accepted a couple of her paintings for the gallery. He hadn't been overly enthusiastic about them, but he said he

would give them a chance and it would allow him to test the market. Lisa had been proud of them, and thought they were the best work she had ever done. She hoped they would sell, and Mark's faith in her would be justified. Sometimes she felt that he held her to higher standards because he was wary of letting his feelings for her colour his judgement. So she had been optimistic as she waited anxiously for some objective feedback.

But as weeks passed without a sale, she became increasingly despondent. She saw Mark's faith in her dwindling, and it undermined her confidence in what she was doing. She had tried to keep her spirits up and persevere with her work. One day, when she had been feeling particularly low and on the verge of giving up, she had dropped into the gallery to look at her paintings to cheer herself up. It had been one of the proudest moments of her life when she had first seen her art hanging on the wall in Mark's gallery. Having her paintings for sale in such a prestigious space – not to mention the hefty price tag attached to them – had felt like a huge achievement, and a real validation of her work. It had made her feel like a proper artist, and she had gone there that day to remind herself of that.

She cringed now, recalling her dismay as she walked around the gallery and found her paintings were no longer on display. She had gone around twice to make sure. Mark had never said anything to her about removing them, just mentioned occasionally that they still hadn't sold. She had left the gallery feeling embarrassed and more despondent than ever, and that night she had confronted him about it. Again he had given her that pitying look. They weren't selling, he had explained, and he simply couldn't afford to give up the wall space to them any longer.

She had felt dazed. 'When?' she had asked faintly. 'How long have they not been for sale?'

'Just the last couple of weeks,' he had said, looking shamefaced.

'Why didn't you say anything?' She had felt like an idiot. She had been taking pride in Mark's endorsement, when in fact he had already given up on her.

'I'm sorry. I just didn't have the heart to tell you. I know how hard you've been working, how badly you want this.'

That was when he had told her that she would never make the grade as an artist. With her confidence already at an all-time low, it had been easy for him to persuade her that she should give up.

'It's just making you miserable,' he had said. 'I hate seeing you so unhappy.'

She had decided he was right. It was making her frustrated and depressed, and for what? She was banging her head against a brick wall. If Mark didn't think she was good enough, she had to accept that it was never going to happen for her.

They had talked for hours that night, making new plans. He had been kind and sympathetic as they gently dismantled her dreams. It was decided that she wouldn't go back to college and finish her degree. Mark insisted that she didn't need to work, that he would continue to support her financially, but when she made it clear that she meant to get a job, he offered to take her on at the gallery. It was the ideal solution, and Lisa tried to feel happy about it, but inside her heart was breaking.

The next day Mark cleared out the studio he had built for her at the top of the house and hired an architect to convert it into a gym. When she came home from a shopping trip a few days later to find all her paintings gone, Mark calmly told her he had thrown them in the skip. Shocked that he would do such a thing, Lisa had howled in

protest and automatically ran outside to rescue them. But it was too late – the skip had been collected while she was out. Mark had been contrite when he saw how distraught she was, but explained he'd thought a clean break would be best for her.

'I never wanted to be the one to shatter your dreams,' Lisa', he'd said soothingly as he held her, while she felt like her heart was being ripped to pieces.

Her stomach still heaved now at the thought of her paintings being destroyed; tossed out like garbage. They may not have had much objective worth, but they had meant something to her. They were a part of her, and she still felt an aching emptiness and an almost overwhelming sense of loss when she thought of them.

Damn Rose, she thought. She'd stirred up all sorts of feelings that were better left alone. Lisa blinked away tears as she hailed a cab, feeling her buoyant mood of earlier evaporate as she headed for home.

12

Even on a busy Friday night, the atmosphere in Locale was hushed. Lisa's heels sank into the thick carpet as the maitre d' led them to their table, the plush furnishings muffling the sounds of conversation. Waiters moved between the tables with balletic grace, accompanied by the gentle tinkle of glass and silverware, carrying out their tasks with calm, unobtrusive efficiency. Mark loved this place. Everything about it appealed to his ego, from the eye-watering prices on the menu to the professional staff who treated him with just the right balance of friendliness and deference. There was an air of exclusivity about it that pleased him. Mark hadn't grown up with money, and being a regular at a place like this was proof that he'd arrived.

'You look amazing, Lisa.' He took her hand across the table when they were seated. 'Every man here wishes he were me,' he said with a self-satisfied smile, his eyes flicking around the elegant dining room.

She was just the icing on the cake – the perfect accessory for the man who had it all. 'Thanks,' she said, faking a loving smile as she opened her menu.

'Don't bother with that,' Mark said, reaching across and whipping it out of her hands. 'I'll order for both of us.'

She swallowed down her irritation at this supposedly romantic gesture on his part. 'Sure. Thanks.'

She hardly listened to what Mark ordered. When her starter was placed in front of her, it was a work of art, the plate decorated with edible flowers and dots of purees and jellies in jewel-like colours. It was almost too pretty to eat, and it tasted as exquisite as it looked.

'Good choice?' Mark asked, smiling at her knowingly.

'Excellent,' she nodded. 'It's delicious.'

Of course she had known it would be. Everything here was always perfect – the food was sublime, the service impeccable. She looked around the elegant dining room, full of wealthy and influential people, taking in the massive brass chandeliers that hung from the high ceiling, and the important and valuable art collection that adorned the walls. She had been so impressed by all this in the beginning. Now she found herself thinking longingly of the bustling Italian restaurant she used to frequent with her college friends, where they had spent long nights filled with noise and laughter, fuelled by pizza and cheap wine. It was a good thing Mark couldn't read her mind, she thought wryly. He'd be outraged at her ingratitude.

'I've got something to tell you,' Mark said, breaking into her thoughts. 'I have to go to China next week, on business.'

'Oh?' She waited for more, wondering what this meant for her. Would he want her to go with him? Socialising was an important part of Mark's business – relationships with clients were forged and deals done over lunches and dinners, and he usually wanted her by his side to help oil the wheels.

'It's a damn nuisance, but there are a couple of big

clients there who I'm trying to woo. It could mean millions of pounds in new business.'

Lisa nodded. 'It would be great for you to get a foothold in China.' She knew Mark was excited about its potential as an important emerging market — he had spoken of it often recently. 'What part will you be going to?'

'Beijing. I'd take you with me, but I'm afraid it's not going to be a holiday. I'll be working twenty-four/seven.'

'That's fine. I don't mind.' She kept her expression carefully neutral, but her heart was racing with excitement at the thought of having some time alone.

'Mr. Wong, who'll be my host, is a bit old-fashioned,' he said with a crooked smile. 'He doesn't like to mix business with pleasure, and to him, business is strictly men-only.'

Lisa silently thanked Mr. Wong for his chauvinism. 'How long will you be gone for?'

'A week,' Mark sighed. 'I wish you could come. I hate being away from you for so long.'

'I know.' She covered his hand with hers, trying to look regretful. 'Me too. But it sounds like we'd hardly see each other anyway. And I wouldn't want to get in the way.'

'I'll make it up to you when I get home,' Mark said, with an indulgent smile.

Lisa didn't have to fake her good mood for the rest of the meal. She felt light-hearted, and almost giddy with excitement at the thought of a whole week of freedom. It was a pity she hadn't saved up enough to leave yet — it would be the perfect opportunity. But she quickly dismissed those thoughts. It was too soon — she would just make the most of this unexpected time to herself and enjoy it for what it was.

'So, you've enjoyed our evenings with Grayson and Isabel?' Mark asked later as they waited between courses.

'Yes,' she said. She felt her heart quicken hopefully at the mention of Grayson.

'Would you like to do more of that?' he asked with a wicked grin, swirling the wine in his glass.

'Yes, if you would,' she answered, careful not to sound too eager.

'I thought when I come home we could continue to … explore other avenues. In fact, we've been invited to a party the weekend after I get back—'

'A—a party?' Lisa asked, a knot of dread forming in her stomach. 'At Grayson's house?' she asked hopefully.

'No,' Mark said with a little chuckle. 'I'm not talking about playing with Grayson and Isabel. I mean, I enjoy their company – don't get me wrong. But the point of this is to be adventurous, not to get stuck in a rut with another couple. You do see that?'

'Yes,' she breathed. 'Of course.'

'Besides, Grayson isn't into exhibitionism, and it was probably good for your first couple of times, to have that one-on-one time with him. But I really want to watch,' he said, his eyes glittering. 'I've met some people through work who arrange these parties—'

'When you say "party",' Lisa began.

'Well, I suppose the technical term would be "orgy", if you want to get specific about it,' he said with a mocking smile.

Lisa struggled to disguise her shock and revulsion – clearly without success.

'Your face!' he laughed. 'You're such a little prude, Lisa.'

'But … an orgy!' she stuttered. 'It's so … *sleazy*.'

Mark's smile faded. 'Don't be ridiculous,' he snapped.

'They're very classy parties, very exclusive, and there's nothing remotely sleazy about it. Guests are chosen very carefully. It's quite an honour to be invited.'

Dear God! How could she talk him out of this? She cast around desperately for some way out. Maybe she could appeal to his ego.

'I just—I hate the thought of you being with another woman,' she said pleadingly. 'It's been hard for me seeing you with Isabel. It makes me so jealous. I try not to be, but I can't help it.'

'Oh, darling.' To her relief, his expression softened and he reached for her hand. 'This has nothing to do with how much I love you. You have to understand that. I hate that you're so insecure.'

'I don't understand why I'm not enough for you,' she said. She knew she was on dangerous ground, testing him, but she was desperate enough to risk it. She couldn't go along with fucking strangers just to please him. She had been lucky with Grayson, but what were the chances of meeting up with another man as kind and understanding as him?

'No,' he said, cupping her face and staring intently into her eyes. 'Please don't think that. It's quite the opposite, Lisa. It's because you're so beautiful and sexy, and I'm so damn proud of you. I want to take you out and show you off. I want other men to look at your body and want you. I want to watch them fuck you, all the while knowing that you'll only ever belong to me.'

She stifled a gasp. Christ, he was sick. He was more twisted than she'd even realised.

'I can't help it,' she said. 'It makes me feel inadequate knowing you want to be with other women.'

'It's not about that,' he said tetchily, withdrawing his hand. 'Don't be so small-minded. Just because I'm interested in exploring sex with other people doesn't mean I love you any less. Don't you trust me?'

'Yes, of course I do. But it's hard to keep feelings out of it when you're intimate like that with someone.'

'You've enjoyed being with Grayson, haven't you?'

'Yes, but—that's different.'

'And it hasn't changed how you feel about me?'

'No—'

Suddenly his expression clouded. 'Or has it? Is that what this is about, Lisa? Has sex with him changed your feelings towards me?'

'No,' she gasped, horrified.

He narrowed his eyes at her. 'You're a liar,' he spat, his eyes hard, flinty. 'You're the one who can't keep feelings out of it.' His lip curled in a sneer. 'You want him, don't you? You're the one who's really being unfaithful, and you're projecting it onto me.'

'No, that's not true.'

'If you were sure of your feelings for me, you'd understand that the sex means nothing. Have you fallen in love with him?'

'Wh—what? *No!*'

'Why is it different then? Why were you so keen to see him again?'

'I wasn't. I only did it for you – you know that.'

'I wish I could believe you, Lisa. But I saw how you responded to him. You loved him touching you. You couldn't get enough of it. I saw how hard he made you come, remember?'

'But that was what you wanted! I only did it to please you.' Tears burned the backs of her eyes. It was unbelievable how he could twist things, so that she always ended up on the defensive. Now he was trying to make her feel guilty for a situation he had engineered himself – a situation in which she had been an unwilling participant. She had only gone along with it to keep the peace, and now he was using it against her.

'Maybe I made a mistake introducing you to him. I should have known a stupid little slut like you wouldn't be able to handle it. I suppose you've developed a pathetic little crush on him?'

'No, of course not.'

'Well, don't get carried away with any romantic notions, Lisa. Don't believe for one minute that he's interested in you beyond a casual fuck. You've seen Isabel.' He gave her a scornful look. 'Do you really think a man who's got a woman like her would be interested in *you*?'

'Mark, please—'

'They probably laugh about you after we're gone – how clumsy and inexperienced you are. So desperate for it, yet so inept.' His voice was silky smooth, taunting her.

He broke off his tirade when the waiter came with their main courses. Lisa's stomach churned as she looked down at her plate of sea bass. She didn't know how she was going to get anything past the lump in her throat. It's not true, she told herself – none of it's true. Don't let him into your head, don't believe him. She imagined herself back in the library with Grayson. He was a good person, a kind man. He wasn't laughing at her.

'No one else will ever love you like I do, Lisa,' Mark continued as soon as the waiter was out of earshot. 'Everything I do is for you. I work my ass off so you don't have to. I give you everything a woman could possibly want, you live a life of luxury that most women could only dream of. God knows, I don't ask for much in return.'

'I appreciate it, Mark,' she said placatingly, putting a hand on his arm.

'You have a funny way of showing it.' He shook her

hand off impatiently. 'I'm going to be away for a week, and I thought we could have a nice dinner tonight, just the two of us, and have a weekend to ourselves. But you have to ruin it, like you ruin everything. I suppose you'd prefer to be with Grayson. Would you rather we just forget this and go over there instead?' He tossed his napkin on the table.

'No, of course not,' Lisa said, stroking his arm soothingly. She felt exhausted and worn down, all the fight beaten out of her. 'I don't care about Grayson. You know I was only with him because it was what you wanted. Other men don't interest me. I just want to be with you – only you.'

He sighed finally, and his features softened, relenting. She hated how relieved she felt. 'I'm sorry, sweetheart. It's just that I love you so much. I'm so scared of you leaving me. I can't bear the thought of living without you, Lisa.'

'I know. But I'll never leave you, Mark.'

'Promise me.' He grabbed her hand, crushing it in his, a fierce intensity in his eyes as he gazed at her. 'I'd do anything to make you happy, Lisa. Just promise you won't ever leave me.'

'I promise.'

'Let's not fight.' He lifted her hand to his lips and kissed it. 'Think about the party idea while I'm away, okay? Will you do that for me?'

She nodded uncertainly.

'It would really mean a lot to me, Lisa.'

'I'll think about it,' she said. But already her mind was on the envelope of cash hidden in her nightstand drawer.

On Monday morning, Mark left for China. He had been on his best behaviour since dinner on Friday, and Lisa caught a rare glimpse of the man she had fallen in love with – as sweet, affectionate and solicitous as he'd been when they first met. But it was a pattern she was familiar with by now. He was always like that after a row, on a mission to win her around again if he felt unsure of her. In the past, she had been taken in by his shows of remorse, accepting his excuses and forgiving his behaviour time and again. He would play on her sympathy, opening up to her about his childhood with an absent father and cold, emotionally abusive mother who had made him insecure and distrustful, feeling undeserving of love. So she had made allowances, and believed him when he promised that things would be different in future.

Now she saw it all for the manipulative behaviour that it was. He had kept her constantly off balance, as she tried to gauge and manage his moods. It was like walking through a minefield, and she never knew what might trigger the next explosion. He would fly into a jealous rage if she so much as glanced at another man. He would accuse her of sleeping around while he was at work, and became obsessive about tracking her movements. One moment he would tell her she was unattractive, ignorant and boring in bed, and that no one else could ever love her; the next that she was the cleverest, sexiest, most beautiful woman he'd ever known, and that he wasn't worthy of her. It was an endless cycle of emotional abuse followed by spells of utter adoration, and it was mentally and emotionally exhausting until Lisa felt so ground down by it that she had no strength left to stand up for herself.

But somehow over the last few months she had found the reserves within her to fight back. She saw Mark clearly now for what he was – an abusive, controlling man, incapable of real love or affection. She believed he did love her in his own sick, twisted way – but it was an unhealthy obsessive fixation that scared her, and she wanted nothing more than to get far away from it. So she had slowly started to build up her confidence and self-esteem along with her hoard of cash, stealthily working towards the day when she could make her escape.

He had left this morning with the promise that he would Skype her every night. She knew what that meant. He would be keeping an eye on her, controlling her even when he was on the other side of the world. There was no respite from him.

'Think about what we discussed on Friday,' was his parting shot. 'The parties? It would mean a lot to me if you could do this for me.'

She hadn't been lying when she had promised to think about it. She could think of little else now, her mind constantly preoccupied with trying to find a way out. It made her more desperate to leave than ever.

As soon as he'd gone, she ran upstairs and took out

her hidden envelope, pouring the notes out onto the bed. But the reassurance she usually felt at the sight of the money eluded her. Instead she just felt frustrated by how little there was. This would be the perfect opportunity for her to escape, while Mark was away. It was the first time he had left her on her own while he was out of the country. Who knew when it would happen again? She picked up the money, counting the notes, but she already knew it wasn't enough. She had to get far away, and she needed enough to live on until she found her feet and established a life somewhere else. If Mark knew where she was, he would follow her. He'd never leave her alone. Women like her ended up dead. She would just have to be patient.

She'd bided her time this long, she told herself – she could do it a bit longer. But she felt a mounting sense of panic at the thought of letting this opportunity slip through her fingers. She looked around the room, her eyes scanning the place for something she could sell, desperation driving her to think like a thief. Any one of the paintings would fund her escape, but they were too traceable – they would lead Mark right to her. The jewellery he had given her was very valuable, and would raise questions if she tried to sell it for cash.

Tears of frustration stung her eyes. What she needed was a fairy godmother, she thought wryly – or just a regular wealthy friend who could lend her the money she needed. But Mark had isolated her until there was no one she could turn to for help – and besides, she had never had friends with that kind of money.

Suddenly her thoughts flew to Grayson. He was wealthy – and he said he wanted to be her friend. He could give her the money she needed and not even miss it. Could she ask him to lend it to her? She chewed her lip thoughtfully. He seemed kind, and she thought he would want to help her if he knew she was in trouble.

But she dismissed the idea almost immediately. Money bestowed power, and she couldn't give a man that kind of control over her ever again, no matter how nice he seemed. Mark had been kind and charming at the start. No, she thought, scooping up the money and stuffing it back into the envelope, she would have to do this herself, no matter how long it took. It would be worth it in the end when she was free and beholden to no one.

On the other hand … She did have something she could sell Grayson. He wanted her. She knew he did. It would be a fair exchange, so it wouldn't be like she was asking him for a favour. It would be more like a business transaction. She wouldn't owe him anything. She didn't think he'd betray her to Mark, so she had nothing to lose – if he turned her down, she'd be no worse off than she was now. But if he took her up on it … She felt a leap of excitement in her chest at the idea. Would Grayson be prepared to pay, she wondered. Did he want her badly enough to pay to have sex with her?

She shook her head as if to dislodge the idea from her brain. It was ridiculous! Desperation was making her fanciful. Grayson was young, attractive and charming – he wouldn't need to pay anyone for sex. She would just end up embarrassing him and humiliating herself when he refused her. No, she would have to continue biding her time for another while, she thought, as she put the envelope back into the box, secreting it once more in the drawer. Mark had agreed to wait until after their holiday for the surgery, and she would find a way to buy herself more time with the orgy thing. She had to be patient for a little longer.

She tried to put the idea out of her head as she got

ready to spend some time in the gym. Since making the decision to leave Mark, she had started to relish her workouts. He had installed the state of the art gym at the top of the house where her studio had been, and always insisted that she exercise daily. But she worked out for herself now, and she trained harder than ever. She had a sense of purpose, getting fit and healthy for her new life, and it gave her great satisfaction to feel herself get physically and mentally stronger with each day. As she headed upstairs, she decided she would focus on that and put all thoughts of propositioning Grayson out of her mind.

But the idea refused to go away, niggling at her brain as she pounded on the treadmill, and firmly taking hold as she watched herself in the mirror pumping weights. As it took root in her mind, she felt more positive and hopeful than she had in years. She was going to do it, she decided, working it over in her head as she lifted the weights, pumping herself up mentally as well as physically, trying to muster the courage she needed.

What did she have to lose? Sure, it would be humiliating if Grayson turned her down, but she would get over it. She never had to see him again. Besides what was a little humiliation compared to the degradation and abuse she put up with on a daily basis? On the other hand, if he agreed, she had a hell of a lot to gain. It was a gamble, but it was a chance she had to take when her freedom was at stake.

There was a far greater risk, of course. If Grayson did turn her down, could she count on him not to tell Mark what she had proposed? He had kept secrets for her before, and she felt she could trust him. She just had to hope she was right.

Once she had resolved to do it, she didn't waste any more time. She abandoned her workout midway through, racing downstairs to change before she talked herself out of it again. She had to do this now before she lost her nerve. If she thought about it too much, she would never go through with it. That meant she would have to go to Grayson's workplace. But it was better that way, she told herself, since this was basically a business proposition she was putting to him.

She did a quick internet search on her phone and found the address of Grayson's offices. Then she showered quickly and dressed with care, trying to choose clothes that would be appealing to Grayson. She picked out a cream button-down dress in a simple, figure-hugging style and a pair of medium-height heels in navy, teaming it with matching navy accessories. Mark liked her to wear this outfit for daytime events and lunches. It was subtly sexy without being overtly provocative. As she carefully applied her make-up, she rehearsed what she would say and tried to ignore the shaking of her fingers as she applied mascara and lipstick, pushing the enormity of what she was about to do to the back of her mind. When she was done, she surveyed herself from all angles in the mirror and was satisfied with her appearance. Then she picked up her bag and raced out of the house before she could change her mind. She walked to the corner of the road and hailed a cab.

The cab dropped her off in front of a large converted warehouse in the east of the city. A silver plate to one side of the door was inscribed simply 'Fielding Architects'. It was a beautiful old building, the yellow brickwork broken up by rows of massive floor-height windows, and Lisa paused for a moment on the footpath to admire it before stepping inside. There was something about it that she found instantly comforting and reassuring, and it brought a smile to her face. Perhaps it was the way it had been so sympathetically restored in keeping with its history and surroundings. It was impressive without being in any way flash or showy, and it reminded her of Grayson.

Inside it had the same friendly feel, despite the cavernous dimensions of the space. A love for original materials and features was evident in the exposed pipes and brickwork, and the vaulted ceilings and enamel light fixtures paid homage to the building's industrial past. Combined with contemporary elements of interior design, the overall effect was vibrant, eclectic and energetic.

Lisa's legs felt wobbly as she crossed the light-filled lobby to the large reception desk, where she was greeted with a smile by an immaculately groomed young woman.

'Good morning. How may I help you?' she asked.

Lisa took a deep breath, trying to appear calm and in control. 'I'm here to see Grayson Fielding,' she said.

'Do you have an appointment?' the woman asked.

'Oh.' This hadn't occurred to Lisa. Of course, she should have realised Grayson would be busy. She felt foolish, wishing she had thought this through. But then, if she'd thought about it too much at all, she'd never have come. 'No, I don't,' she said with an apologetic grimace.

'I'm sorry, but Mr. Fielding won't be able to see you without an appointment.'

'Could you just tell him I'm here? I'm a … friend.'

'What's your name, please?'

'Lisa Matthews.'

'Why don't I send you up to his personal assistant, and perhaps she can help you?' The woman smiled pleasantly, picking up the telephone as she spoke. Lisa could tell she was just passing the buck, happy to hand over the unpleasant task of getting rid of her to Grayson's PA. 'It's on the fourth floor.' She pointed to a bank of lifts at the other side of the lobby. 'When you come out of the lifts, it's straight ahead at the end of the corridor. I'll ring her and tell her you're on your way.' She punched a couple of numbers into the phone.

'Thank you.' Lisa gave her a grateful smile and turned to the lifts.

She emerged on the fourth floor and followed the receptionist's directions to a large office at the far end of the corridor. Beyond the open door, a glamorous woman with wavy blonde hair sat behind a desk in front of a small seating area with squashy leather sofas and chairs grouped around a low glass coffee table. She stood as Lisa approached her, holding out her hand.

'Hello, I'm Gaby, Mr. Fielding's PA. How may I help you today?'

'Hello,' Lisa said as they shook hands. 'My name is Lisa Matthews. I just wanted to see Grayson. I'm a—a friend of his.'

Gaby raised an eyebrow at Lisa's slight hesitation over the word 'friend', but said nothing, her polite smile never faltering. 'I'm afraid he's with clients at the moment,' she said. 'But we can set you up with an appointment for another time?' She sat back down and waved Lisa to a seat in front of the desk.

'Oh.' Lisa remained standing, twisting the strap of her bag nervously in her hand. 'I, um … it was a spur of the moment thing,' she said with a conspiratorial laugh. 'I was in the area and I thought I'd surprise him. I should have thought …' She trailed off, biting her lip. 'Maybe I could wait?'

'I'm sorry, but he's tied up all day.'

Lisa glanced at her watch. It was almost one. 'I thought I'd take him to lunch,' she said, forcing a bright smile. 'Doesn't he take a break?'

'Unfortunately, he has a lunch meeting today.'

'Can't you just get a message to him that I'm here?' Lisa persisted. She hated making a nuisance of herself, but she'd never get up the nerve to do this again. 'I think he'd want to see me. It won't take long. I only need a couple of minutes with him.'

Gaby shook her head. 'Sorry, but he doesn't want to be disturbed. Look, why don't you leave your number and I'll tell him you called.'

Lisa sighed in frustration. Gaby clearly thought she had 'crazed stalker' written across her forehead in large letters. No doubt she was just doing her job, keeping people like her from wasting Grayson's time. 'Could I just wait here?' she asked, waving to one of the couches. Surely he had to finish work some time.

'There's really no point,' Gaby said, barely hiding her irritation now. 'He won't be able to see you. But I'll tell him you called, and I'm sure he'll be in touch.'

Lisa nodded. 'Okay. Thank you,' she murmured, swallowing over the lump forming in her throat.

'If you'd like to make an appointment for another time, leave your number with me and we'll get back to you as soon as we can,' Gaby added helpfully.

'No, that's … that won't be necessary,' Lisa said. She couldn't risk having Grayson's office number on her phone. If Mark were to discover it, she would never be able to explain it away. 'I'll try him at home later,' she said, backing out of the office, her lip trembling.

Blinking back tears, she turned and stumbled back down the corridor towards the lifts. She didn't know what to do now. She felt ridiculous and deflated. She had worked so hard psyching herself up to come here, and it had all been for nothing. It was stupid of her to think she could just walk in and see Grayson in the middle of the working day.

'Lisa?' Startled, she turned in the direction of the voice to see Grayson walking towards her, frowning at her curiously. She had been so wrapped up in her misery, she hadn't even heard him approach.

'Lisa?' he said again as he came close. 'What are you doing here?'

'I— I came to see you.'

'Well, this is a surprise – a very pleasant one,' he added with a smile. 'Why did no one tell me you were here?' he asked, glancing back towards Gaby's office with a frown.

'I … um … I know you're busy. I'm sorry. It doesn't matter.' She shook her head. She turned away as the lift arrived with a ping.

'I'm not too busy for you,' he said, taking her hand as the lift doors opened. 'Come into my office.' He jerked his head in the direction from which she had come.

Lisa hesitated for a second, then nodded, relieved that all her effort wouldn't be wasted after all.

'I'm sorry, Gaby didn't tell me you were here,' he said crossly as he led her back down the corridor.

'She didn't think you'd want to be disturbed,' Lisa said, not wanting to get the woman into trouble.

Grayson sighed. 'She's just doing her job,' he said more reasonably. 'I do pay her to keep people out. But sometimes she's too bloody good at it.'

Gaby's eyebrows shot up as they reached the entrance to her office, and she rose from her desk. 'Sorry, Grayson,' she said, with a wave towards Lisa. 'You said you didn't want any interruptions.'

'It's all right, Gaby,' he said with a wry smile. 'You weren't to know, but Lisa is an exception.'

Gaby nodded. 'Sorry,' she said to Lisa with a more genuine smile than she'd had before.

Lisa smiled back. Then Grayson led her through

another door off the corridor and into a vast office with breathtaking views over the river. He waved her to a seat in front of a large desk that was covered in plans and drawings.

'So, you wanted to see me?' he asked, leaning against the desk and folding his arms as he looked down at her.

'Yes.' Lisa licked her lips. 'I wanted to— I mean, I have a ...' She trailed off, all her rehearsed words failing her now that she was actually here in front of him.

She took a deep breath and started again. 'I wanted to make you a proposition,' she said.

'A proposition?' He raised his eyebrows, seeming taken aback.

'Yes. Well ... an offer, really.'

'I see. And what is it that you're offering?'

Lisa looked at the floor, screwing up her courage. Then she lifted her head and looked him in the eyes. 'Me.'

14

Grayson was taken aback, she could tell. He just looked at her, and the silence was agonising. 'You?' he asked eventually.

'Um … yes.' God, what if she'd read him all wrong? Maybe he wasn't interested in her in that way at all.

He frowned, looking perplexed. 'I'm sorry, I'm not sure I understand. Are you saying what I think you're saying? I just want to be clear.'

She took a deep breath, steeling herself to look him in the eye. 'I mean sex. I'll sleep with you – if you want me, that is.'

A small smile tugged at the corners of his lips. 'I think it's pretty clear that I want you – very much.' His eyes were warm on hers, and she realised that he didn't yet understand exactly what she was proposing.

Damn! She chewed her lip nervously, not sure how to introduce the subject of money. She should have started with that. He thought she had simply changed her mind, and had decided to have an affair with him. 'How much exactly?' she asked.

'How much?' He frowned in confusion. 'Sorry, I don't understand.'

'I mean, how much do you want me? What's it worth to you?'

Something flickered in his eyes and the smile was wiped from his face. He was silent for what seemed like an age. 'You're talking about money?' he asked finally. 'You want me to pay you?'

'Yes. I don't see why I shouldn't get something out of it,' she said more boldly.

Grayson looked baffled, and a little intrigued. She had taken him by surprise. She got the impression that didn't happen often.

'Well,' he said, with a crooked smile, his eyes roving over her body, 'I like to flatter myself that you'd get a lot of pleasure out of it.'

She shrugged. 'I'm not interested in having sex with you for pleasure,' she said coolly. 'But I'll sleep with you if you pay me.'

He narrowed his eyes at her. 'How much?'

The question felt like a slap. For the first time she felt like a whore and the brutal reality of what she was doing hit her. But she couldn't betray her nerves and risk this all falling apart. This was a gamble and she was playing with the highest stakes of her life. If she succeeded, she could win big – she could win her freedom. She assumed her best poker face. 'A thousand pounds,' she said. She was pleased with how steady and firm her voice sounded. It took all her nerve to maintain eye contact as she said it.

Grayson raised his eyebrows and gave a low whistle under his breath. 'That's a lot of money.'

She shrugged. 'You're a wealthy man, aren't you?'

'Yes,' he said matter-of-factly. 'Very.'

'Well, then. It's all relative, isn't it?'

'You don't get rich – or stay rich – by throwing money away.'

She forced herself not to react to the implied insult. It took all her will not to flinch or lose eye contact, but it was vital that she brazen this out.

'You really think you're worth that much?'

'It depends how much you want me,' she said without emotion. 'I'm worth whatever you're prepared to pay for me. That's how the market works, right?' She had to stand her ground. She had nothing to lose. If he wanted her badly enough, he would pay what she asked. If he didn't, she would be no worse off than she had been before.

He laughed softly to himself. 'Yes, that's how it works. What would I get for a thousand?'

'Me.'

'Yes, but for how long? One time? One night? What acts exactly would you perform?'

'One night,' she said. 'And I'll do whatever you want.'

He drew in a harsh breath. 'Whatever I want?' he asked. He seemed almost angry. 'What if I want to be rough with you? Hurt you even?'

She bit the inside of her lip, willing herself not to show her panic. Could she really let him do whatever he wanted to her? What if he was sadistic? Still, she reasoned, it could hardly be worse than what she'd had to endure from Mark. And it would just be for a week at the most.

She nodded. 'That would be all right.'

His eyes widened. 'Please tell me you're not in the habit of making offers like this to men you barely know.'

'I've never made anyone an offer like this before.'

'Thank Christ for that!' He sighed.

She frowned, wondering why he'd care.

'I hate to think of someone taking you up on it,' he said, as if he understood her confusion.

'Does that mean you're not going to take me up on it?'

He sighed. 'Are you in some kind of trouble, Lisa? If you need money, I could help you.'

'I don't want a handout.'

'I could give you a loan.'

'I don't know when I could pay it back – maybe never.'

'That doesn't matter.'

'It matters to me. I do need money, but I have to earn it.'

Grayson frowned at her. She could tell he was torn.

'I can't accept a gift or a loan from you. The money has to be mine, free and clear. I can't explain, but this is the only way I can do this. If you don't want to accept my offer, I'll go away and I won't bother you again. I'd just ask that you please forget that this ever happened and don't mention it to anyone.'

'Lisa, I don't want to feel I'm exploiting you. If you're in some sort of trouble—'

'It's nothing like that.'

'But you won't tell me what it is?'

'No, I can't. But I promise you it's nothing sinister. I just want to make some good money quickly, and this is an easy way for me to earn it. After all,' she added with a sudden flash of inspiration, 'it's not as if I'm not attracted to you.' She thought of their kiss in the library. He had left it up to her to make the first move and she had initiated it. She hoped he was remembering it too, and that it would ease his qualms about taking advantage of her. 'You know I want you too,' she said, looking up at him seductively from under her eyelashes.

Grayson looked at her for a long time, his eyes dark and unreadable, but she thought she saw desire hidden in their depths, and she felt sure he was remembering that kiss too.

'But you won't act on that unless I pay you?'

'No.'

'What about Mark?' he asked. 'Are you leaving him?'

'No, this has nothing to do with Mark.'

'But you can't ask him to help you out?'

'No. I can't.' She twisted her hands in her lap. 'He—he gives me enough as it is. I can't ask him for more.'

His eyes narrowed. 'You still love him?'

'My feelings for Mark haven't changed,' she said, choosing her words carefully. She didn't want to lie any more than was necessary. 'We're still together. But he's away on business this week.'

'So you're available to have a fling with me?' His mouth curled up at one corner.

'Yes, for one week only,' she said brightly. 'It's a limited time offer. Like I said, I want you, Grayson. This way, I can get you out of my system, and it won't seem so much like cheating if you're paying me.'

He gave a startled laugh. 'Interesting logic,' he said with a quirk of an eyebrow.

She shrugged. 'We can both get what we want, and no one gets hurt. It seems like a win-win to me.' She kept her tone light, insouciant.

Finally he sighed and leaned back on the desk, his hands gripping the edge. 'Okay,' he said. 'I accept.'

'You do?' Lisa smiled, relief flooding through her body.

He nodded, his eyes already heated as they rested on her face. 'Yes, so help me. I do.'

'There are a couple of conditions. First, this has to be a secret. You mustn't tell anyone. Mark can't ever find out.'

His jaw clenched as he nodded. 'Understood.'

'And I'll need the money in cash.'

'That's not a problem,' he said, but he looked concerned.

'Okay, great!' she said with a smile. 'Thank you.'

'So when is this … transaction going to take place?' he asked.

'Any time you like this week. Mark is away until Tuesday. But I always have to leave by midnight.' Mark had told her that he would Skype around six each evening Chinese time, which would be about one in the morning in London. She couldn't risk missing that call. 'Apart from that, it's up to you. When would you like to do it?'

He pushed away from the desk and came towards her. He took her hand and pulled her to standing, their bodies almost touching. Then he cupped her face, his eyes burning into hers as his thumb stroked her cheek.

'I'd *like* to do it right now,' he said, his gaze fixed on her mouth. 'I'd like to take you to the hotel down the street — or have you right here on my couch.' She followed his gaze as his eyes flicked to the leather sofa across the room. 'The possibilities are endless.'

His hands pushed up into her hair as he bent to kiss her. His lips were soft and warm on hers. He wrapped his arms around her, pulling her closer as his tongue slid across her lips and into her mouth. She pressed herself against him, waves of heat and pleasure washing over her as she buried her fingers in his hair.

Finally he lifted his head, his eyes dark with desire. 'What if I want more?' he asked.

'More?' Her voice was shaky. She already felt she was losing control of this situation.

'More than one night.'

'You can have me as often as you like in the next seven days,' she said. 'But it will cost you more.'

He smiled sadly, his eyes crinkling. 'Lisa,' he said softly, one finger lightly tracing the curve of her jaw. 'You're not who I thought you were.'

His words and the look in his eyes saddened her. She wished she could be herself with him. She wished she could just let this happen naturally between them – no money, no agenda. But she couldn't. It was her only hope, and she couldn't afford to be sentimental right now.

'How much for a lunchtime quickie?' he asked with a crooked smile.

'Two hundred,' she blurted, before she had a chance to second guess herself.

Grayson raised his eyebrows. 'You know I could get a professional for a quarter of that?'

'That's your choice,' she shrugged, determined to keep her cool and not let him shame her into backing down. 'But this offer isn't open to anyone but you. You pay more for exclusivity.' She was gambling on him wanting *her* specifically, but the heat in his eyes reassured her that it wasn't a big risk.

'Agreed,' Grayson said. 'Can you start right away?'

She gulped and nodded, her heart starting to race. She hadn't expected this to happen so fast. She'd thought she'd have more time to prepare. But she didn't want to put him off.

'But don't you have a lunch meeting?' she asked.

'Damn!' He threw his head back and closed his eyes in exasperation. 'And I have a site visit in Scotland in the morning. I'm flying up there tonight.' He sighed. Then suddenly he grabbed her hand. 'Come with me,' he said urgently, his eyes dancing with excitement.

'I can't,' Lisa said regretfully. 'I have to leave by midnight, remember?'

'Shit! I wish I'd known you were going to turn up today with this fantastical proposal,' he said with a wry smile. 'I would have arranged my week around it.'

'Sorry.' She hated having to say no, afraid he would

regret his decision. She wished she could tell him that if she had a choice in the matter, she would much rather be in Scotland with him than at home Skyping with Mark.

'I guess I'll just have to wait until tomorrow evening,' he said, trailing a finger lightly along her jaw. 'But it's going to be torture.' His eyes were dark, his tone brooding. 'I'll spend the whole time thinking about you – the feel of your naked body against mine, the taste of you ...'

Lisa felt her nipples tighten, heat spreading through her at his words. He wrapped his arms around her, pulling her closer, so she felt the hardness of his erection. He smelled amazing, of citrus and sandalwood, and she was consumed with longing.

'Do you have any time before your meeting?' she asked breathily.

He raised his eyebrows. 'Only about fifteen minutes. What are you suggesting?'

She answered him with actions rather than words, her hand going to the bulge in his trousers. His breath hitched as she began stroking him. She dropped her eyes to watch the movements of her hand, licking her lips suggestively as she felt his cock harden beneath her fingers.

She looked up at him questioningly, and he nodded, his eyes burning into hers. 'Just give me a moment.' He pulled away, then went to his desk and picked up the phone. 'Gaby, I don't want to be disturbed for the next fifteen minutes. There's no need to let me know when the guys from Global Tech arrive. Just keep them out there, and I'll join them at two. Thanks.'

He put down the phone, swiftly crossed to the door and locked it. Then he went to the sofa and took a cushion from it. His eyes were on Lisa as he walked back to her and tossed it on the floor in front of him.

Lisa sank to her knees on the cushion, grateful for his

thoughtfulness. Her hands went to his belt, unfastening it deftly.

'Can you open your dress?' he asked huskily. 'I want to see you.'

She nodded, her hands shaky as she quickly unbuttoned the top of her dress and let it fall to her waist. Then she reached around and unfastened her bra, taking it off and tossing it aside. She knew it wasn't just the cool air hitting her skin that caused her nipples to feel tight and achy, longing to be touched. She couldn't remember when she had last felt this turned on, but she still recognised the feeling, and she knew it was down to wanting Grayson, and the way his eyes darkened and burned when she exposed her body to him.

His gaze fixed on her breasts as she unzipped his trousers and pulled them down along with his boxers. He was hard and thick, his erection straining against his stomach, and she was taken aback by how much she wanted this. She wanted to touch him and taste him, she longed to feel the warm fullness of his cock in her mouth. She wanted to please him, but what took her by surprise was the realisation that she wanted this for herself – it would be for her as much as it was for him.

She cupped his balls, stroking them softly while she licked the length of his shaft. His breathing deepened as she curled her hand around his cock and licked around the head, feeling it twitch and throb in her fist as she swirled her tongue around the tip. He groaned deeply as she cupped his balls in one hand and pumped his shaft with the other, while she licked and sucked. He pushed his hands into her hair as she took him into her mouth, slowly at first, sucking him rhythmically as she took him deeper and deeper. He felt warm and heavy in her mouth, and she couldn't get enough of him. She waited for him to grab her hair and start fucking her mouth like Mark would, pushing himself down her throat until she gagged. But his hands were gentle, his fingers tugging lightly as they clutched her hair, and she felt a surge of excitement as she realised that he wasn't going to take over. She felt powerful and sexy knowing that she was in control, she was in charge of his pleasure. She felt his body shake as she hollowed her cheeks and increased the suction, and she swelled with pride at his sharp intake of breath as his cock hit the back of her throat, glad that she could do this for him, that she could take him so deep, give him such pleasure.

'Oh, fuck!' he groaned, his hands fisting in her hair as she sucked him deep again and again, driven on by his helpless moans of pleasure. She felt him throb and knew he was close.

'Lisa,' he said urgently, his voice shaky as he pushed firmly on her forehead. 'I'm going to come.' He pulled away, and she looked up at him in confusion.

'That's okay,' she said, opening her mouth and leaning towards him, but he shook his head, and then his whole body jerked and he came over her breasts with a groan.

He stood looking at her dazedly as his breathing returned to normal, his eyes blank and unseeing. He seemed stunned. Then he blinked hard, as if waking himself up.

His eyes widened as they raked over her chest. 'Sorry,' he said with an apologetic grimace. 'I hope I didn't mess up your dress.' He hastily pulled his trousers back on. His belt still hanging loose, he held a hand out to her and helped her up.

Lisa blushed as she glanced down at her bare chest covered in his cum. 'It's okay,' she said shakily.

He ran a hand through his hair, throwing her another

apologetic look. 'There's a bathroom through here,' he said, grabbing her hand and leading her across the room. 'You can get cleaned up.'

She didn't pull her dress back up, holding it at her waist as he led her through to a small bathroom. It was decorated in keeping with the rest of the building, with lots of exposed brickwork and pipes, and industrial style light fittings. A wall of glass panels framed in black metal separated a large concrete shower stall from the rest of the room. Distracted by taking in her surroundings, she hardly noticed as Grayson lifted her onto the countertop and ran a washcloth under the tap.

'I love your office,' she said absently.

'Thank you,' Grayson said, smiling at her as he turned off the tap. His obvious pleasure at her remark made her smile – he was clearly very proud of the building. 'I didn't have much money when I started out here, but I think it worked to my advantage – forced me to be more creative with the design and materials.'

Before she realised what he intended, he started wiping her chest with the warm cloth.

'Oh!' she blushed, putting a hand over his to still it. 'I —I can do that myself.'

'Of course, sorry.' He withdrew his hand immediately and she took the cloth from him. 'There are clean towels,' he said, nodding to a shelf. 'I'll give you some privacy. Come out whenever you're ready.'

Lisa nodded dumbly and he left the room, closing the door behind him. She was relieved to be alone – she needed a moment to pull herself together. She realised her hands were shaking as she washed herself. She felt disoriented, still reeling from what had happened – and Grayson had seemed almost as flustered as she was. It had taken them both by surprise, she supposed – it had all happened so suddenly, before either of them had had time to adjust to the idea. When she had towelled herself dry, she refastened her bra and buttoned up her dress. Her hands trembled as she smoothed her hair in the mirror, and she looked tense and nervous. She took a few deep breaths, trying to calm herself down before she stepped back into the office.

Grayson was standing with his back to her, looking out the window. He turned as she came into the room.

'Ready?' he asked, raising a querying eyebrow. His clothes were once more in order, and he looked smooth and unruffled, every inch the professional, totally in control. It was hard to believe that just moments ago he had groaned helplessly as she sucked him off.

Lisa nodded, still not able to find her voice.

He crossed the room to her. 'Are you okay?' he asked, his eyes full of concern, and she saw the anxiety in his face then, the uncertainty, and she knew he wasn't as calm as he appeared. He wasn't unaffected by what had happened between them.

'Yes,' she said faintly as he took her hand lightly in his. To her surprise, he raised it to his lips and kissed it, and she was taken aback by the sweetness of the gesture.

'I feel a bit wobbly, to be honest,' she admitted with a small smile.

'I know,' he said. He pressed a soft, lingering kiss to her forehead, his hand ghosting against her waist. 'Me too.'

She was surprised to find her eyes filling with tears, but she was touched by his open admission of vulnerability. 'Sorry,' she said, smiling as she blinked the tears away. 'I don't usually do this sort of thing.'

'I know.' He smoothed her hair, tucking a stray strand behind her ear. 'You were amazing, Lisa,' he murmured.

He leaned in and kissed her softly on the lips. 'I wish I didn't have this meeting,' he said as he pulled back.

Lisa glanced at her watch. It was almost two. 'Oh yes, I'd better go.'

'I'll show you out,' Grayson said, taking her hand and leading her to the door.

He led her back down the corridor, a hand resting lightly on her back. Gaby flashed Lisa a friendly smile as they passed her office, and Lisa held up a hand in a quick wave.

Grayson pressed the button for the lift and stood beside her waiting.

'I can make my own way out,' Lisa said, turning to him. 'You don't have to wait.'

'No, I'll come down with you,' he said, just as the lift pinged and the doors opened.

They stepped inside and Grayson pressed the button for the lobby. 'We still have some arrangements to make. Like when I'll see you again. Can you come to my house tomorrow evening, around seven?'

'Yes, that's fine.'

'You remember the address? I can pick you up if you'd like.'

'No,' she shook her head. 'Thank you, but that's not necessary. I know where it is. I'll make my own way there.'

He nodded. 'Do you—' He broke off and frowned, looking uncertain. He swallowed and began again. 'Do you want me to pay you now?'

'Oh!' Lisa felt herself blush furiously. She had completely forgotten about the money! Some whore she'd make, she thought wryly.

'If you need money today, I can arrange—'

'No, there's no hurry,' she said quickly, her eyes sliding

away. She was mortified to be having this conversation – discussing taking money for sex.

Grayson's eyes narrowed. 'Are you sure you're okay?' he asked. 'If you don't want to go through with this—'

'No, I do. I'm fine.' She smiled to reassure him. 'I really want to do this.'

'Good.' He sighed. 'I wish I could blow off this thing tomorrow. I can't wait to see you again.' He drew her into his arms and kissed her softly, tantalisingly on the mouth, pulling away with a groan as the lift reached the lobby. Grayson hit the stall button.

'Well, I'll see you tomorrow night,' she said as she stepped out of the lift. 'Seven o'clock.'

'I'll look forward to it.'

'So will I.'

She nodded goodbye and turned to the door. Out on the street, she stumbled towards the Tube as if in a dream, her mind racing with what had just happened – and with what lay ahead for the rest of the week. As she walked, she tried to sort out the jumble of conflicting emotions that battled inside her. She was shaken by how she had felt with Grayson. What happened between them should have been humiliating for her, but she hadn't experienced any loss of dignity or self-respect. On the contrary, when she was with him she had felt powerful and cared for rather than used and degraded. She had *wanted* to touch him that way. She had been as desperate for him as he had been for her, and she realised she had forgotten what that felt like – mutual desire. They wanted each other. She had said the words automatically, but she realised now she hadn't been lying when she'd told Grayson she was looking forward to seeing him again. She couldn't wait.

15

THE FOLLOWING NIGHT, Lisa's heart was hammering as she got ready to go to Grayson's. She had spent the day preparing. She had had a wax, and got her hair and nails done. Then she had come home and had a long soak in the bath and massaged scented lotion into every inch of her skin. She had put on the red slip dress that she had worn the night she first met Grayson, and she was wearing the hated Louboutin heels too. They were hellishly uncomfortable, but Mark was right – her legs looked fantastic in them. This was the sexy, sophisticated image she had always presented to Grayson, she thought as she surveyed herself in the mirror, and it was what he would expect. He was paying a lot of money for her, and she was going to do her best to make sure he wasn't disappointed.

She tried to ignore the nervous fluttering in her stomach as she put the finishing touches to her make-up. But she was pleased with her appearance as she took a final look in the full-length mirror, and she was glad she had chosen to wear the spiky heels and skimpy dress. They helped her look the part and gave her confidence. She took

157

a deep, calming breath. Then she threw her keys into her bag, slung it on her shoulder and left, wondering what was in store for her tonight.

To her relief, Andrew had taken the opportunity to go on holiday while Mark was away, so she didn't have to find excuses to dispense with his services for the week. She walked to the main road and flagged down a taxi to take her to Grayson's.

Her nerves returned as she stood on his doorstep, but she had barely touched the bell when the door swung open.

'Hi!' Grayson beamed. He looked really pleased to see her, and she was touched by the warmth of his smile. 'Come in.'

Her legs felt shaky as she stepped into the hall.

'I've been looking forward to seeing you all day,' he said as she unbuttoned her coat and he stood behind her to take it from her. She was taken aback by this frank admission, instantly disarmed by his friendliness. She had thought he would be cool and aloof, but there was a tenderness in his eyes that was disconcerting, and a warmth and enthusiasm in his demeanour that took her by surprise. She had been half expecting him to slam her against the wall as soon as she arrived, or to order her to take off her clothes and get on her knees, like Mark often did. Grayson was paying her, after all – he'd be entitled. She was here as his paid whore, and yet he was treating her with more care and respect than her boyfriend. It was nice, but unsettling.

'You look beautiful,' he said, his eyes travelling over her body as he took her coat.

'Thank you,' she said breathily.

'Well, come through.' He placed a hand lightly on her back and guided her across the hall to the library. 'I thought we'd be more comfortable in here.' He ushered her in ahead of him. A cheerful fire blazed in the grate, and in front of it a small table set for two was placed between the deep armchairs. Lisa was taken aback – and touched. It was intimate and romantic, like a seduction scene – almost as if he was wooing her – and once again she felt knocked off balance.

'Have a seat.' He waved her to one of the chairs, and she sat, perching nervously on the edge.

'Wine?' He took a bottle from an ice bucket on the table, holding it aloft.

'Yes, please.'

'I made pasta,' he said as he poured two glasses. 'I hope that's okay?'

'You—you cooked?'

'Yes,' he smiled, handing her a glass. 'I'm not completely useless.'

'Oh, no, it's just—I didn't expect—'

'Oh, have you eaten?' He frowned.

'No.' The truth was she had barely eaten all day – she had been too nervous. But she hadn't expected him to cook for her – this wasn't a date. 'Pasta would be lovely. Thank you.'

In fact, it would be wonderful. She couldn't remember when she had last eaten pasta. Mark didn't allow it – yet another thing that he claimed made her 'bloated'. But Mark wasn't here – and with a bit of luck, he would never see the effects of the pasta on her figure.

'Good.' Grayson picked up an envelope from the mantelpiece. 'Why don't we get this out of the way first, so we can relax,' he said, crossing to where she sat and handing it to her.

'Oh! Thank you.' She blushed, realising this was her payment, as she took the slim white envelope from him, her fingers brushing against his.

He nodded. 'I'm just going to finish up,' he said, going to the door. 'It'll be ready in a moment.'

'Is there anything I can do?' Lisa asked.

He shook his head. 'Just relax,' he said with a gentle smile. 'It won't be a moment.'

Lisa slipped the envelope into her bag as soon as he was out of the room, grateful for how discreetly he had handled that. She sipped her wine, trying to relax. But she was aware that she had just crossed a line. She had taken money for sex. Grayson had upheld his end of the bargain – now she had to hold up hers. There was no going back, she thought, wrapping her arms around herself, unconsciously seeking comfort.

Unable to sit still as she waited for Grayson to return, she stood and took the opportunity to get a proper look at the artwork in the room. There were some amazing pieces, and most of the artists she recognised and admired. She was studying a large abstract by one of her favourite painters when Grayson came into the room carrying a tray. He placed two large white bowls of steaming pasta on the table, then came to stand beside her.

'You like this?' he asked, nodding at the canvas.

'Yes, very much.'

'You have excellent taste.' He smiled. 'It's my favourite.'

'You're very lucky to own it.' She knew the artist's work fetched very high prices. 'I love his stuff, but it's way beyond my means.'

'I'm sure Mark could afford it.'

'He's not such a fan as I am, unfortunately,' she said with a sigh. 'And it's his house, so …' She shrugged. Mark wasn't about to buy art that wasn't to his taste just to please her. She would have been happy with a print of something she loved, but Mark didn't approve of prints. 'Maybe one day …' She trailed off wistfully.

'Well, let's eat before it gets cold,' Grayson said. He took her hand and led her back to the table. He pulled out a chair for her, and as she sat, his fingers brushed lightly against her arm.

'Bon appétit,' he said, dropping a kiss on her bare shoulder. He was being very tactile, but not in an aggressive, brutish way like she had expected. He was gentle and lover-like, as if he was trying to seduce her – which didn't make any sense in the circumstances. It was a little unnerving.

'Are you warm enough?' he asked as he took his seat opposite.

'Yes. Thank you.' She lifted her fork and spoon. 'This looks wonderful.'

It tasted every bit as good as it looked. The silky linguini was coated in a delicate sauce of lobster and cream, and Lisa ate hungrily. It had been too long since she'd had pasta, she thought, closing her eyes to savour the texture of it in her mouth. It was heaven. When she was on her own again she would eat pasta all the time. She could have it every day – twice a day if she wanted. And pizza! She should start making a list of foods she could indulge in when she was no longer with Mark, she decided, and add it to her mental picture of what her future would look like. She couldn't have a physical inspiration board, but she kept one in her head, and it helped her to stay motivated and focused on her goals. When she was having a bad day and slipping into despair, visualising her future life buoyed her up.

She suddenly became aware of Grayson watching her, smiling indulgently, and realised she had zoned out. 'This is really good,' she said to cover her embarrassment.

'I'm glad you like it.'

'You're a good cook.'

'I enjoy it. I don't get to do it often enough.'

'So, where's Isabel tonight? Doesn't she mind you having another woman here?'

'No.' He smiled. 'I told you, Isabel and I aren't like that. We're just friends.'

She nodded. 'Friends with benefits. I remember.' Once again she felt hopelessly naive. She didn't understand these casual sexual relationships – and she didn't think she ever would.

'You don't approve,' he said.

Damn! She must have let some of what she was thinking show in her face. *Fix it, Lisa!* 'No,' she said hastily, 'it's not that. It's like Mark said – I'm very parochial.' She gave a self-deprecating laugh. 'I'm just not very sophisticated, I'm afraid.'

'Yet here you are,' he said softly. The implication was clear – here she was, ready and willing to have sex for money. She could hardly claim to be a wide-eyed innocent.

She shrugged. 'Well, I'm learning.'

'What about you and Mark? You seem to have a pretty open relationship.'

'Not as much as you'd think. Mark is … quite possessive. If he knew I was here—' She stopped abruptly. She had been going to say *If he knew I was here, he'd kill me*. Still, even if she had said it, Grayson wouldn't take it literally. People said that all the time. It was just an expression.

'Don't worry, I won't say anything.' He covered her hand with his in a reassuring gesture.

'Thank you,' she smiled. As they ate, Lisa felt herself relax. The heat of the fire, Grayson's easygoing manner and the comfort of the food all combined to soothe her and put her at ease.

'Dessert?' Grayson asked as he got up and started clearing their plates.

'No, thank you,' Lisa said automatically. She never ate dessert. Mark didn't allow it. Then she remembered the first night they had met, and blushed. Maybe he didn't mean dessert literally …

'There's chocolate mousse,' Grayson said temptingly, a teasing smile playing about his lips. 'I made it specially.'

'Oh. Well, in that case …' Lisa relented with a smile, feeling very reckless.

Grayson grinned and left the room, and Lisa's smile faded as it struck her how ridiculous it was that she should feel so daring simply for saying yes to dessert. God, she was pathetic!

She shook off her gloomy thoughts as Grayson returned with two little individual pots of mousse topped with whipped cream.

'Oh my God, this is amazing!' Lisa said as she swallowed the first mouthful. It was rich and indulgent, and tasted so good, she almost wanted to cry. Chocolate was another food that was going on her list, she decided.

Grayson smiled at her. 'Well, it's nice to have such an appreciative guest.'

A loaded silence fell between them as they finished eating. Grayson pushed back from the table and sipped his wine, and Lisa felt his heavy, hooded gaze on her.

'Come here,' he said finally, holding out a hand to her, his dark eyes glittering with intent.

She took his hand and stood. Time to pay the piper, she thought, about to sink to her knees in front of him. She was startled when instead he pulled her onto his lap, wrapping his arms around her.

'I can't believe you're finally here, like this,' he said, one hand stroking her cheek softly, while he gazed at her. He dropped a kiss to her bare shoulder. 'I've thought about having you here so often,' he said, nuzzling her neck. 'What I'd like to do to you.' He kissed her ear, tugging lightly on the lobe, his hot breath tickling her skin and fizzing along her nerve endings. 'All the places I want to kiss you,' he whispered, his hand sliding up her thigh under her dress. He kissed her mouth, parting her lips with his. He cupped her bottom, pulling her closer as his tongue slid into her mouth. She felt the hardness of his erection as he pulled her tighter, thrusting his hips against hers, and she rocked into him, wanting more. His breathing deepened, and his hands became more urgent, stroking her thighs and brushing over her breasts until her nipples were taut and hard. She gasped as he bent and sucked one through the thin material of her dress, cradling his head to her, her fingers digging into his hair. He groaned deep in his throat as he slipped a finger inside her knickers and stroked along her folds. 'You're so wet,' he gasped, lifting his head, his eyes dark with desire as they met hers. He watched her face as he continued to stroke, and Lisa clutched him tighter as her excitement mounted.

He withdrew abruptly, placing both hands firmly on her waist as he pulled back a little.

'Come upstairs,' he said.

Lisa nodded, and he stood, gripping her hand tightly in his as he led her from the room and up the stairs almost at a run.

The bedroom he took her to was large and airy, moonlight streaming in from two floor-to-ceiling windows, illuminating the imposing king-size bed of rich, dark wood that dominated the room, its intricately carved headboard adding a touch of drama. Grayson pulled the curtains and flicked on a lamp that bathed the room in a warm yellow light. Then he pulled her into his arms, holding her tight into his body, so she could feel how much he wanted her, his erection pressing into her stomach as he kissed her, his mouth hot and demanding on hers. His fingers shook as he fumbled with the tie of her dress at her neck. She shivered as he opened it and the material slid against her skin as it fell to her waist. Grayson pulled back slightly, his eyes dark and hungry as they dropped to her naked breasts. Then he undid the zip and pushed the dress off so it landed in a pool at her feet and she was naked except for her thong and high heels.

'You're so beautiful,' he breathed, his eyes following his hand as it stroked across her shoulder and down over her breast, lingering there, caressing, his fingers lightly pinching her nipple as he bent to kiss her.

Lisa started fumbling with the buttons of his shirt, surprised by the intensity of her desire. She wasn't just playing a part. She wanted Grayson. Seemingly just as impatient as she was to feel his bare skin against hers, he helped her with the buttons and shrugged out of his shirt. Lisa ran her hands over the planes and hollows of his chest, loving the warm, solid feel of him. He pulled her into his body as he deepened the kiss, the touch of skin against skin setting her nerves tingling. He made a guttural sound in his throat as her fingers brushed across his taut stomach and she reached for his zipper.

She felt the tension in his body as he broke the kiss, his movements urgent as he quickly removed the rest of his clothes. Then he stood before her naked, and for a long moment she just gazed at him. He was beautiful – lean and muscular, his golden skin lightly dusted with dark hair. His cock was already hard and thick, standing proud against his taut stomach. Waves of heat washed over her as she drank in the perfection of his naked body, while his eyes devoured her in turn.

He bent and scooped her up into his arms, and Lisa kicked off her shoes as he carried her to the bed. He pushed her down onto it and crawled over her, and she stifled a gasp as he hovered above her, feeling momentarily overwhelmed by him and what was about to happen.

Then he lowered his mouth to her, kissing his way down her neck, along her collarbone to her breasts. She whimpered as he flicked his tongue lightly across one nipple before sucking it into his mouth, while his fingers teased the other until she writhed beneath him. His mouth moved lower, kissing and nuzzling along her sides and across her stomach, his tongue dipping into her belly button while he continued to caress her breasts. She dug her hands into his hair as his mouth travelled down her body, the softness of it in her fingers contrasting with the rasp of his stubble on the soft skin of her thighs. His groans of pleasure were interspersed with whispered praise, telling her how beautiful she was and how much he wanted her. He tugged down her panties, and she lifted her hips to help him. He slid them off and dropped them on the floor.

'You're so wet.' His voice was husky as he buried his head between her legs, his words exciting her as much as his touch. She got even wetter as he licked along her folds, simultaneously stroking her with two fingers before sliding them inside her. Her body arched towards him reflexively and she curled her hands around his head, clamping him to her. The heat that was building inside her became almost too intense as his mouth latched onto her clit, sucking and licking mercilessly while he pumped his fingers inside her. She clutched at the sheets, whimpering help-lessly as she came, her body bowing off the bed as the waves of pleasure consumed her. Still he didn't stop, keeping up the relentless onslaught until he brought her to another juddering climax and she cried out with a raw, primitive sound.

He knelt up and grabbed a condom from the nightstand, his eyes burning into hers as he slid it on. She knew the fire in her eyes matched his, silently communicating to him that she wanted this as much as he did. He bent to kiss her as he hovered over her again. Then in one swift movement he grabbed her hands and held them over her head as he drove into her. Lisa felt suffocated, and tried to stifle her panic at the feeling of helplessness as the weight of his body pinned her to the bed, his hand holding hers immobile. But she couldn't help the instinctive jolt of fear, the hitching of her breath or the panicked widening of her eyes.

'Sorry,' Grayson whispered, instantly releasing her hands, frowning in concern as he withdrew, his body stilling over hers.

'No, it's okay,' Lisa reassured him, clasping her hands together over her head where he had placed them. She had said she would let him do whatever he wanted. If he wanted to hold her down, she would just have to tough it out. She waited for him to grab her wrists again. But instead he put his arms around her and flipped them over so that she was on top.

'Okay?' he asked, bringing her down onto his cock and settling her so she was sitting astride him.

She nodded hesitantly, worried that she had displeased him. But he didn't look remotely unhappy, his eyes appreciative as they raked over her body.

'This is better, actually,' he said with a smile, his hands stroking along her thighs and over her bottom, pulling her tighter into him. 'I can see you better when I'm inside you. I can touch more of you.' His hands came up to cup her breasts, teasing the nipples as he pushed up into her.

Lisa felt powerful as she began to move up and down on him, the naked desire in his eyes emboldening her as he held her waist and thrust up to meet her. He groaned as Lisa wiggled her ass, grinding her hips into his, and his thrusts became faster and more urgent. His breathing was heavy and ragged as he put his hands on her shoulders, bearing down so he could push deeper inside her, his face contorted with tension as his cock began to twitch. Then, with a ragged moan, his whole body shuddered as he came inside her.

16

When his body went limp, Lisa collapsed on top of him, and he wrapped his arms around her, kissing her softly as his breathing returned to normal. Then he pulled out of her, easing her onto the bed beside him. They lay side by side, their bodies slick with sweat, just gazing into each other's eyes. Lisa wondered what Grayson was thinking. Did he regret spending so much money on her? Was he disappointed that she'd shown fear when he held her down? Would he want to do it again? He'd paid to have sex with her as many times as he wanted until she had to leave at midnight. But maybe he'd had enough of her already.

'Grayson?' she began in a small voice.

'Hmm?' He traced a finger lightly along her cheek.

'I didn't mean to stop you – when you were holding me down. I'm sorry.'

'No, *I'm* sorry.' He frowned. 'It scared you.'

'You took me by surprise, that's all. But you shouldn't have stopped. It's okay if you want to restrain me—'

His eyes narrowed. 'Why would I want to do that? You clearly don't like it.'

'I said you could do whatever you wanted. If that's what turns you on—'

'You think dominating you and overpowering you excites me? That doing something that scares you is a turn-on for me?' He seemed almost angry, his jaw tense.

She shrugged. 'I don't know …'

'Well, it's not. I don't want to do anything you're uncomfortable with. I want to please you.'

'But … why?'

'*Why?*' he asked, aghast, his eyes widening. 'Isn't that what sex is about – mutual pleasure and satisfaction?'

'Well … yes.' She did know that in theory at least that was what sex was meant to be about. She wasn't so naive as to think the way Mark treated her was how it should be. 'But this is different.'

He tilted his head to the side, regarding her curiously through narrowed eyes. 'Why?'

'Because … you're paying me.'

'Ah, the money.' He gave a wry smile. 'I wish we could just forget about that. It's not part of the equation for me – and frankly, I'd rather not be reminded of it.'

'Why not?' Did he regret paying so much money to have sex with her? It was hardly surprising. He was almost bound to be disappointed.

'Because I'd rather not be reminded of the fact that I had to pay you to sleep with me. It's not very good for my ego.'

'That's not personal,' she said, keen to reassure him. 'When I said I wasn't interested in having sex with you for its own sake, I meant it. But that's not just with you. The same goes for anyone.'

'Still, I'd rather indulge in the fantasy that you like me

for myself,' he said with a crooked smile.

'I do like you, Grayson. But you don't have to seduce me or try to please me. I'm not your girlfriend or your wife. I'm just a—a paid whore in this situation.'

He frowned. 'Don't say that,' he snapped.

'It's what I agreed to. You've kept up your end of the bargain, and I'll keep up mine. I said you could do whatever you wanted. So if you want to be rough with me or hold me down, that's fine. You took me by surprise, that's all. I wasn't prepared.'

'I don't want to be rough with you. I don't want to do anything you don't like. I just want to make you feel good.'

'I don't understand why.'

He shrugged. 'Call me old-fashioned. It's how I was raised.'

'Your mother taught you how to treat women in bed?' she asked, eyebrows raised.

He chuckled. 'No, of course not! Thank God.' He mimed a shudder. 'But she taught me to be considerate and sensitive to other people's feelings. And she taught me how to treat a guest in my home – to make them comfortable and put them at ease.'

She looked at him curiously. 'Is that how you see me? As a guest in your home?'

'You're here in my home, aren't you? What else would you be?'

'I don't know,' she shrugged. 'A paid worker?'

He huffed in exasperation. 'Even if that were true, do you think the fact that I'm paying you gives me the right to intimidate you and push you around? To make you do things that obviously freak you out?'

'Yes, if it's in my job description,' she said hesitantly, not wanting to anger him. 'I mean, if it's what I signed up for …'

'Well, I don't agree. I wasn't brought up to abuse my power over people, where I do have power over them. Have I ever done anything to make you think I would?'

'No,' she said quickly. 'You're a credit to your parents.' She saw that he found the idea that he would treat someone badly insulting and she risked offending him. He had treated her with nothing but kindness and consideration, even though she was here as a paid whore. 'You've been very sweet to me. Your mum would be proud.'

He gave a relieved smile. 'Thank you. I'm glad to hear it.'

'Though I'm not sure she'd be impressed with your table manners the first night we met,' she teased.

He frowned. 'God, I'm so sorry about that. But I'm not actually in the habit of stripping and groping my female guests at the dinner table.'

'You're not?' She quirked an eyebrow.

'If I'd known—'

'Hey, I'm just teasing,' she said. He looked so pained, she was sorry she'd brought it up. She had only meant to tease him, to lighten the mood.

'I want you to tell me if I do anything you don't want, Lisa,' he said seriously.

'Okay. I will.'

'You want to know what turns me on?' he asked softly, tracing a finger down her neck and across her collarbone, so lightly it almost tickled.

She shivered, nodding.

'Watching you come,' he said, his finger brushing across her nipple, 'and knowing I did that to you. Knowing that I'm giving you pleasure – making you wet,' he said, his hand sweeping down between her legs. 'Feeling you want me as much as I want you.' One finger began gently stroking the soft flesh of her folds. 'Hearing you moan and scream because of what I'm doing to you. That's what turns me on more than anything, Lisa.'

Her breathing became jagged as she felt the heat building inside her again at his words, the touch of his hands working its magic on her.

'I want you so much.' He bent and gave her a soft kiss on the lips while his finger continued its stroking. 'I've wanted you since the first moment I saw you.' He was working her clit now, tantalisingly slowly and languorously, and she rocked against his hand in frustration, seeking more friction. He kept up the relentless torture, gazing into her eyes as she whimpered and clutched at him as she came.

This time when he reached for a condom, she urged him on top of her.

'I like you on top,' she said when he hesitated. 'Just don't hold me down.'

He supported his weight on his hands and drove into her, moving slowly at first, rhythmically, and then picking up the pace. She stroked his back, loving the feel of the muscles beneath his warm, smooth skin as he drove them both to another mind-blowing orgasm.

He rolled off her and they collapsed, panting side by side on the bed. Grayson reached for her, but she pulled away.

'I should go,' she said, glancing at her watch. It was almost midnight. She sat up and turned away from him, disconcerted by how much she wanted to stay – to let him wrap her in his arms and pull her close. This was just a business transaction, she reminded herself. She couldn't get involved.

'I wish you could stay,' he said, echoing her feelings. She felt the bed give as he sat up behind her. He dropped a wet kiss on her shoulder.

'I have to go.'

'I'll pay you double if you stay the night.' He kissed her neck. 'And I'll make you breakfast in the morning.' He wrapped his arms around her and rested his chin on her shoulder. She felt the roughness of his stubble against her skin.

She longed to be able to say yes, but she shook her head. 'Sorry. I can't.'

'Just sleep with me,' he whispered. 'We can just sleep.'

She sighed. 'It's not that. I need to be home when Mark calls.' Tempting as the money was, she couldn't risk missing Mark's call. He mustn't have any reason for suspicion.

He sighed. 'Will you come again tomorrow?'

'If you'd like,' she said, pleased that he wanted her again. If he wanted her often enough, she could be gone by the time Mark came back. 'I can come any night this week,' she said, turning her head to look at him.

'Come *every* night this week,' he said, smiling at her.

'Really?'

'Absolutely. What about days too?'

She nodded. 'Whenever you want me.'

'Be careful what you agree to,' he said. 'Because I want you all the time.'

She steeled herself to talk about money. She couldn't let a few moments' embarrassment stop her from getting what she wanted. 'I'm sure I can handle it,' she said with a shrug. 'But it will cost you.'

She saw his slight flinch, though he tried to disguise it. But she couldn't afford to feel bad for him. She had to be tough, businesslike.

'Of course,' he said. 'But as you pointed out, I'm a wealthy man. I can afford it. How much?'

She tilted her head, looking at him questioningly.

'How much for the whole week – all your available time, day and night? Unlimited access?'

Her breath hitched. She knew she should be ashamed to be negotiating like this for the use of her body, but her heart was already racing at the thought of all that money. She could tell he was desperate for her. She could name her price. She took a deep breath. 'Ten thousand pounds,' she said steadily.

'Deal.'

Just like that. Grayson had just agreed to pay her ten thousand pounds in cash as if it was nothing! With one word, he had guaranteed her freedom, given her a future. She was reeling, but she struggled not to betray any emotion. She would absorb all this later when she was alone.

'Unlimited access up to midnight,' she amended, just to make sure everything was clear between them.

'Done,' he said. 'My little Cinderella.' He tucked a lock of hair behind her ear.

She was amazed at how easy it was – that he'd agreed so readily, without trying to negotiate or haggle. It was an obscene amount of money to pay for a few nights with her. She was just an ordinary woman – not particularly skilled in bed, nor especially beautiful – and nowhere near as sophisticated and experienced as the women she imagined he was used to. She couldn't understand what drove him to it. He was kind, smart, drop-dead gorgeous – there must be plenty of desirable women who would be only too eager to sleep with him and wouldn't charge for the privilege. And if he wanted to pay, he could find someone much more skilled in bed who would charge a lot less. Still, he was also very wealthy and could afford to indulge his every whim. If he wanted something, he could buy it. Fortunately, he wanted her.

'You shouldn't waste your money on me,' she said, the words coming out of her mouth before she even realised what she was saying. Damn it, she didn't want to talk him out of this. But she couldn't help feeling guilty towards him. He was a nice man. He deserved to be with someone who wanted him for himself, not for what they could get out of him.

'It's not a waste,' he said. 'You're worth it.'

She highly doubted it, but she refrained this time from telling him how deluded he was. 'I'm glad you think so,' she said simply.

'I'll have the money ready the next time you come – in cash.'

'Thank you.' She sat awkwardly on the edge of the bed, clutching the sheet to her, feeling very aware of her nakedness now. Considering everything she'd done with him, it was ridiculous to be shy of him now, but she suddenly felt very exposed. 'Um … could I have a shower?'

'Yes, of course.' He threw back the sheet and got out of bed. 'Come on, I'll show you where everything is.'

Reluctantly she dropped the sheet and stood. He was paying her a fortune for unlimited access to her body for a week; the least she could do was let him look at it. She would just have to get used to being naked around him.

Grayson had no such inhibitions as he took her hand and led her to the bathroom. When he had shown her how to work the shower and given her clean towels, he left her alone – though Lisa got the feeling he would have liked to get in the shower with her. She wouldn't have minded that herself, if she had enough time. But she needed to get home quickly now.

As she washed Grayson's saliva from her skin, she tried to dismiss him from her thoughts equally briskly. She liked him a lot, and he made her feel amazing, but he was just a means to an end, and he could never be more than that. It would be all too easy to fall in love with him, but she couldn't let that happen. She had to remain detached – there was too much at stake to allow herself to give in to feelings that might weaken her resolve and risk losing the freedom she had endured so much to achieve. She was here for one thing only – his money. She had to remember that. Still, she couldn't help wishing that things were different – that she could have met Grayson under different circumstances. If only she'd met him before Mark. Maybe something would have happened between them. She could have allowed herself to have feelings for him …

She was grateful that Grayson wasn't there when she got back to the bedroom and she got dressed and dried her hair in privacy. Then she called a cab on her mobile and sat on the bed as she waited for it to arrive. Only when she heard the doorbell did she go downstairs. Grayson was in the hallway, dressed in a bathrobe.

'Well, I'll see you tomorrow,' she said as she went to the door.

Grayson went ahead of her and opened it. 'See you tomorrow. Thank you for coming, Lisa.' He bent and gave her a soft kiss on the lips.

'Bye. You have my mobile number. Call me if you … change your mind.'

'I'll see you tomorrow,' he said firmly as she turned to go.

Grayson watched the taxi pull away, then closed the door and went into the library. He poured himself a large whiskey and settled into one of the big armchairs by the fireplace, wishing Lisa were sitting opposite him in the other one. He didn't want to go back to bed just yet – not when she wasn't in it. He felt conflicted by this arrangement they had. On the one hand, he was getting everything he wanted – and on the other hand, nothing. Lisa would be sexually available to him every day this week, as often as he wished. She would give him her body, but she wouldn't give herself to him – and he was beginning to realise that that was what he most wanted.

And what about when the week was over? He would be left with nothing – less than nothing, because he had a feeling that the more he had of Lisa, the more he would want from her, and when they were done, he would be left with this empty, gnawing hunger that she had created and that no one else could satisfy.

He didn't like what the money said about either of them. If it made Lisa a whore, what did it make him? He wasn't happy about exploiting her in that way, despite her assurances that it was what she wanted. He couldn't shake the feeling that she was in some sort of trouble, and though he knew this was the only way she would let him help her, his conscience still nagged at him. He wished he could talk to Isabel about it, get her advice. But he had promised Lisa he wouldn't tell anyone about their arrangement.

At least he knew she wanted him. He could console himself that she wasn't hating every minute of it when she was with him, just enduring it for the money. He couldn't have agreed to it if he thought that, no matter how desperate she was. But she had wanted him that night in the library. He had left it up to her, and she had made the first move. And she had wanted him tonight – there had been nothing fake about that look in her eyes. It was small comfort when they had only just begun and he was already starting to feel the pain of losing her.

17

THE NEXT MORNING, Lisa woke feeling happy and optimistic for the first time in ages. She could finally see light at the end of the tunnel, and the chance to restart her life seemed almost within reach. She couldn't ignore the fact that part of her feeling of wellbeing was down to the warm glow she felt whenever she thought of last night with Grayson – the way he had touched her, how his eyes had burned when he looked at her. But she tried not to dwell on that. Still, she couldn't stop the images that occasionally flashed across her mind and brought a little smile to her face. And try as she might, she couldn't deny that she was looking forward to seeing him again tonight. It had been a long time since she had felt such eager anticipation.

Even Mark's callous boorishness last night hadn't been enough to crush her spirits. He had Skyped about half an hour after she had got home. He had only spoken to her to issue a series of orders about how she was to spend her time while he was away, and to quiz her about her day, checking up on how long she had worked out, what she had eaten, who she had spoken to. If only he knew, she thought, experiencing a little thrill of spiteful glee at having a secret from him.

Then he had told her to strip and touch herself for him, and they had had Skype sex. She had been alarmed to find that she felt dirty after it in a way that she hadn't after having sex for money with Grayson. She was just glad that Mark was on the other side of the world and she didn't have to actually endure his touch, his teeth tugging and biting at her skin, his hands rough as they pinched and dug into her flesh.

'Oh, baby,' he had panted when he was finished. 'I miss you so much. That was great, but I can't wait to get home and fuck you properly.'

Never, she thought. If she had her way, he would never touch her again.

'Me too,' she had said, smiling sweetly. Then she had closed the laptop and gone upstairs, relishing having the bed to herself. She had slept peacefully in blissful solitude, and sprang out of bed this morning feeling determined and purposeful. She ate breakfast, and worked out extra hard in the gym, challenging herself to run longer, to lift more weight – not for Mark's sake, but for herself. She was on the treadmill when her mobile pinged with a message from Grayson. She was almost afraid to open it, suddenly afraid he might have changed his mind about their arrangement. But instead it said:

Have an hour free at 1.00. Meet me for lunch?

She answered yes immediately, and he texted back telling her to meet him at his offices.

This time she was immediately admitted to Grayson's offices. The receptionist was obviously expecting her, and Gaby greeted her with a friendly smile.

'I'm here to meet Grayson for, um … lunch,' Lisa told her with a shaky smile. She couldn't help feeling discomfited. She didn't think for a minute that Grayson would have informed Gaby that she would be stopping by to provide sexual services for him when he had an hour to spare. But it probably wouldn't take her long to figure out what was going on when the two of them were locked up in his office for an hour with a 'do not disturb' order in place.

'Yes, I know. Whatever you're doing to him, keep it up,' Gaby said cheerfully. 'He doesn't take a break often enough.'

Lisa blushed, feeling more embarrassed than ever. She doubted she'd get such wholehearted approval from Gaby if she knew exactly what it was she was doing to Grayson.

'I'll just tell him you're here,' Gaby said, picking up the phone.

Lisa expected to be told to go through to his office, but after speaking with Grayson, Gaby said 'He'll be with you in a moment,' and waved her to a chair.

'Oh. Thank you.' Thinking about it, Lisa decided it made sense that they would go somewhere else. Yesterday she had taken him by surprise and it had been spontaneous. But he wouldn't want to risk having sex in his office on a regular basis, and today he'd had time to plan. She was glad that he was being discreet, and she could at least preserve her dignity with Gaby.

'Hi,' Grayson appeared at the entrance to the office, pulling on his jacket. 'Ready?'

Lisa nodded and stood. 'Bye,' she said to Gaby as she joined him.

'I'll be back in about an hour, hour and a half,' Grayson said to Gaby.

'No rush. Enjoy yourselves,' Gaby called to them as they left.

Grayson took Lisa's hand as they walked to the lifts.

'Thank you for coming,' he said as they stepped into the lift.

Lisa shrugged, knocked off balance once again by the way he treated her as if she was a girlfriend. 'It's what you're paying me for,' she said.

'Thank you anyway.' He leaned in and gave her a soft kiss on the lips. 'It's really nice to see you again.'

He led her across the lobby with a hand at her back and out through the revolving door into a waiting car. She was surprised when Grayson told the driver where they were going – a five-star landmark hotel in Mayfair. She hadn't expected him to take her somewhere so up-market. It certainly wasn't the sort of place that would rent rooms by the hour. But then, Grayson could easily afford to take a room there for the day, even if he only intended to use it for an hour or so. Besides, he was a classy guy – he wouldn't want to go anywhere seedy, even for a lunchtime quickie. She was glad he was taking her somewhere nice – it made the whole thing feel a little less sordid and sleazy. At least she was a high-class hooker, she thought wryly.

But her heart sank when they arrived at the hotel and Grayson led her straight past reception and into the ritzy restaurant. She zoned out as he told the maitre 'd that he had a reservation and they were led to their table. So much for not feeling sleazy, she thought, her heart pounding. She had thought they would have the privacy of a hotel bedroom. She wasn't prepared for getting it on in a crowded restaurant.

The place was busy with the lunchtime rush, and the walls reverberated with the buzz of conversation and the clatter of plates and glasses. The clientele was mostly made up of suited businessmen and women. They looked high-powered and professional, and Lisa began to feel very uncomfortable and out of place. She didn't imagine any of the other women were here to get felt up under the table or to give their man a little light relief over lunch. Certainly none of them looked like prostitutes – but then, hopefully neither did she.

They were shown to a corner table, and she felt very far from her comfort zone as Grayson sat beside her on the banquette. The waiter handed them menus and bustled off. She took in the room with its plush furnishings, crisp table linen and sparkling glasses and bit her lip, feeling nervous. Glancing around, she tried to judge how much she and Grayson could be overseen from the other tables, and how easy it would be to touch him under the table without anyone knowing what was going on. Her stomach curdled at the thought. Mark sometimes liked to play games in public, discreetly finger fucking her in a restaurant, or getting her to give him a blow job under his desk at the gallery. But she found it humiliating and embarrassing, and she had always hated it.

'What's wrong?' Grayson asked, breaking into her thoughts. She looked up to find him frowning at her in concern.

'Nothing,' she said, noticing that she had been twisting her napkin into a knot and her shoulders were up around her ears. She clasped her hands together to stop them fidgeting. This was work, she reminded herself. She didn't have to enjoy it. She just had to suck it up and get on with it.

The gesture didn't escape him. 'It's something,' he said, placing a warm hand over hers, stilling them. 'What is it?'

'I just—I'm not sure what you want me to do.'

He looked bemused. 'Well, it's a restaurant.' His lips twitched in a smile.' I want you to choose something to eat.' He indicated her menu.

'Oh, right. Okay.'

'Hungry?'

'Not very.' She had been – she was always hungry – but now she felt too tense, her stomach in knots. She gazed unseeingly at the menu, unable to concentrate. She doubted she'd be able to eat anyway – the prospect of performing sexual acts in public had taken away her appetite.

'Are you ready to order?' Grayson looked queryingly at her as the waiter stood by their table, notebook and pen poised.

'Oh, yes. I'll have the prawn salad. Thank you.' She handed the waiter back her menu. She had automatically zoned in on what Mark would have ordered for her if he were here, she realised.

Grayson ordered roast sea bass, and a bottle of sparkling water, declining wine as he had a busy afternoon ahead, including a site visit for one of his latest projects. 'But you have some, if you like,' he told Lisa.

'No, thanks. I'll just have water too.'

She was distracted, waiting for Grayson to make some move to let her know what he wanted, expecting every moment to feel his hand on her leg.

'Lisa?'

She jumped at the sound of his voice, aware that she hadn't been listening to him. 'Sorry, what did you say?'

'I just asked what you've been up to this morning.'

'Oh, I just hit the gym.'

'You work out a lot?'

'Yes, every day for two or three hours.'

'That's very dedicated. You like it?'

'No, not really,' she said absently.

Grayson laughed. 'Why do you do it so much if you don't enjoy it?'

She shrugged. 'For the results, I guess. It keeps me fit

and in shape.' She felt edgy and nervous, wishing he would just dispense with the small talk and do what they had come here for. Their food arrived and he continued to chat as he started to eat, telling her about the new project he was working on. He was clearly excited about it, but Lisa barely listened, just toying with her salad. Finally, she could bear it no longer.

'What do you want me to do?' she asked in a whisper, putting down her fork.

His brows knitted in confusion. 'What do you mean?'

'I mean, um …' She decided maybe it would be better if she initiated things. Perhaps that was what he expected. She put a hand on his thigh under the table, sliding it up to his crotch, her fingers finding his zipper.

'Jesus!' he gasped, grabbing her hand and pushing it firmly away.

'Sorry,' she blushed. 'I thought—'

He narrowed his eyes at her. 'What do you think I brought you here for?'

'Well … sex,' she whispered, leaning towards him so she wouldn't be overheard. 'I mean, that's what you're paying me for. I thought we'd go to a room, but—'

His eyes widened, and he looked horrified.

'I'm not objecting,' she said hastily. 'If you want to do it here, that's fine. Just tell me what you want and I'll do it.'

'Christ!' He leaned back against the banquette. Then he turned to her and took her hand. 'I'm sorry,' he said, looking into her eyes earnestly. 'I guess I should have made myself clearer. I didn't bring you here to have sex, or so you could get me off under the table. I just want to spend time with you.'

'Oh.'

'Is that okay?'

'Yes, of course,' she said faintly. 'Whatever you want.'

But she wasn't sure that it *was* okay. She almost wished he would make her get on her knees and suck him off under the table. It would be easier if they didn't blur the lines, if he just treated her like his sex toy, bought and paid for to cater to his every demand. The nicer he was to her, the harder it was going to be not to fall for him.

'Are you sure? I like you, Lisa. I'd like to spend time with you, not just in bed – though obviously I want that too.'

'But … you're paying me.'

'Yes, I'm paying you.'

'Just to have lunch with me?'

'Just for the pleasure of your company.'

'Why?'

'Would you be here if I wasn't paying you?' he asked, his eyes telling her he knew the answer.

'No,' she admitted, looking away.

'I'd like to get to know you better, Lisa. I'm paying you for your time. Does it matter how I choose to use it?'

'No, I guess not,' she said, fighting the warm feeling it gave her that he wanted to get to know her as a person, that he had said he liked her. 'It's your dime,' she added, mentioning the money to remind him of the nature of their arrangement. They may like each other, but this wasn't a date. It wouldn't lead anywhere. They would never have a relationship. She was on a job. Whether they were having sex or just talking, it was still just a business transaction between them.

'Understood,' he said with a sad smile, and Lisa felt a pang. She got the impression she'd hurt his feelings. 'I just want you to relax and enjoy lunch.'

'Okay,' Lisa said, picking up her fork again, her appetite returning as her tension melted away. 'I can do that.'

It didn't have to mean anything, she told herself. As long as they both understood it was nothing more than a business arrangement, they could enjoy each other's company in or out of bed. She would be like Vivian in *Pretty Woman*. After all, she had been a hooker, but Richard Gere's character had paid her to spend time with him in other ways besides having sex. She tried to silence the little voice inside her head that reminded her that story had ended with them falling in love.

18

WHEN SHE ARRIVED at Grayson's that evening, he took her straight into the library. A blanket was spread in front of the fireplace, where a blazing fire roared, throwing cheery warmth into the room.

'Are you hungry?' he asked her.

'You took me out for lunch,' she reminded him. 'I didn't expect you to cook for me tonight as well.'

'It was just prawn salad. And you hardly ate a thing.' He led her over to the blanket. 'Anyway, I haven't cooked – just bought a bunch of stuff from the deli. I thought we could eat in here picnic-style, and have a game of chess.'

Lisa eyed the blanket warily. On it was a bottle of wine and two glasses, and an assortment of cheeses and bread, pâtés and chutneys, and little savoury tarts. It looked delicious. Beside it, the chess board was already laid out on the little table between the two deep armchairs. It seemed like such a lovely, sweet gesture, so thoughtful and … romantic, she thought, alarm bells going off in her head. It was the sort of thing a man might plan for an evening with his girlfriend – not a woman who was charging by the hour.

'Lisa? Is something wrong?' She looked up to find him frowning at her in concern.

She took a deep breath. She needed to put a stop to this now. 'This all looks lovely,' she said, nodding to the blanket. 'But I'm not here to play chess and have picnics, and we both know it.' Her fingers went to the buttons of his shirt and she smiled up at him flirtatiously. 'I'm on the clock here, Grayson. Why don't we just get on with it?'

He grabbed her hand, stilling it as she started opening the buttons of his shirt. 'I thought we agreed that I could use your time however I want as long as I'm paying?'

She sighed. 'But we both know what this is, Grayson. You don't have to dress it up. I won't think any less of you, I promise,' she said dryly.

He frowned, pushing her hand away. 'Did you think I'd just take you straight to the bedroom to fuck? Or order you to strip and get on your knees for me the minute you came through the door? Did you expect me to push you around and treat you like trash?'

She bit her lip. Honestly, when she had started this, that was exactly what she had expected. And it would have been easier if he had just used her like a whore and shown her the door when he was done with her. She wouldn't have to think of him as a person then – a person who was kind and considerate, who treated her with respect ... a person she liked more and more as she got to know him. That was the problem. It would make things so much easier for her if she could despise him – if he was just another callous, manipulative asshole who she could leave behind along with Mark when this was all over.

'You'd be entitled,' she said in a small voice. 'It's what you're paying me for.'

He shook his head. 'You said I could do whatever I want, remember?'

'That was when I thought you might want to be rough.'

Grayson let out a harsh breath. His expression was horrified. 'So it's okay for me to hurt you, but not to cook for you or play chess with you?'

'It's very nice, Grayson,' she said reasonably, nodding to the blanket. 'I appreciate it, really I do. But we both know that's not what I'm here for. We're not lovers, except in the most basic sense. I'm not your girlfriend. You can buy my body, but you can't buy *me*.'

'I know that.'

'I'm here to fuck, pure and simple. I mean, you don't *really* want to play chess and have picnics with me, do you?'

'What if I do?'

'It's not what I agreed to.'

'Do you want me to pay you more?' he asked, frowning.

'No. You're already paying me far more than I'm worth.'

'That's not true.' He tucked a lock of hair behind her ear, looking down at her in concern. 'And yes, I want to have sex with you. But I also want to do this,' he nodded to the blanket. 'Okay?'

She sighed, giving in. 'It's your money,' she said with a shrug. She kicked off her shoes and let him pull her down on the blanket beside him. As he poured them both wine, she wished she could relax and enjoy this. It had all the ingredients of a perfect evening. She liked Grayson's company, she enjoyed playing chess with him, and the food all looked delicious. Mark was far away on the other side of the world, and she should be able to make the most of the opportunity to spend an evening in the company of a nice man, who seemed intent on pleasing her. But she felt tense and off-balance, wary of the growing attachment she felt to Grayson. She had to be on her guard against it. She couldn't give in to it and let it weaken her resolve.

Grayson handed her a glass of wine and a plate. 'Help yourself,' he said, gesturing at the food spread out on the blanket.

It all looked so tempting – doubly so because just about everything here was on Mark's forbidden list. But she felt too tense to eat. She took a small piece of cheese and nibbled at it, struggling to swallow past the lump in her throat. She felt Grayson's eyes on her and looked up to find him frowning at her in concern.

'I'm sorry,' he said. 'Is this making you uncomfortable?'

'No,' she shook her head. 'It's lovely. It was just … unexpected.'

'Don't you like the food?'

'Yes, it all looks wonderful. I just … I guess I'm not very hungry.'

He looked down, thoughtfully watching his thumb as it played with the stem of his glass. She almost felt him steeling himself to say something. 'Would this be easier for you if I treated you like a whore?' he asked finally, looking up at her.

Christ, he was so intuitive! It was as if he could read her mind. She tried to gauge his expression, considering how she should answer. His gaze was tinged with sadness, but open and direct, and she could tell he really wanted to know.

'Yes,' she admitted, her voice barely above a whisper. 'I think it would.'

His eyes flickered away, and now he was the one to look uncomfortable. Then he nodded, as if to himself and put down his glass. 'Okay, we can—'

'But I'm really glad you don't,' she interrupted hastily, and she was rewarded with a gentle, relieved smile.

She suddenly knew she didn't want that from him. However difficult this was for her, she didn't want him to compromise himself for her sake. He was courteous and kind, and he shouldn't be punished for being a good person. She knew he would hate himself if he were to treat her badly.

'I'm sorry, you just took me by surprise, that's all,' she smiled, eager to reassure him, and to show her appreciation for his thoughtfulness. 'This all looks wonderful.' She helped herself to a mini quiche with salmon and asparagus. She felt her tension seep away as Grayson smiled at her, his body relaxing. She took a big bite, all thoughts of Mark and calorie counting forgotten as she focused on making up to Grayson for her earlier ingratitude. The pastry burst on her tongue in rich, buttery flakes, and it tasted divine.

'Oh, my God, this is amazing!' she said when she had swallowed.

Grayson gave her a huge grin, and she was relieved that he appeared totally relaxed again. 'I don't think I've ever seen a woman enjoy food as much as you,' he said. 'I wish I knew where you put it all.'

He wasn't to know that eating with such abandonment was a rarity for her. She hadn't indulged her appetite like this in years. The thought made her sad. Her grandmother had always considered a hearty appetite a very good thing. She had loved cooking for Lisa and her grandfather, and their enthusiastic enjoyment of her food had given her great satisfaction. She'd hate it if she knew how Lisa restricted herself now. It would make her very happy to see Grayson providing all this delicious food for her. Lisa could hear her pronouncing him a 'mensch' – her highest compliment.

'What are you thinking?' Grayson broke into her

thoughts. He was watching her curiously, his head tilted to one side.

'Nothing.' She shook her head. 'I was just thinking my grandmother would have approved of you.'

Grayson raised his eyebrows in surprise.

'Oh, not the whole paying me for sex thing, obviously,' Lisa said, blushing. 'But she'd like you for feeding me like this.' She took a sip of her wine to cover her embarrassment.

Grayson smiled gently at her.

'This wine is lovely,' she said, raising her glass. Then she remembered the first night they had met, and laughed. 'If Mark could hear me, he'd be appalled,' she said. 'It's probably some fine vintage, and I should be swirling it around my glass and saying something clever about its bouquet.'

'Well, it *is* rather good,' Grayson said with a smile. 'But don't worry, there won't be a test. All that matters is that you enjoy it.'

After that, the atmosphere changed and they were completely relaxed with each other, chatting easily as they ate. Lisa decided to let go and enjoy indulging in the rare treats of rich, tasty food and the luxury of being spoilt. She found herself opening up to Grayson as he drew her out about her upbringing with her grandparents, her art, and her college years. He listened attentively as she talked, and in turn he told her stories about his family. He spoke of them with such affection; it was obvious they were close.

'You're so lucky to have sisters,' Lisa said wistfully. 'I'd love to have had a sister – or even a brother,' she conceded teasingly.

'I know. I do appreciate it. It must be hard not having any family.'

'Yeah, it can be pretty lonely. I miss my grandparents

so much. I miss having that closeness, you know – the acceptance, the unconditional love. You only really get that with family. And sometimes I think the loneliness led me to make some bad choices.' Oh God, she shouldn't have said that. She was revealing too much. The wine had loosened her tongue, and Grayson's gentle coaxing had broken through her defences. The trouble was he made her feel safe, and then she lowered her guard and said things she shouldn't.

Grayson was looking at her expectantly, as if waiting for her to say more.

'Sorry,' she said, shaking her head as if to clear it. 'I'm talking too much.'

'No, you're not. I like listening to you talk.'

'Well, I like listening to *you*. Tell me more about your-self. Have you ever been married?'

He was silent for a long time, just looking at her care-fully, and for a moment she thought he wasn't going to let her switch the focus to him. Finally he answered. 'No.'

'Ever come close?'

He shook his head. 'No. I've had a couple of long-term relationships, but no one I've felt I wanted to make a life-time commitment to.' He was silent for a moment. Then he said 'What about you? Will you marry Mark?'

'He hasn't asked me,' she said, glancing away, aware that she wasn't answering his question. She thought about what she had said earlier. Her grandmother wouldn't have approved of Mark – not one bit. She couldn't help thinking she would have seen through him from the start. How different things might have been then …

'Tell me more about your family,' she said, anxious to shake off her dark thoughts.

He seemed to pick up on her discomfort because he quickly obliged, making her laugh with stories about his three older sisters, who he complained bossed him around terribly, but who he clearly adored. She relaxed again as she listened, warmed by the heat of the fire, and drunk on the sensual pleasures of good food and wine, and the attention of the beautiful man opposite her.

When they were finished their picnic, they moved to the chessboard, and continued to sip wine as they played. But neither of them was really concentrating on the game. Lisa could feel Grayson's eyes on her the whole time, and whenever she looked up, he seemed to be focused on her rather than the board, his dark, hooded gaze lingering on her lips or breasts. She felt flustered by his closeness and played recklessly, too distracted to think strategically. Instead her attention wandered to the curve of his jaw or his beautiful full mouth. She watched his fingers as he moved a piece, her skin tingling as she imagined them on her body. The air seemed super-charged between them, and when their hands brushed over the board, they both started as if they had received an electric shock.

Lisa quickly surveyed the board, then looked up at Grayson. 'I offer a draw,' she said breathily.

'I accept,' he said without taking his eyes off her. Then in one fluid movement he surged to his feet and took her hand. He tasted of wine as their lips met hungrily and he wrapped his arms around her, not breaking the kiss as he pulled her down onto the rug in front of the fire. His hands were urgent but gentle as he peeled off her clothes. Then he kissed her all over, his mouth hot and wet and fervent on every inch of skin he exposed. Lost in a fog of lust, Lisa wasn't even aware of him removing his own clothes. She just knew that suddenly they were both naked and moving as one, hands stroking and caressing, mouths sucking and kissing and licking, bodies grinding against each other, desperate to get closer and closer. Grayson held her hand as he moved inside her, his eyes wide open and gazing into hers with a look that was almost worshipful. When he came, he said her name, and there was such tenderness and passion in his tone that Lisa wanted to cry.

Still he never stopped kissing and touching her, bringing every nerve ending in her body to life again and again. Every time she thought she was done he would coax her to a new peak of pleasure. He made love to her slowly, thoroughly, making her come over and over until she couldn't take any more and lay shaking and dazed in his arms. They lay like that, knotted together, not speaking, just breathing each other in, until they were brought back to earth with a jolt by the buzz of the alarm on Lisa's watch signalling it was time for her to leave.

Grayson looked pained as she moved out of his embrace, gazing at her longingly as she dressed and called a taxi. He pulled on his clothes and saw her out. On the doorstep he took a thick white envelope from his pocket, throwing her an almost apologetic look as he handed it to her. Lisa's hand shook as she took it from him.

'Thank you,' she whispered.

He gave her a soft kiss on her forehead. 'I'm busy all day tomorrow,' he said. 'But come tomorrow night – same time?'

She nodded and turned to go.

Lisa felt fundamentally changed in some way as she left his house, instantly bereft the moment she walked out the door, and longing to turn around and run back into his arms. It was crazy, but she missed him already; missed his arms around her, his mouth on her skin, his eyes looking into hers and really seeing her. She felt dazed on the cab ride home, her mind constantly replaying images of their lovemaking, or just of Grayson's face, the way he smiled at her, how his eyes glowed with tenderness sometimes when he looked at her. Tears rolled down her cheeks before she even realised she was crying.

She felt so lonely without him, wrapping her arms around herself for comfort. This was what she had been afraid of. It was why she had tried to put up barriers between them. She didn't want to like him, but she did – she liked him so much it hurt. What made it harder to bear was the fact that she knew he felt the same way. It was there in his eyes, in the way he touched her – it was unmistakable. It would have been so much easier if she didn't like him – and if she didn't enjoy the sex so much. She hadn't expected that.

She had enjoyed sex before, but it had been a long time ago, and she had thought that Mark's brutality had put her off sex for good. With him, it had become a chore, just one more thing she had to get through to please him and keep some semblance of peace. It hadn't always been like that. He had been a good lover in the beginning; less selfish, more giving. He had made her feel good. He hadn't treated her like his plaything, only existing for his pleasure.

But over time he had chipped away at her confidence and self-esteem until sex had become something she dreaded. He had become more demanding; more contemptuous and critical. He told her she was a lousy lay, and she started to believe him. He thought she should be able to orgasm to command, and he would get angry with her if she didn't, calling her frigid and accusing her of deliberately holding back. So now when he said 'Come for me' she went through the motions and faked an orgasm. It worked for them both. Mark was satisfied that he was some kind of sex god who could control her orgasms, and she was glad to get the whole thing over with, so he would leave her alone.

She hadn't expected to ever feel lust or take pleasure in

sex again. She thought her libido was dead, that she was numb to desire. But Grayson had shown her that wasn't the case. She really wanted him – she had been dismayed to discover how much. Not only did she crave his kisses and caresses, she wanted to please him too. She was stunned by how proud and glad she felt when she made him groan and shiver with pleasure, bemused by the dawning realisation that she wanted his satisfaction as much as her own.

What was that? Was it love? It couldn't be love, she told herself firmly as the cab pulled up outside Mark's house. And if it was, she just had to ignore it. She couldn't afford love, not now – not when there was so much at stake.

19

Lisa tried to dismiss the giddy feeling she had as she left Mark's house the following evening. But there was an undeniable spring in her step as she walked to the main road to flag down a cab. She felt buoyant and excited, looking forward to seeing Grayson. She had tried to shake off her disappointment that he couldn't see her at lunchtime and get on with other things, but without success. She had basically spent the whole day thinking about Grayson and waiting for the moment she would see him again. She had dressed with special care, and she felt light-hearted and excited, like any young woman going to meet her lover.

The traffic was moving slowly, crawling bumper-to-bumper up the hill in the high street, but she waited for the pedestrian light to turn green before stepping into the road. She was halfway across when she saw the car coming towards her in her peripheral vision and realised it wasn't slowing down. She knew it was going to hit her seconds before the impact.

The next thing she knew she was on the ground at the

side of the road, one shoe missing and tears streaming down her face. A crowd was starting to gather around her, voices asking was she all right, but she was too dazed to answer. A man held a hand out to her and helped her up. The car that had hit her was parked at the side of the road now and a woman emerged from it and rushed up to her.

'I'm so sorry,' she said to Lisa. 'Are you all right? The sun was in my eyes and I didn't see the red light. It's all my fault. Are you okay?' She spoke in a breathless rush, and she was so obviously distraught that Lisa felt sorry for her.

She made a mental check of her body. She didn't seem to be injured, apart from a few cuts and grazes. She realised she was lucky the traffic had been moving so slowly. She nodded reassuringly at the woman, still struggling to speak. 'I'm okay,' she managed finally, her voice sounding tearful and shaky, she supposed from shock.

Somebody handed her her shoe, and she thanked them, and then the woman was offering to take her to hospital. 'You should get checked out.'

Lisa shook her head. 'I'm fine, really.'

'Well, at least let me give you a lift,' she said, putting an arm around Lisa and steering her towards the car.

Lisa was grateful to let someone take over. She sank gratefully into the leather upholstery, and concentrated on trying to calm and reassure herself. She felt wobbly. She was shaking, and tears were still flowing from her eyes.

'Are you sure you don't want to go to the hospital?' the woman asked as she passed Lisa a tissue.

Lisa thought about it, but she would probably have to wait ages to be seen, and she didn't want to spend hours alone in an emergency department. Besides, she wasn't worried about her injuries. She hadn't been badly hurt.

'I'd rather just go home, thanks,' she said, wiping her eyes.

'Okay.' The woman nodded. Then she pulled a piece of paper and a pen from her bag. 'I'll give you my number and address, in case you want to contact me,' she said as she wrote. 'My name's Sheila,' she said, handing the paper to Lisa.

For insurance, Lisa realised, taking it from her – in case she wanted to sue. 'Thanks,' she said. 'But I'm fine, really.'

'Well, just in case. Sometimes complications take time to set in.'

'It's just a few scrapes. You didn't hit me hard.'

'Thank God,' Sheila said, looking horrified. 'I got such a shock. I just didn't see you. The sun is so low, and it was in my eyes, but that's no excuse—'

'It's okay, really. I'm fine,' Lisa said, feeling sorry for Sheila, who was obviously shaken up herself. 'It's lucky the traffic was jammed and you were moving so slowly.'

Sheila heaved a shaky sigh. 'Well, where would you like me to take you?' she asked, as she started the car.

Lisa considered giving her Mark's address. But the thought of going back to that cold, empty house was depressing. She wasn't badly injured, but she was in shock and she wanted the comfort of being with someone – someone who cared about her and would be concerned and sympathetic. She wanted Grayson. Besides, he was expecting her, and he'd already paid her for the whole week. She wasn't badly injured, and she would be perfectly able to have sex with him, so there was no reason to cancel. She gave Sheila his address.

'I hope there'll be someone at home to look after you.'

'Yes, my … boyfriend.'

'Good. Maybe he'll insist on taking you to the hospital.'

If it were Mark, he probably *would* insist on taking her to hospital. He would make sure she had the best care possible, but he would also want to make Sheila pay. She shuddered to think how he would react if Sheila were to turn up at his door taking responsibility for Lisa's accident.

'Thanks,' she said, turning to Sheila as they pulled up outside Grayson's house.

'Well, you have my number if you need to contact me. Anything you need, don't hesitate to call.'

'Thanks. But I'm sure it won't be necessary.' Lisa unbuckled her seatbelt.

'Well, take care,' Sheila said. 'I'll just wait here until you get inside.'

Lisa glanced at her watch as she got out of the car and saw that she was late. It was almost seven-thirty. Grayson opened the door seconds after she rang the bell, as if he had been eagerly awaiting her arrival. His welcoming smile vanished as soon as he saw her, taking in her cut, grazed knees, her legs streaked with dirt and her tear-stained face at a glance.

'Lisa!' he gasped, his eyes wide with alarm. 'What happened?' His eyes drifted behind her to Sheila's car still parked at the gate with the engine running.

Lisa turned and waved to show she was okay, and Sheila raised a hand in acknowledgement before driving off.

'I was knocked down,' she said to Grayson as he ushered her inside.

'Oh my God, are you okay?' he asked, his eyes sweeping over her.

Lisa nodded, but she was so touched by his concern, her eyes welled with tears again and her chin started to wobble.

He put an arm around her and led her into the sitting room and over to the sofa. Lisa sank down on it gratefully as she was starting to shake uncontrollably. She supposed it was a mixture of delayed shock and relief.

Grayson hunkered down in front of her and took her hands.

'Was that the woman who hit you?' he asked, jerking his head towards the window.

Lisa nodded.

'Did you go to hospital? Have you seen a doctor?' he asked as his eyes raked over her.

'No.' Lisa shook her head. 'I'm fine. I just have a few cuts and grazes. The traffic was moving really slowly, so I wasn't hit hard. I just—' She drew a ragged breath. 'I just got such a fright,' she finished on a sob, tears spilling from her eyes.

Grayson sat beside her and pulled her into his arms gently. 'Ssh,' he whispered as he stroked her back soothingly. 'You're okay now.'

'It's just shock,' Lisa gulped.

'Should I take you to the hospital?' Grayson asked when her tears subsided. 'You should probably get checked out.'

She shook her head. 'No, I'm fine, really. The only reason to see a doctor would be if I wanted to sue, and I don't.'

Grayson looked at her uncertainly for a moment. 'Well, if you're sure,' he said finally. 'You didn't hit your head?'

'No.'

His features relaxed a little. 'Okay, then. Let's get you cleaned up.' He took her hand and led her upstairs to the bathroom. There, he sat her down in a big comfy chair by the sink while he rolled up his sleeves and filled the basin with warm water. He wrung out a washcloth and handed it to her, and she washed her face while he moved around the room gathering towels and medical supplies. Then he knelt in front of her, removed her shoes and deftly attended to her cuts, washing them with cotton wool before swabbing them with antiseptic. His hands were so gentle on her that Lisa felt like crying again, and her eyes welled up with tears. It had been a long time since anyone had touched her in such a caring, non-sexual way.

'Sorry,' Grayson winced sympathetically, looking up into her eyes, 'am I hurting you?'

'No,' Lisa said in a choked whisper. 'I'm just—it's just delayed shock, I guess.' She couldn't admit that she was moved to tears because he had made her feel cherished simply by looking after her like this.

'Better?' he asked, smiling up at her when he had applied strips of plaster to the cuts.

'Yes,' she nodded, smiling back. 'Thank you.'

He stood and dropped a soft kiss on her forehead before helping her up. 'Come on, you need something to eat. And I think we could both do with a drink. I was going to make risotto. Is that okay?'

She nodded. 'That would be lovely. Don't go to any trouble, though.' She felt she ought to tell him that it wasn't necessary to cook. He had already wasted enough of his time taking care of her. But she still felt shaky, and food would be comforting and help steady her nerves. She knew it would make her feel better. She would make it up to him later.

So she let him lead her downstairs and into the library, where he made her comfortable on one of the big armchairs in front of the fire, piling up cushions around her until he was satisfied she was snug. He went to a side table and poured them both glasses of wine.

'Thank you,' she said as she took it from him. 'Can I do anything to help?'

'No.' He shook his head. 'You just relax. It won't take long.' He strode from the room, carrying his glass.

Left alone, Lisa sat sipping her wine, listening to the

distant sounds of Grayson moving about in the kitchen while he prepared dinner. As the heat of the fire seeped through her, she felt herself relax completely and an overwhelming feeling of wellbeing and contentment washed over her. Grayson made her feel so cherished and safe. He was so attentive and solicitous towards her. He would be a wonderful boyfriend. Not for the first time, she wished they could have met under different circumstances. Who knew what might have happened then? Maybe this could have been her real life. She allowed herself to indulge the fantasy for a moment that Grayson was her boyfriend and she lived with him in this beautiful house and shared his life – and when they had sex later, it would be because they loved one another. She sighed sadly. If only it could be like that between them, with no financial transaction involved. But there was no point in wishing for what could never be. She had to put aside any feelings she might have for Grayson. If she was to earn her freedom, she needed to remain cold and mercenary in her dealings with him. She was glad she had him to come to tonight instead of going home to an empty house, and she was grateful for the way he cared for her. But she would just enjoy it for what it was and accept that it couldn't be anything more. Meeting Grayson was the best thing that had happened to her in a long time, and she wouldn't let it be a source of dissatisfaction or unhappiness by wishing for what could never be.

Grayson brought dinner into the library. He set up a little table between them and they ate in front of the fire. The risotto was soothingly creamy, rich with butter and cheese, and Lisa ate hungrily. She couldn't remember when food had ever tasted so good. As she finished her bowl, she looked up to find Grayson watching her, an indulgent smile on his face.

'What?' she asked.

'I love how much you enjoy your food,' he said. 'It's a pleasure to cook for you.'

'The pleasure is all mine,' she grinned at him. 'That was absolutely delicious. Thank you.'

'You're welcome.'

He began clearing away the things, insisting she stay where she was when she offered to help.

'Are you sore?' he asked when he returned to the library. 'Do you want some painkillers?'

'No, thanks. I'm a little stiff,' she said, stretching her arms out to test them. 'But I'll be fine. I'm sure I'll loosen up once I move around a bit.'

'Would you like to go to bed?' Grayson asked.

'Yes,' she said, smiling up at him. Glancing at her watch, she saw that it was just after nine. He wasn't getting great value for money, she thought wryly.

All her muscles had seized up, and she felt stiff and sore as she stood. The food and wine had made her feel sleepy, and she suppressed a yawn.

'Are you okay?' Grayson frowned in concern.

'Yes, I'm fine. Just a little—oh!' she yelped in surprise as Grayson swept her off her feet and scooped her up into his arms. She didn't protest, wrapping her arms around his neck and nuzzling into his shoulder. He carried her up the stairs as if she weighed nothing.

Lisa didn't unwind her arms from around his neck as he set her on her feet in the bedroom. She pressed herself closer to his body and kissed his mouth, one hand drifting to the waistband of his jeans. Grayson went very still. As she popped the button, she realised he wasn't kissing her back.

'Lisa,' he said hoarsely, stopping her hand and pulling away. 'What are you doing?'

'I'm—' She looked up at him in confusion. Wasn't it

clear what she was doing? That was what she was here for, after all. 'Do you want … something else?'

He reared back, looking shocked. 'You think I expect you to have sex with me tonight?'

She shrugged, completely thrown off balance. 'Well … yes. That's why I'm here, isn't it?'

He looked like she had hit him, but she couldn't understand why he seemed so upset.

'And what do you think all that was earlier – me fixing up my sex toy? Jesus!' He raked a hand through his hair.

'No. I know that you care about me. But I hope you don't think I expect you to look after me. I'm not your responsibility, Grayson. I mean, I wouldn't have come here tonight if I didn't think I could … do what you're paying me for.'

'Christ! Please tell me that's not true.'

'What do you mean?'

'That you wouldn't have come here if you didn't think you'd be up to having sex.'

'No, I wouldn't. It wouldn't be fair on you. I'd have cancelled.'

'And done what? Gone home to your big empty house and spent the night alone, with no one to look after you? Mark isn't even home. Would you have called anyone? A friend?'

'No, I don't—' She broke off, biting her lip. She had been about to say that she didn't have any friends, but she didn't want his pity. 'No. I'd have been fine on my own.'

Grayson sighed heavily, and when she raised her eyes he was looking at her sadly. 'Lisa.' He shook his head. 'You do know I … care about you, don't you?'

She nodded. 'I know,' she mumbled.

'I like to think that we're friends, apart from our … arrangement. Despite our arrangement, maybe,' he added with a wry smile. 'And friends take care of each other when they're hurt or in trouble. I'd like you to feel you can rely on me.'

'I don't really like relying on anyone else,' she told him honestly.

He nodded. 'Okay. But just know that if you ever need anything, I'd always do my best to help you.'

Her eyes welled up with tears again at his words, and she swallowed a sob. 'I know you would.'

'You only have to ask.'

She wiped her eyes in frustration as the tears started to flow again. 'Sorry, I'm just—'

'You're just exhausted,' he said, with a look of such tenderness and sympathy that she thought her heart might break. He pulled her into his arms. 'I think you should stay here tonight. Just to sleep,' he added as she drew breath to protest. 'I don't want you going back to that empty house and spending the night alone. I'd like to keep an eye on you.'

There was nothing she would have liked more as she relaxed into the warmth of his body. 'I can't. I need to leave by midnight – I want to be home when Mark calls.'

'Can't you take his call here?'

She shook her head. 'We Skype, and I don't want him to know I'm here.'

'You wouldn't have to tell him about our arrangement – just that you didn't want to be alone. I'm sure he'd understand in the circumstances.'

She shook her head. 'I'm not going to tell him about the accident.'

Grayson frowned. 'You're not?'

'There's no point in worrying him when he's so far away and there's nothing he can do. I'm absolutely fine and he'll get in a big panic about nothing.' There was no way Mark would understand. He'd be furious if he thought she had turned to another man, even if only for comfort.

Grayson sighed. 'Maybe you're right. I can imagine how I'd feel if …'

He didn't finish the sentence, but Lisa knew what he meant, and tried not to feel touched by the sentiment. 'I am exhausted, though,' she said, yawning again. 'If we're not … doing anything, maybe I should just go home and go to bed.'

'Why don't you just lie down here and have a rest? I'll drive you home later.'

'I don't know …' The bed looked so inviting, but could she risk it?

'Or let me come with you. I hate to think of you all alone in that house when you've just been in an accident.'

'Okay. I'll lie down here for a while.' Her eyes were drooping closed already, and she really couldn't resist the pull of that bed.

'Good.' He went to the bed and turned back the duvet.

Lisa kicked off here shoes and crawled between the sheets. Grayson pulled the duvet over her, then sat on the edge of the bed and gave her a soft kiss on the forehead. Lisa buried her fingers in his hair, clinging to him. She wanted him to stay with her, but was afraid to ask.

'Do you want me to lie down with you?' he asked, looking down at her.

She nodded. 'Yes – if you don't mind.'

Without another word, he kicked off his shoes and crawled into the bed beside her, pulling her into his body.

Lisa laid her head on his chest and breathed a contented sigh as she closed her eyes and snuggled into him.

20

Lisa woke with a start. It was dark, and for a moment she couldn't remember where she was. Disoriented, her eyes darted around the unfamiliar bedroom, and she remembered she was in Grayson's house. She turned to find him lying in the bed beside her, fast asleep, his chest rising and falling rhythmically. His long eyelashes rested softly on his cheeks, his features soft and relaxed in sleep. He was still fully dressed, his arms wrapped loosely around her.

Oh God, what time was it? How long had they slept? Her heart hammering, she shot up in bed in a panic, the ache in her limbs as she did so reminding her of yesterday's accident. She turned on the bedside light and checked her watch. She gasped when she saw it was almost twelve-thirty. Mark could call any minute, and she wouldn't be there. She threw back the cover and scrambled out of bed. How could she have been so stupid? She'd never make it home in time, she thought, as she fumbled for her bag.

'What's going on?'

She turned to see Grayson had woken and was sitting up in bed, blinking dazedly at her. He looked sleepy and confused, his hair tousled.

'I fell asleep!' she whined as she stepped into her shoes, simultaneously pulling her phone out of her bag to call a cab. 'It's twelve-thirty. I have to get home.' Tears pricked the backs of her eyes, and her voice trembled.

'Jesus, what's wrong?' he asked, glancing at the phone in her hand. 'Are you okay? Has something happened?'

'I'll miss Mark's call.' She heard the accusation in her tone, but she couldn't worry about that now. She was struggling to concentrate on finding the cab company's number in her phone, her mind a blur.

'Sorry,' he sighed. 'I didn't mean to fall asleep. I can't believe I slept so long.' He rubbed his eyes and relaxed back against the pillows with a little smile. 'Why don't you call him on your phone?'

She felt like hitting him for not taking this seriously. 'No, I have to be at home. If I'm not there when he rings —' She knew how hysterical she sounded, but she couldn't help it. She was in a blind panic, oblivious to everything but the thought of Mark ringing and finding her not at home. Her fingers were useless, clumsy and shaking, and she kept pressing the wrong buttons as she tried to dial the cab company. She clutched her hair agitatedly. Then she swiped tears from her eyes, forcing herself to breathe and focus on her phone.

Grayson's expression changed suddenly as he watched her. His smile faded and was replaced by a look of alarm. He threw back the duvet and got out of bed. 'I'll drive you.'

Lisa was relieved that he seemed to understand her

urgency now. He was looking at her with real concern. No doubt he thought she was acting like a crazy person, but she didn't care if it meant he'd get her home in time.

'Would you?' She raked shaking fingers through her hair. 'I'd really appreciate it.' They might actually make it in time. 'I'm sorry to be such a nuisance, but by the time a cab gets here—'

'No problem,' he said, shuffling into his shoes. 'Don't worry, you'll get there in time,' he said, stroking her arms soothingly. 'Just calm down, okay?'

She nodded, still breathing rapidly. Then she grabbed her bag, Grayson swiped his car keys from the nightstand, and Lisa followed him wordlessly down the stairs.

Grayson opened the car doors and they got in simultaneously. He pulled out of the drive while Lisa was still fastening her seat belt, hoping that his urgency would reassure her somewhat. Her movements were jerky, her tension palpable. He could tell she was miles away. He was taken aback by her distress. When he woke to find her in such a panic to leave, he thought she must have had bad news or that she was suffering some after-effects from the accident yesterday. So he'd been relieved to discover she was just worried about missing Mark's call. But then he saw how upset she was, her voice shaking, her eyes welling with tears. The cool mask she often wore with him was gone, replaced by naked panic and fear. He didn't understand it, but he knew it was very real and he had to take it seriously.

'It'll be okay,' he said to her once they were out on the open road, trying to put her mind at rest. She was so agitated. 'What time does Mark usually call?'

'Any time after twelve-thirty. Usually around one or a quarter to.'

He glanced at the clock on the dashboard. 'Don't worry. We'll get there in time.'

She threw him a grateful glance, but she still looked absolutely terrified. Christ, what had that asshole Mark done to her to make her so scared of missing one fucking phone call? He wanted to ask her why Mark couldn't call her on her mobile for once, why she had to be in the house to take his call, why she didn't want to tell him about her accident. But he knew now wasn't the time for questions. It would only make her more stressed than she already was, and the last thing he wanted to do was add to her anxiety.

'I'm sorry I fell asleep,' he said. 'I didn't realise how important it was for you to be home.'

'It's okay,' she said, her voice tense and breathy. Her fists were clenched on her legs, and she looked so tightly wound she might burst. It was anything but okay. Shit! She'd told him she wanted to be home when Mark phoned. He should have listened. He just hoped he could get her there on time – then she might forgive him.

Fortunately, the traffic was light and they made good time – aided by Grayson racing through every amber light. It was almost twelve forty-five when they pulled up outside the house. Grayson prayed Mark hadn't called yet.

'Thanks,' Lisa said as she unlocked her seatbelt. She sprang from the car and raced to the door without a backward glance.

Grayson turned off the ignition, not sure what to do. Should he follow her in or just drive home? He didn't like the idea of leaving her here alone in the state she was in, particularly after her accident yesterday. He at least wanted to make sure she was okay. He got out of the car and followed her at a more leisurely pace to the door.

As she opened it, she turned, looking startled to find him behind her.

'Can I come in?' he asked.

'Oh.' She looked at him unseeingly, her eyes darting around, perhaps looking for a way to get rid of him.

'I'd like to make sure you're okay. I can wait until you've finished your call.'

'Sure,' she shrugged, more he suspected because she didn't have time to think up an excuse to say no than because she wanted him there. She let him in and closed the door behind them, then walked ahead of him down the hall. 'You can wait in there,' she said briskly, waving to the kitchen. 'Help yourself to anything.'

He watched as she continued to the end of the hall to the dining room where they had eaten when he and Isabel had come to dinner, shedding her coat on the way. Seconds later she came out armed with a laptop. She was turning it on as she hurried back down the corridor and disappeared in the direction of the stairs.

Alone in the kitchen, Grayson decided to make himself some coffee. He had driven here still half asleep, and he didn't want to risk driving home again in the same state. He rummaged around in the cupboards and found everything he needed, then used the high-tech coffee machine. He drank two shots of espresso, so strong it made him shudder. Then he sat at the kitchen counter and waited. He had left in a hurry and hadn't even taken his phone, so he had nothing to occupy him. He became increasingly restless as time passed and there was still no sign of Lisa. Eventually, he got up and started to explore the house, drifting in and out of the downstairs rooms aimlessly.

The dining room brought back vivid memories of the night he and Isabel had come to dinner, when Mark had used a vibrator on Lisa at the table. He remembered the helpless need in her face as she came; how soft and warm she had felt in his arms when he pulled her into his lap; how hard it had made him. In the study, he smiled to himself as he remembered their chess game. She had worn that sheer shirt, her gorgeous breasts clearly visible, and he had struggled to concentrate on the game, when all he wanted to do was touch her. And then later, miraculously, *she* had kissed *him*. He had left it up to her and she had made the first move. He got hard now just thinking about it – how soft and yielding she had been, how responsive when he had kissed her breasts, sucking her hardened nipples through the silky material, her soft moans and gasps as he had stroked and caressed her. He could almost feel her in his arms, taste her on his tongue.

He shifted uncomfortably, wanting her again. He glanced at his watch. It was almost two. He wondered if Mark had called yet. Perhaps Lisa had gone to bed forgetting he was here, or assuming he would let himself out and go home. Maybe he should go in search of her. He didn't want to leave without letting her know. If she was expecting him to still be here, she might be upset if she came down to find him gone.

Hesitantly, he made for the stairs, unsure he was doing the right thing. He treaded softly, feeling like an intruder. Several doors faced him on the landing, but one was slightly ajar and there were noises emanating from it. He tiptoed across the landing, recognising Mark's voice as he got closer to the door. He was relieved he had got Lisa home in time. He knew he should turn around and go back downstairs to wait for her, but instead he found himself creeping to the door, unable to stop himself. He peeked through the gap and he had to stifle a gasp as he took in the scene before him. Lisa was kneeling naked on the bed, the laptop propped up on a dressing table opposite. He could just make out Mark's face on the screen from where he stood, but he could hear his words all too clearly.

'That's it, baby,' he said, his voice ragged and breathy with excitement. 'Touch yourself for me.'

Lisa's hands stroked her breasts, her head thrown back.

'Pinch your nipples,' Mark said. 'Come on, baby. Do it hard. Really make it hurt. I want to hear you moan.'

Grayson's stomach lurched sickeningly as Lisa whimpered, a sound that was somewhere between pain and pleasure. He shouldn't be seeing this. It was private. He ought not to be watching, yet he felt frozen in place, holding his breath.

'I can't wait to get home and fuck you properly,' Mark was panting. 'Spread your legs for me, baby.'

Grayson reared back from the door, suddenly overcome with revulsion for himself as voyeur and for the scene he was witnessing. Noiselessly, he darted for the stairs and ran down them like a man being hunted.

He was sitting in the kitchen when Lisa came back down fifteen minutes later.

'Oh, you're still here.' She was wearing a robe, and she seemed surprised to see him there, as if she had forgotten him.

'I just wanted to wait, to make sure you were okay.'

'I'm fine.' She smiled at him. 'I'm sorry for freaking out like that.'

He was relieved she appeared more relaxed now. 'No, *I'm* sorry. I wouldn't have let myself fall asleep if I'd known how important it was for you to be here.'

'It's okay. Anyway, I got here in time, so thank you for that. Sorry for dragging you out of bed.'

'Well, I'll leave you to sleep,' he said, reluctantly getting up. 'Unless …'

'Unless?'

He studied her face. She looked so weary and drained. She had had such a stressful day – first the upset of the accident, then the panic about over-sleeping and the rush over here for Mark's call, all so that asshole could treat her like his own personal peep show, making her perform for him and telling her to hurt herself for his gratification. The thought of what he had overheard sickened him. She probably just wanted to be left alone. He should leave her in peace. 'Nothing,' he said, shaking his head. 'I'll go. You should rest.'

'It's late,' she said, glancing at her watch. 'You can stay here if you like.'

He looked at her questioningly, trying to decipher if she really wanted that or if she was just being polite, hoping he'd refuse. As he watched, she nodded to herself as if deciding something.

'Come on,' she said, taking his hand and looking up into his face. 'We're both exhausted. We were just going to sleep anyway. And …' She bit her lip, looking down. 'I think I'd sleep better with you there,' she said to the floor, so quietly he had to strain to hear her.

'Me too,' he said, his fingers curling around hers. He dropped a kiss on her forehead, and she looked more relaxed when she looked back up at him. 'Lead the way.'

In the bedroom, Lisa slipped off her robe. She was completely naked underneath and Grayson willed himself not to stare at her body. She quickly got into bed and covered herself with the duvet, and he stripped to his boxers and got in beside her. Then he turned to her and wrapped his arms around her, pulling her into his body, her back to his front, praying that he was too tired to get an erection. Her bare skin felt amazing against his, so soft and silky.

'Goodnight,' he said, planting a soft kiss on her shoulder.

She sighed contentedly and nuzzled into his body. 'Goodnight,' she whispered.

He didn't know who fell asleep first.

21

Lisa woke the next morning feeling more content than she had in a long time. Mark's presence was always so oppressive and crushing, but it was different knowing it was Grayson next to her in the bed; his arm slung across her body, his warm breath on the back of her neck. She didn't feel trapped and anxious with him – just warm, safe and happy. She yawned sleepily and turned gently towards him, careful not to disturb him. She let her eyes linger on his face, taking the opportunity to gaze at him unashamedly while he slept. He was so beautiful, she thought, drinking in his sleep-softened features; his long eyelashes and strong, chiselled jaw; his full, sensual lips slightly parted; all the lines of his face relaxed in slumber.

But he wasn't just beautiful, he was *good* – kind and decent and sincere. He was always so sweet to her, so protective of her. When she was with him she felt safe and cherished. She was more at ease than she'd been in years, and at the same time she'd never felt so alive. She sighed, nestling closer to him. She'd been touched by the way he took care of her yesterday after her accident, and she was glad he was here now.

She had hated having to leave the warmth and comfort of his bed last night to rush over here so that Mark could treat her like his sex toy. All the security and wellbeing she had felt when she was with Grayson had been stripped away in an instant at the sound of Mark's voice, the old familiar sense of despair and depression creeping over her once again as she obeyed his harsh commands. Even from the other side of the world he spoiled everything for her, and she felt like weeping even now as she thought of how she had stripped and touched herself for him, while she tried to hide how humiliated she felt and how disgusted she was by him. He claimed to love her, but he got off on degrading and dehumanising her, and it galled her that she had given him such power over her that she would leave Grayson, a man who genuinely cared for her, to come running whenever Mark snapped his fingers. It frightened her when she was faced with the stark reality of what she had become, how low she had sunk.

When the call ended, she had allowed herself to shed a few tears of self-pity. She had felt so lonely and sad, longing to crawl back into Grayson's bed and sleep wrapped in his arms until morning. She regretted that she hadn't stayed with him and risked Mark's anger. What could he do to her, after all, when he was thousands of miles away? She had berated herself for being such a coward. So when she had come downstairs and found him still there, waiting for her in the kitchen, it was like she had been given a do-over, and she wasn't going to let a second chance to spend the night with Grayson slip through her fingers.

It was ridiculous how much courage it had taken to ask him to stay, but Mark's conditioning went deep, and it felt empowering to make a simple decision and carry it out without worrying about his reaction. She wasn't used to acting on her own wishes and desires. Asking for what she wanted seemed daring and reckless, and even though Mark was so far away, even though she wouldn't be here when he got back and would never have to face his wrath, it still felt brave to defy him by letting Grayson spend the night. She knew how pathetic that was, but at least she had done it – it was a start.

As she watched Grayson sleep, she made a decision. She had lost so much already because of Mark, but she was done losing. She wasn't going to let Mark take one more moment of happiness away from her if she could help it. She was going to take back control of her life, and she would start right now, with Grayson.

She wanted him. Trying to resist her feelings didn't make them go away, and denying them wasn't going to make it any easier to leave him. So why not grab whatever fleeting happiness she could and make the most of what little time she had left with him? From now on she would stop holding back, trying to protect herself from the pain of losing him. Instead she would just let go and allow herself to enjoy being with him. For the next two days, she would live in the moment and soak up every kiss, every touch, every affectionate gesture and loving glance that he offered her, and she wouldn't worry about the future or allow her thoughts to dwell on what might have been. Two days wasn't much – it wasn't near enough – but it was something. It was more than she'd had in a very long time.

She felt Grayson stir beside her as he woke. His eyes flicked open, looking straight into hers.

'Good morning,' she smiled.

His eyes darted between hers with a slightly puzzled

look, as if he was struggling to recognise her. She wondered had he sensed the change in her.

'Good morning.' He glanced around the room, seeming surprised to find himself here. His gentle smile was bemused. 'Wow, I slept really well,' he said, propping himself up on one arm.

'Me too.'

'How are you feeling?'

'Fine. Never better, in fact.' They were so close, she could feel his warm breath on her face, and she was suddenly overcome with shyness. They had had plenty of sex, but they'd never slept together, and it seemed strangely intimate to be waking up beside him – which was crazy, considering all the things they'd done together.

As if sensing her withdrawal, Grayson sat up. 'Thanks for letting me stay last night,' he said. 'I'll get out of your hair.'

As he pulled back the duvet, she put a hand on his arm. 'You don't have to go, do you? It's Sunday, so we've got all day. I'm completely at your disposal – if you want me, that is.'

'Of course I want you. But you should rest.'

'I feel fine, honestly. And I have some time to make up for yesterday.'

'You don't owe me anything, Lisa. I got to spend the whole night with you last night.'

'But you were asleep. We didn't … do anything. It doesn't count.'

'It counts to me,' he said with a little shrug. 'I liked sleeping with you.'

'I liked it too,' she said, looking up at him shyly from under her lashes. 'I liked you being here last night, and waking up with you this morning.'

His eyes darkened, desire flickering in their depths.

'And I'd like to spend the day with you,' she continued, lifting her gaze to his.

'Really?' His eyes lit up.

She nodded. 'Yes, really. We can do whatever you want.'

He smiled teasingly. 'Even if I just want to hang out with you?'

'Even then.'

'What if it involves picnics or conversations? Or if I want to play chess?'

'That would be fine,' she smiled.

He said nothing, studying her face closely as if he was trying to decipher how she really felt.

'I like spending time with you, Grayson. We only have a couple of days left of this arrangement. I thought we should make the most of them.'

He frowned. 'I thought you were uncomfortable with the romantic stuff?'

'Well, I've changed my mind. You can be as cheesy as you like.'

'Cheesy?' He grinned, his features softening and relaxing. He settled back into bed beside her and leaned in to kiss her, and her lips clung to his, wanting more. Too soon, he pulled away. 'What's brought about this change of heart?' he asked.

'I don't know,' she shrugged. 'Maybe the accident yesterday was a wake-up call – made me realise life's too short, and you have to grab it by the balls.'

He laughed. 'So you decided to grab me by the balls?'

'Something like that.' She giggled. 'Or maybe you've just got under my skin.'

'It's very nice skin,' he said, trailing a finger down the length of her arm. It ghosted over the side of her breast, and she shivered as it grazed her nipple.

'Anyway, I'm supposed to be getting you out of my system, remember?' she said teasingly.

'And how's that going for you?' His voice was husky and seductive as his finger continued to stroke tantalisingly along her arm.

'It's going to take a bit more time.' She took a deep breath. 'I guess I decided you have to go after what you want. And I want you.'

Something flickered in his eyes, some intense emotion that she couldn't quite decipher – a mixture of desire, pain and pleasure.

'I want you too, Lisa,' he whispered, leaning in to kiss her. 'So much.'

His lips brushed hers softly. 'If I had all the time in the world with you, I don't think I'd ever get you out of my system.'

Then his mouth was on hers, hot and needy. She felt the hardness of his erection as she kissed him back, and she moaned into his mouth, giving his tongue access. He lifted her so she was straddling him, his hands gripping her waist as he deepened the kiss, his tongue tangling erotically with hers.

She tore her mouth away and kissed her way down his neck and over his chest, feeling the rising tension in him as she slid down his body. His breath hitched as she kissed his taut stomach and dipped her tongue into his navel. His hands slid from her waist, his fingers digging into her flesh as he clutched her shoulders, then sliding into her hair as her head moved lower. She grabbed the hem of his boxers, and he lifted his hips to help her slide them off.

His erection was hard and thick, and he groaned deep in his throat as she wrapped her hand around it. She licked along the shaft from base to tip, swirling her tongue around the head before sucking it into her mouth. She loved the taste of his skin, the warm, heavy feel of his cock, swelling and twitching in her mouth as she sucked harder. His hips flexed, thrusting to meet her, and she felt his body tauten, all his muscles clenched as she took him deeper and deeper, until his cock was hitting the back of her throat.

'Lisa!' he groaned, his hands fisting in her hair. 'I'm going to come.'

She knew it was a warning, but she didn't stop, hollowing out her cheeks and sucking harder as he twitched and came in her mouth, his whole body shuddering as the thick, warm liquid hit the back of her throat. She swallowed every drop, then licked him clean as she felt him soften.

'Wow, that was amazing,' Grayson said breathlessly as she looked up at him with a triumphant smile, feeling very pleased with herself. She was confident of her oral skills, and she knew she could please him that way. But it had surprised her how much she had wanted to do it – not like when Mark would push her onto her knees and violently fuck her mouth. With Grayson it was about giving rather than something being taken from her. It was so different with someone you loved …

The thought brought her up short. *Love*? She couldn't *love* Grayson, could she? She liked him a lot, but she had only known him a few weeks. They had never spent more than a few hours together. People didn't fall in love that quickly, did they? She dismissed the thought as she collapsed onto the pillow beside Grayson. She wasn't going to over-think this. She had resolved to live in the moment and she wasn't going to waste any more time analysing her feelings.

'That's a hell of a way to start the day,' Grayson murmured. He pulled her into his arms and kissed her face, light butterfly kisses on her eyes, her nose, her cheeks.

'How do you feel?' he asked, his breath moist and warm on her skin as he nuzzled her jaw.

'Fine,' she said. 'A little stiff.'

He stroked her body gently, his hands sweeping from breast to hip, his knuckles brushing over her nipples, his warm palm stroking her stomach. His touch was tantalisingly slow and leisurely, slowly waking up every nerve ending, gently caressing until every inch of her skin was tingling and alive with desire, and she trembled with need, her body crying out for release.

He drew back, his eyes sweeping over her body from head to toe. He frowned as his gaze rested on her legs. 'Is this sore?' he asked, touching her lightly just over her knee.

She shook her head and looked down to see that she had a large purple bruise on her right thigh. God, she looked a mess, she thought, laughing inwardly. With a plaster on her knee and a bruised leg she looked more like a scrappy kid than the high-class hooker Grayson was paying her to be. She blushed.

'It's fine.' Embarrassed, she pulled the sheet over to cover herself. 'But it's not a very sexy look!' she said with a laugh.

Grayson tossed the sheet aside again. 'Let me kiss it better,' he said huskily. His lips were infinitely gentle on the tender flesh as he pressed soft kisses over her bruises. He nudged her legs apart as his mouth trailed higher, and she gasped as he reached the aching flesh between her thighs, her body bowing off the bed as he licked along her folds.

'You're so wet,' he groaned, his voice thick. He slid a finger inside her, then two, pumping them in and out while his tongue flicked over her clit. She pushed her hands into his hair, holding him in place there, where she needed him. Her breathing was ragged, her body tightening as he increased the pressure of his fingers, angling them to press against her G spot while his mouth worked her clit, kissing, nibbling and sucking until she came with a scream, her head thrashing helplessly on the pillow. Still he didn't let up, relentlessly pleasuring her and making her come again and again, her body arching off the bed with each onslaught, taut as a string on a violin. Each orgasm was more powerful than the last, the pleasure so intense it was almost unbearable, and her hands clutched frantically at the sheets or fisted in his hair.

Just when she thought she couldn't take any more, his mouth gentled on her, and his fingers withdrew from her still pulsing flesh. He crawled back up her body and pulled her to him, holding her tightly and stroking her hair while she trembled in his arms. It had been the most intense sexual experience of Lisa's life and she felt dazed and shattered by it.

'Better?' Grayson whispered softly, kissing her hair.

She nodded, too shaken to speak. 'How will I ever get over you now?' She hadn't meant to say it out loud. She thought the words were only in her head, and she was horrified to hear them coming out of her mouth. What was she thinking? She wasn't thinking, that was the problem. She couldn't think straight after what had just happened – not when Grayson's arms were still wrapped around her, his naked body pressed against hers, when she was surrounded by the smell and taste and feel of him.

'You don't have to, you know.' He stroked her hair, looking into her eyes.

'Yes, I do,' she said firmly. 'You know I do. I can't see you again after tomorrow.'

'After Mark gets home.' His voice was leaden and it was as if a light had gone out in his eyes.

'Yes.'

'Because you don't want to? Or because you can't?'

'It's … complicated. I can't explain.' *Please don't ask me*, she begged him silently.

'What's happening here, Lisa?'

'Wh—What do you mean?'

'What's happening between us?'

She looked away, frightened by the depth of feeling in his gaze. 'Nothing,' she said faintly, hardly able to find her voice.

'Really? It doesn't feel like nothing to me.'

'You know what this is, Grayson. We both know. We're just two people fucking, that's all.'

'That's all?'

'Yes.' She kept her gaze averted. She couldn't look into those beautiful eyes and lie to him.

'Are you sure?'

'Okay, sometimes we play chess,' she said, trying to lighten the mood. 'Sometimes we have dinner. But mostly we just fuck because we want each other and because I want the money.'

He took her chin in his hand and turned her face to him. 'Why do you need the money?' he asked with a frown. 'Mark's a wealthy man. I know I've asked you this before, but are you in some kind of trouble?'

'No, of course not. Nothing like that.'

His eyes narrowed. 'Are you leaving him?'

'No.' She trusted Grayson, but she still didn't want to confide in him. The less he knew, the better it would be for him. If Mark suspected Grayson had helped her get away, she dreaded to think what he might do. Besides, she didn't want to give Grayson any reason to think he could change her mind. She didn't know how long she could hold out if he tried to persuade her to stay with him.

'I wish you would. I wish you'd leave Mark and come to

me,' he said tentatively, his arms around her tightening, and she felt a pang, already tempted to give in to him. 'If you're —' he hesitated, biting his lip. 'I've seen how he treats you, Lisa,' he continued. 'I could protect you, if you're afraid of what he might do. I could take care of you.'

She knew he could, she thought yearningly. Grayson was a very wealthy man, and she knew the protection money could buy. But she also knew how it could make you a prisoner. She didn't want to be protected anymore, because depending on someone else for your security made you weak and vulnerable, and she never wanted to put herself in that position again. She had to stand on her own two feet and take care of herself.

She didn't believe Grayson would ever try to control and manipulate her, but then she had trusted Mark in the beginning. He had been charming at the start too – sweet, thoughtful and affectionate. He had made her feel loved and special; and safe, she thought bitterly. It was the ultimate irony. Mark had made her feel as if nothing bad could ever happen to her when she was with him. But the truth was she'd been safe all along until he'd come into her life.

She would never again let her head be turned by a man with money, no matter how nice he seemed. She trusted Grayson, but she no longer had any faith in her own judgement. If she had met Grayson in another lifetime, things could have been very different. But she had to deal with how things were, not how they might have been, and she needed to be on her own now. She was just a shell of a person, in no state to start a relationship. She had to find herself again before she could think about being with someone else.

'Of course I'm not scared of Mark,' she said, the hard

edge to her voice sounding false even to her own ears. 'I love him.'

'Why all the secrecy about the money, then?'

'Because …' She cast around for a plausible reason. 'I want to buy him a present, that's all. And I want it to be a surprise. But I don't have any money of my own, so …'

He was frowning at her and she suspected he didn't believe her. But it was at least partly true – she did want to surprise Mark, and she needed the money to carry it off.

'What are you getting him? It must be expensive.'

'I was thinking maybe a boob job,' she said, affecting a playful tone.

'What?' He reared back with a horrified expression, his eyes wide and panicked. 'Please tell me you're not serious.'

She was startled by his reaction, but she didn't let it show. 'Mark's always wanted me to have one,' she said with a casual shrug.

'Fuck him!' Grayson said harshly, his eyes sparking with anger. 'Lisa, you don't need a boob job. Please don't do that to yourself. You have a beautiful body, gorgeous breasts.'

'Mark thinks they're too small.'

A muscle twitched in Grayson's jaw. 'Don't let him make you think you have to mutilate yourself to—'

'Hey, calm down.' She placed a finger lightly on his lips to silence him. 'I—I was just joking,' she said with a reassuring smile. She felt guilty for upsetting him so much. 'I mean, Mark really does want me to have the operation. But I'm not going to.'

He gave a relieved sigh, his eyes closing briefly. 'Thank Christ! I'd never forgive myself if I thought I'd provided the money to fund that.' He bent to give her a soft kiss. 'You're perfect just as you are, Lisa.'

'Hardly,' she huffed.

'You are. And you're with someone who doesn't even appreciate you. How can you love someone who—'

'All these questions,' she interrupted, desperate to change the topic. 'I wouldn't have agreed to spend the day with you if I thought you were going to spend the whole time giving me the third degree.'

'Ah, but you already agreed,' he said with a grin, pulling her closer. 'You can't back out now. Besides—' he began, but stopped himself.

'Besides, I'm yours to do with as you please – bought and paid for,' she said with a playful smile, wanting to lighten the mood. 'So I'm on the clock here, Grayson. Is this really how you want to use the time we have together?'

He gave her a gentle smile. 'No, you're right. It's not.'

'So, what would you like to do?' she asked, trailing her fingers down his abdomen suggestively.

'First, I'd like to have a bath,' he said, throwing back the duvet and swinging out of bed, his back to her.

'Oh!' It wasn't the answer she had been expecting. 'Okay, then,' she said, watching as he stood and made his way to the en suite. He had such a beautiful body. She could look at him all day.

He disappeared into the bathroom and she flopped back against the pillows, listening to the sound of splashing water as he filled the tub. Moments later, he appeared again in the doorway.

'Well, aren't you coming?' he said, jerking his head to the bathroom.

'Oh, you want to have a bath together?'

He rolled his eyes playfully. 'Of course. You don't think I'm going to wash myself when I've got you to cater to my every need?'

Lisa grinned as she got out of bed and ran around to join him.

'Besides,' he said, taking her hand, 'I'd be lonely without you.'

She would be lonely without him too, she thought with a pang – the day after tomorrow. She was going to miss him so much. Then she dismissed such gloomy thoughts, and let him pull her into the bathroom, determined to enjoy what time she had left with him.

22

In the bath, Lisa lay back against Grayson's chest, his legs on either side of hers, while he soaped her languidly, his hands gentle on her skin and in her hair. He was taking care of her again, treating her like she was precious. The hot water soothed and eased her stiff muscles as his hands glided lazily over her wet skin. He dropped occasional soft kisses on her neck and shoulders, and when his hand moved between her legs, he found her clit and made her come again, softly and silently, her body rising out of the water before sinking back against him, sated.

'So, what do you want to do today?' she asked.

'This,' he said, wrapping his arms around her tighter and sighing contentedly. 'We could just stay here all day.' He dropped a kiss on her shoulder.

She twisted around to look at him. 'We'll shrivel up!' she laughed, lifting a hand out of the water to show him her pruned fingers.

'I'd like to stay and get shrivelled and wrinkly with you.'

Her breath hitched at the intensity in his eyes, the

meaning behind his words. She turned in his arms to face him, lifting herself so she was straddling him.

'I'm falling in love with you, Lisa,' he said huskily.

'Ssh.' She placed her fingers on his lips, silencing him. 'Don't say that.' She hated the wounded look in his eyes.

'You said I could do whatever I want today. I want to tell you how I feel. I know you don't want to hear it.'

'Ssh.' She took his hands and placed them on her breasts. He was already hard, and they gazed into each other's eyes as she lowered herself onto his cock, taking him inside her. She needed to make this about sex again. It was just sex, nothing more – just two people fucking.

'I've never felt like this about anyone before,' he whispered, his hands caressing her breasts as she began to move up and down on his shaft. She silenced him with a kiss, burying her fingers in his damp hair. He tugged gently on her bottom lip and she opened her mouth to him, moaning as he sucked on her tongue. Their kisses grew wilder, sucking and biting, fucking each other's mouths as Lisa moved rhythmically, Grayson thrusting his hips up to meet her. Water splashed out onto the floor as their movements became faster and more frantic.

I'm falling in love with you too, Lisa thought, wrapping her arms tightly around him as his mouth closed over her nipple. His hand moved between her legs and she felt the quickening inside her, and then she was lost, drowning in the smell and taste of him, until everything else disappeared and there was nothing in the world but him and her, the feel of the muscles and sinews of his back flexing and straining under his slippery skin as he pounded into her, the animalistic sounds of his grunts and moans, the slap of flesh and splash of water.

A violent shudder shook through him and he bore down on her shoulders, grinding his hips into hers. She felt his cock jerk inside her and he looked right into her eyes as he came at the same time as she did. Then they collapsed against each other, both of them dazed and silent, except for their heavy breathing and their pounding hearts.

Hunger finally drove them to get dressed and head down to the kitchen together. It was early afternoon and they'd missed breakfast, so they were both starving.

'I don't have much food in, 'Lisa said apologetically, peering into the fridge. 'But I could make scrambled eggs?' she turned to Grayson questioningly.

'Hmm, I think I'm up for something more substantial,' he said. 'And I wouldn't mind swinging by my house to grab a change of clothes, if that's okay with you?'

'Yes, fine,' Lisa smiled, relieved. She didn't like being with Grayson in this house – it made their time together feel tainted. What she had with Grayson felt pure and good – paradoxically in the circumstances – and she wanted to keep it that way, completely separate from her twisted relationship with Mark.

'Besides,' he said, smiling, 'you cooking for me wasn't part of the deal. We can go out to eat. There's a pub just down the road from me that does a fantastic brunch.'

'Sounds great!'

It was a warm, sunny spring afternoon when they walked from Grayson's house to the pub on the corner. Lisa didn't protest when Grayson took her hand out on the street, and he gave her a boyish, triumphant grin as she curled her fingers around his. He looked so damn happy, she couldn't help grinning back at him. She loved the feeling of his big hand enveloping hers, and the affectionate, lover-like gesture felt more precious than all the more intimate ways he'd touched her.

The pub he took her to was a converted church, the restaurant area furnished with large unvarnished oak tables and cushioned pew-style benches. They sat side by side, so close their thighs touched.

'This is lovely,' Lisa said, looking around. The room was flooded with light from the high, vaulted ceilings and the many slender Gothic windows, the stained glass adding colour and interest. It was obviously a very popular place, and was doing a brisk weekend brunch trade. There were people of all ages, family groups and friends, but despite the bustle, it had a bright, airy feel and a relaxed atmosphere.

'You sound surprised.' Grayson looked at her questioningly.

She shrugged. 'It just doesn't seem your style, I guess.' Mark would never take her to a place like this. Their local pub had an excellent reputation for food, but they hadn't been there once the whole time she'd lived with him.

'What, you think I only frequent Michelin-starred establishments?' he asked, smiling as his hand smoothed over the surface of the table. She could tell the simplicity and integrity of the chunky aged wood pleased him. 'I really like it here,' he said. 'And it's fantastic what they've done with the building.' He looked up at the rafters and she smiled fondly, loving his enthusiasm for good design.

He did look at home here, she thought – it suited him. He was just as wealthy as Mark, but that was where the resemblance ended. Grayson wasn't in the least pretentious or snobbish, and seemed quite at home in the casual surroundings of the pub.

'And the food is great,' he nodded at her menu.

He wasn't wrong about that. They both ordered huevos rancheros, and they were delicious. They could hardly keep their hands off each other as they ate, Grayson resting a hand on her thigh, or Lisa laying her head on his shoulder between forkfuls. Lisa couldn't remember when she'd been so happy. This was how it should be, she thought, wishing this day could go on forever.

When they left the pub, they joined the crowds of Sunday morning shoppers on the high street, and Lisa felt a little thrill of excitement to be doing something so normal. They were just like any other couple they passed, enjoying a leisurely Sunday morning together, strolling lazily along hand-in-hand, stopping occasionally to look in shop windows. But whereas those other women could take a day like this for granted, for her it was special and something to treasure.

They wandered slowly through a little open air craft market, the stalls a jumble of quirky jewellery, colourful clothing and original artwork.

'I'd love to see some of *your* paintings,' Grayson said as they stopped in front of an artist's stall, draped with canvases. A woman perched on a stool to the side gave them a nod and a smile. Lisa assumed she was the artist. 'Do you have any at the house?'

Lisa shook her head. 'No.'

'None?'

'There was … a fire. They were all destroyed.'

'Oh.' He frowned. 'When was this?'

'About two years ago.'

'And you haven't done any since?'

'No. I don't paint anymore.'

'Not even just for yourself? For pleasure?'

'No.' But I will, she thought. I'll start again when I'm away from here, away from Mark. She felt a familiar pull as she stood looking at the paintings, and she could almost feel the brush in her hand, smell the heady mixture of oil paint and turpentine.

'That's a shame. I'd love to have seen some.'

She shrugged. 'I wasn't very good anyway.'

'You were good enough to go to art school,' Grayson said as they moved on. 'Good enough for Mark to take an interest.'

Maybe he was right, she thought. Perhaps she should have had more belief in her own talent, and not let Mark discourage her.

She paused to look at a stall selling hand-painted silk scarves. They were really beautiful, she thought, fingering the material.

'Let me buy you something,' Grayson said suddenly, squeezing her hand.

'Oh, no. Thank you, but I couldn't let you do that.'

'Please. I'd like to.'

Her thoughts automatically flew to Mark. What would he think when he saw it? He would be suspicious. He'd demand the receipt, and when she couldn't produce it, he'd become angry and jealous and accuse her of having a secret lover. Then she remembered – Mark would never see it. God, it was pathetic how completely conditioned her thinking had become, so her first thought was always of him.

'Lisa?' Grayson prompted her.

She shook her head. 'Sorry, I was miles away.'

'Which one would you like?'

'No, really – you've given me too much already.'

He frowned. 'I've never given you anything.'

She raised her eyebrows at him, wordlessly reminding him of the money. Ten thousand pounds was hardly nothing.

'That doesn't count,' he said. 'That was payment. I want to give you a gift.'

She smiled. He didn't know it, of course, but he'd already given her plenty of gifts. Today was a gift, and all the time they'd spent together; their chess games; the way he made love to her. He'd given her the only moments of happiness she'd had in a very long time. It was more than enough.

'Please,' he said. 'Choose one. I'd like you to have something to … remember me by.'

His words took her by surprise. Could he have guessed that she was going away, she wondered. Or did he simply mean that he wouldn't see her again after tomorrow because she would be back with Mark? Whatever he meant, she suddenly realised she wanted to have a physical memento of him, a reminder of this lovely day and how happy she'd been. Besides, she would like to have the simple, normal pleasure of getting a present from the man she loved.

'Okay,' she said. 'Thank you.' She was rewarded with his sweet smile.

She took her time choosing, studying each one carefully. The girl who made them brought more from under the counter for her to look at.

'This one,' she said finally, picking up a long, narrow scarf with an abstract design in splashes of green and pink.

'Good choice,' the girl said with a bright smile. 'That's my favourite.'

Lisa smiled. She knew it was just sales talk, and that whatever one she'd chosen would probably have turned out to be the girl's 'favourite'. But she admired her cheery, easy way with customers and wondered at her self-confidence as she kept up a constant stream of patter with Grayson while she took his money and gave him change. She tried to imagine herself having such self-assurance, chatting light-heartedly with strangers, but she couldn't. She felt a little frisson of anxiety at the thought of being on her own in the world soon, starting anew with no one else to rely on and no one familiar around her. It had been a long time since she had been independent, and while she longed for it, it scared her a little at the same time.

'Will I put it in a bag or do you want to wear it now?' the girl was asking.

Grayson looked at her enquiringly.

'I'll wear it now,' she said, taking it from the girl with a smile. 'Thank you.'

'The colours suit you,' Grayson said as she put it around her neck.

'I love it. Thank you.'

'Thank *you*.' He kissed her on the forehead.

'What for?'

'For letting me buy it for you,' he said, taking her hand as they walked away. 'For letting me treat you like my girl-friend today.'

It was late afternoon when they got back to Grayson's house. They were on each other as soon as they got through the door, and spent the rest of the evening in bed.

'I'll have to go soon,' Lisa said later as they lay naked in each other's arms. Outside darkness had fallen, and a feeling of gloom descended on her at the thought of talking to Mark tonight.

'I wish I could sleep with you again,' Grayson sighed, playing with her hair.

'Me too.' Lisa said. 'But we still have tomorrow evening.'

A shadow passed across Grayson's face, a flicker of anguish. 'Lisa,' he began warily, 'I know you don't want any more questions, but can I just ask one more?'

'Okay.'

'I'm not going to see you again, am I? After tomorrow?'

'No. You know that. We already talked about it.'

'But what if you and Mark came over together, like before? Couldn't I see you then?'

She took a deep breath, hardly able to say the words out loud. 'No,' she said, her voice barely above a whisper. 'That won't happen.'

He nodded. 'That's what I thought.'

She couldn't bear the hurt look in his eyes, and she wished there was something she could say or do to make things better.

He took her hand and turned it over in his, kissing the palm. 'I hope you'll be very happy, Lisa,' he said, his blue eyes grave.

'Hey, why so serious?' she asked, forcing a playful laugh. 'It's not goodbye forever. I'll see you tomorrow.'

'I know. I just want you to know – in case I forget to tell you tomorrow. I hope you're really happy.'

She blinked away tears. 'Thank you.'

'Sorry, I didn't mean to upset you.' He kissed her forehead, and then he pulled her into his arms, moulding her body to his, and making her wish midnight would never come and they could stay like this forever.

She was in a sombre mood that night as she got ready to Skype with Mark, aware that it would be the last time she would speak to him. Tomorrow night he would be flying home, and when he got back on Tuesday, she would be gone. If everything went according to plan, she would never see him again.

She even felt a slight stab of pity for Mark as she thought of him arriving home from his trip to find the house empty, and her gone. He had been a big part of her life, and she believed he did love her in his own twisted way. But she wasn't in any danger of being swayed from her decision to leave. The man she felt sad for only existed in her memory now. She had no sympathy for the monster he had become.

She felt a mixture of excitement and fear as she thought about the next couple of days. While she planned and prepared for leaving, she had never allowed herself to think far ahead, because it was too daunting. But occasionally the enormity of what she was undertaking hit her, and she felt overwhelmed. She was leaving behind the life she knew, not knowing what the future might hold, and she couldn't help being nervous. However stifling this house and her life with Mark had been, there was a certain safety and security in its familiarity. Now she was facing into the unknown with no map or blueprint, no friendly face to turn to, no one to hold her hand and guide her.

There were things here that she would miss too – things she resented having to leave behind. She was sad to be leaving London, the city where she had grown up. It had always been home to her, and it held so many happy memories of her childhood with her grandparents. And then there was Grayson … She had been desolate leaving him tonight, and he had been just as loathe to let her go. Whenever her mind strayed to thoughts of him, she carefully steered it away. She couldn't bear to dwell on them.

Instead she had concentrated on mechanically making preparations. She had eradicated every trace of Grayson from the house. Then she had busied herself packing. Her suitcase was stashed under the bed, ready to go. There was just this final call with Mark to get through, one more night with Grayson tomorrow, and then she would walk out of this house and her life would change forever.

As she waited for his call, she undressed, put on a sheer black baby-doll that Mark loved, and retouched her make-up. Her lip curled in contempt at the image that stared back at her from the mirror as she applied a final slick of lip-gloss. There she was – the perfect sex doll, ready to do her master's bidding, to serve his every need. She hated what she had become – what Mark had made her. She consoled herself with the thought that after tonight, this person would no longer exist. She would never have to be this pathetic creature again. But for now it was show time, she thought, as she settled herself in front of the laptop.

'Hi, baby,' Mark grinned at her from the screen, his eyes glittering as they raked over her body. 'You look so beautiful,' he said, his voice thick with lust.

'Thanks.' Lisa licked her lips provocatively and slipped the straps of her babydoll off her shoulders, preparing to go through this hated performance one last time. She undid the ribbons at the front and parted the material, exposing her breasts, then peeling it off in a slow striptease. Just one more show, she told herself, closing her eyes as she began stroking her body.

23

Lisa woke at dawn the following morning, too keyed up to sleep any longer. It was a fresh, sunny day, and it already felt like a new beginning as she threw back the duvet and sprang out of bed. She was full of nervous energy, and by mid-morning she had finished making the final preparations for leaving tomorrow. She wasn't due to go to Grayson's house until six, so she decided to make the most of her last day in London and revisit some of her favourite places, saying goodbye to the city. She started with a visit to the Tate Gallery and enjoyed wandering through the rooms at a leisurely pace, soaking up the amazing collection of art. She lingered over the pre-Raphaelites, which she had been drawn to since the first time her grandmother had brought her here as a child. Her grandparents had always been so encouraging of her interest in art. Tears filled her eyes as she stood in front of Rossetti's *Annunciation*, her gran's favourite.

When she left the gallery, she crossed to the other side of the river and strolled along the embankment in the sunshine. It was a warm, bright day, the sun sparkling on the water. She was going to miss all this, she thought as she leaned on the parapet and looked across the river, the city spread out before her. Boats chugged up and down the river with their cargoes of tourists. To her left the London Eye turned slowly, starkly white against the blue sky, while in the distance the palace of Westminster was a potent reminder of the city's past. Downriver on the other side, the imposing dome of St Paul's stood proud alongside futuristic glass skyscrapers. That juxtaposition of the ancient and contemporary was one of the things she loved about London, the weight of its history sitting comfortably alongside the vibrant modernity of the city. She would miss the bustling crowds and the cultural life, the sweep and energy of it all.

She stopped for a coffee at one of the cafes along the embankment, and as she sat outside, taking in the view, her thoughts turned to Grayson. She wished he were here to share her last day with her. It was crazy. She'd only known him a few weeks, but she wanted him with her all the time now, sharing every experience. She touched the scarf at her neck. It had seemed symbolic to wear it today. It was a mark of her new beginning and a small gesture of defiance, openly flaunting something a man other than Mark had given her. She owed so much to Grayson. She wouldn't be here today if it weren't for him, and it wasn't just the money. His regard for her had helped to restore a little of her self-confidence and strengthened her courage to see this through. If only there were something she could give him in return, she thought, stirring her coffee broodingly. She would like him to have something to remember her by. But she had nothing of her own to give. Her paintings, the only things that were truly hers, were gone.

Or were they? It suddenly occurred to her that that may not be true. Mark had never brought her two unsold paintings home from the gallery. She had no reason to think they weren't still there. She hadn't thought of them in such a long time. She had detached herself from that part of her life and put it behind her. But talking about art with Grayson had reminded her how much it had meant to her – and how much she had believed in her work before Mark's criticism crushed all her ambitions and dreams. Maybe she shouldn't have taken his judgment as the last word on her talent. Had she been wrong to give up so easily?

Even if Mark was right and those paintings had no objective merit or commercial worth, they were a part of her, and having all but forgotten about them, she suddenly had a compelling urge to get them back now if she could. She felt the need to see them, to reconnect with the person she had been when she made them, as if by gathering the scattered pieces of herself together, she could start the slow process of making herself whole again.

She had started to envision her life after Mark, and she wanted art to be part of it. Even if she would never make it as an artist, she wanted to try. Painting had always made her happy. She missed it, and she wanted to feel the joy of creating something again, the sense of achievement of finishing a piece she was satisfied with, regardless of anyone else's opinion.

She paid for her coffee and hurried back to the street, excited at the idea of retrieving her paintings. No doubt when she saw them now they would seem naive and crude. But nonetheless, it was what she wanted to give Grayson, and she felt sure he would appreciate the gift. She was always holding back with him, and she wanted to finally give him something of herself before she left.

. . .

Mark's assistant Greta was alone in the gallery when she entered. A tall, attractive blonde in her mid-thirties, Greta had only been working for Mark for about six months. Lisa knew her slightly, having met her occasionally at openings and parties.

'Hello, Lisa,' she smiled, looking up. 'It's nice to see you.'

'You too, Greta.' Lisa smiled. 'I was just passing and I thought I'd pick up my paintings while I was here.'

Greta frowned. 'Your paintings? I'm sorry, did you buy something recently?'

'No, I mean *my* paintings – the ones that were on sale here.'

'Oh.'

Something about Greta's blank expression struck dread in Lisa's heart.

'I'm sorry, I don't know anything about them. Maybe you should wait until Mark gets back. He's home tomorrow, isn't he?'

'Yes, but I'd rather pick them up today, if possible,' Lisa said, forcing a smooth smile. 'It was a couple of years ago …'

'Oh,' Greta brightened, grasping at this explanation. 'Before my time, then.'

'Yes. They didn't sell, but I'd like to have them back. I just thought I'd collect them since I was in the neighbourhood.'

'Well, they're probably in the storeroom. You're welcome to have a look, if you like.'

'Thank you.'

Greta opened a drawer in the desk and produced a key. 'Do you want me to help you?'

'No, thanks,' Lisa said, taking the key from her. 'I know where it is.'

She crossed the floor and went upstairs to the private part of the gallery. She unlocked the door to the store room with a sense of foreboding. It was a large room, with canvases covered in bubble wrap stacked ten deep against the walls. She started by the door and began methodically raking through the paintings, many of them familiar to her. It was a real treasure trove, and she could have happily spent the afternoon poring over the contents of the room. But she didn't linger, quickly moving on to the next stack when she didn't find what she was looking for. She was ready to give up hope as she flipped through the final pile, barely glancing now, no longer expecting to find her paintings. Mark had probably tossed them in the skip with the rest, she thought despondently.

But then, suddenly, there they were — the very last two, tucked away in the furthest corner of the storeroom. Her hands shook as she lifted them out. She picked one up, feeling a sudden rush of pride and satisfaction as she looked at it through the filmy wrapping. She had expected to see it now as Mark did, recognising all its flaws and realising that his assessment had been accurate. Instead she felt a glow of pride, and a sense of relief that she hadn't been deluding herself all those years. She still believed in this, she still felt it was good — more than good, in fact. It had been a long time since she had done anything she felt proud of, and it was a good feeling. She turned the painting over in her hands, and as she did so, her eye caught a little green sticker fixed to the back of the frame with the words: Not for Sale.

She sank to the floor, dazed, a feeling of dread settling in her stomach as the meaning of this edged into her consciousness. She wasn't even sure what it meant. Had it been put there when Mark had removed the paintings from display after they failed to sell? Or had they never been offered for sale in the first place? She lifted out the second painting and turned it over. It had the same sticker.

She shook herself out of her reverie. She could think about what this meant when she was home alone. She stood, gathered up both paintings and left the room with them, locking the door behind her.

'Ah, you found what you were looking for?' Greta asked as she marched back to the desk.

'Yes, thanks.' Lisa handed her back the key. 'Is it okay for me to take them?' It suddenly occurred to Lisa that as far as Greta was concerned, she could be walking out of here with something that didn't belong to her.

'I'm sure it's fine. We know where you live,' Greta laughed. 'I'll just need to mark them off the inventory.' She tapped her computer keyboard. 'Let's see. Your surname is Matthews, yes?'

'That's right.'

Greta frowned at the screen. 'I can't seem to find you here. Let me see the paintings.'

Lisa placed them on the desk side by side.

'Oh yes, of course.' Greta smiled as she picked one up and turned it over. 'They're not in inventory, so it's fine to take them.'

'They're not in the inventory?' Lisa asked, trying to stop her voice shaking.

'No.'

'Why not?'

'They're not for sale,' Greta said, pointing to the sticker.

'But they were.'

Greta shrugged. 'Yes, but Mark told me you decided you couldn't bear to part with them when it came to it. I guess he didn't want to risk them getting mixed up with stock, so just took them off the system altogether.'

'Oh. Right.' Lisa nodded, trying to appear calm while she felt like she had been punched in the gut.

'I'm not surprised you didn't want to sell them,' Greta said. 'They're beautiful pieces – very powerful.'

'Th—Thank you.'

'I'm surprised it doesn't happen more often, to be honest. I mean, art is so *personal*, isn't it? It must feel a bit like giving away one of your children.'

'Um … yeah,' Lisa said faintly.

'Would you like me to wrap them in paper for you?'

'Thank you. That would be great.'

'Lovely weather, isn't it?' Greta made cheerful small talk with her as she wrapped the paintings, but Lisa was hardly aware of what was being said. She just wanted to get out of the gallery and be alone to think this over.

Outside, she walked along the street in a daze, trying to get her head around what had just happened. Mark had lied to her. He had never tried to sell her paintings. Did he simply think they weren't good enough, and pretended to accept them to spare her feelings? Greta had said nice things about them, but maybe she was just being polite to her boss's girlfriend. But deep down, she didn't believe that. He had done it to keep her down, to have her where he wanted her, dependent on him for everything. She couldn't bear it. Tears sprang to her eyes at the thought of all she had lost, the career she might have had. She would never know how different things could have been.

She hugged the paintings to herself. At least she had something worthwhile to give Grayson now, she thought, wiping away a tear. There was no point in crying over what might have been. She would make more paintings – better ones.

Her thoughts were interrupted by her mobile ringing.

She fished it out of her bag, startled to see that it was Mark calling. It would be the middle of the night in China.

'Hi, Mark,' she said warily.

'Lisa, are you okay? You sound—'

She took a deep, shaky breath. 'You didn't try to sell my paintings.' She was surprised to hear the words coming out of her mouth. She hadn't planned to say that. But she would never have another opportunity to confront him about it. Even over the phone, she hardly had the nerve to challenge him.

'What?' His voice snapped like a whip.

'I was at the gallery. I thought I'd pick up those paintings you took to sell. But they weren't in the inventory. You told Greta I didn't want to sell them.'

He sighed heavily. 'Oh baby,' he said, his voice dripping with pity, 'they just weren't good enough. I didn't know how to tell you.'

Once she would have believed him.

'I'm sorry. I should have been honest, but I knew how much it meant to you. I didn't want to be the one to shatter your dreams.'

But you *were*, she thought.

'Lisa? You're not going to sulk about this, are you?'

'No, I just— No.' She swallowed hard, tried to sound calm. 'It doesn't matter.'

'Look, we can talk about this later, when I get home. Okay?'

'Yes, fine. We'll talk about it tomorrow.'

'Well, maybe it would be best to leave it until tomorrow.' She could hear the smile in his voice. 'I'm sure we'll have better things to do tonight.'

'Tonight?' Her heart started to pound and her mouth felt dry suddenly. 'What do you mean?'

'That's why I called. Good news, baby – I got my business finished early and I'm on my way home.'

Lisa's heart slammed into her chest and she could hardly breathe. 'What? Wh—When?'

'I'm in Paris, just about to get on a flight to London.'

'But last night … we Skyped.'

'I was in the Mandarin Oriental on the Rue Saint-Honoré,' he chuckled. 'I was going to surprise you.'

'Oh!' She felt sick at the thought of all her carefully laid plans being thwarted at the last minute.

'But then I couldn't wait to tell you. Besides, I want you to come out to the airport to meet me.'

Lisa struggled to remain calm, but her insides felt like they were on fire. Her mind was racing as she tried to process a thousand thoughts at once. How long did she have? She needed to stay focused, find out exactly where she stood.

'So what time does your flight get in?'

'Andrew's got all the details. I've told him to pick you up. He should be with you in about an hour.'

'Great!'

'Yeah, so cheer up and get your glad rags on. I can't wait to see you, baby. I've missed you so much.'

'Me too.' Lisa gulped, fighting to stem the tears that were stinging the backs of her eyes, trying to swallow down the rising panic. She had no time! And what about Grayson? She would never see him now. Her mind was a blur and she could hardly concentrate on what Mark was saying, just aware that she was losing precious time every minute he stayed on the phone.

'Wear something sexy,' he said. 'And no underwear. I can't wait to fuck you again.'

Lisa just nodded dumbly, not able to speak past the lump in her throat, desperate for him to end the call so she could think. She flagged down a taxi as they spoke. She had to get home and out again before Andrew turned up.

'I have another surprise for you,' Mark was saying in her ear as she opened the taxi door and slid inside. 'But you'll have to wait for that until I get home.'

'I can't wait,' she said, her mouth feeling like sawdust.

'Well, they're boarding my flight. Got to go. See you soon, baby. I love you.'

'I love you too.'

She ended the call and flopped back against the seat, trying to calm her breathing and collect her thoughts. She couldn't let this faze her. It wasn't a disaster, she told herself. She was all ready to go, her bags packed. She just had to get home, grab her stuff and get out again before Andrew arrived. There was plenty of time. Still, she couldn't help growling inwardly with impatience at every red traffic light.

When they got to the house, she leapt out of the taxi and dashed for the door, fumbling with the keys in her haste. In the bedroom, she gathered up her things on automatic. She felt hunted and she wouldn't feel safe until she was out of the house. She had cut it too fine already. As she threw the last of her things into the case, her thoughts flew to Grayson. She would have to stand him up tonight, and she felt a pang of guilt as she thought of him waiting for her.

But there was no time to dwell on that now, she told herself as she flung last-minute things into her bag with trembling hands. She could think about that later. When she was safely away from here, there would be time to indulge in missing him and longing for him, in thinking of what might have been. Right now, she had to concentrate on getting away.

When she had shut her case and checked her bag one

last time for passport and money, she surveyed the room with a quick sweep of her eyes. Most of her clothes still hung in the wardrobe. She looked at the rails of silky tops and strapless cocktail dresses, the rows of spiky heels beneath them. She wouldn't need clothes like those anymore. She wouldn't wear clothes like that ever again, she thought, with a shudder of distaste.

She picked up her handbag, grabbed her wheelie case and raced down the stairs. Her heart was in her mouth as she pulled the door closed behind her. She strode down the path – and froze as she reached the gate and saw the car waiting there.

Andrew – he was already here. She was too late. She stopped dead in her tracks, her knees feeling like they were going to give way. She looked around wildly for some escape route, but Andrew had already seen her and was getting out of the car.

'A—Andrew,' she stammered.

'Miss Matthews,' he said with a deferential nod, not looking right at her as usual. Lisa saw his eyes drift to her suitcase, and he gave a puzzled frown.

'I—I wasn't expecting you so soon,' Lisa gulped. Tears stung her eyes and burned the back of her throat. She felt her body slump despairingly, and she was struggling not to cry. 'I was just …' But she couldn't think of any excuse.

'I was expecting the traffic to be heavier. I got here earlier than I should have.'

Lisa nodded, hanging her head.

'Would you like me to call you a cab?'

She looked up at him, hope blooming inside her chest.

'I'd give you a lift, but I won't get here for another half hour or so. The traffic's bad.'

'Thank you, but that won't be necessary,' she said,

weak with relief. 'I'll get one at the end of the road.' She turned to go, pulling her case behind her.

'Good luck, Miss—Lisa.' She stopped, startled – he had never used her first name before. She turned back to him, and he made eye contact with her for the first time since she had known him.

'Thank you,' she said on a sob, wiping away a tear.

He simply nodded in response, giving her a gentle smile.

'He's going to be so mad, Andrew.'

He shrugged, unperturbed, then got back into the car. He was still sitting there when she got to the end of the road.

She quickly hailed a cab, and asked the driver to take her to Euston Station, still feeling spooked as they sped away. She only started to relax a little as they got into the busy streets of central London. She checked her watch. Mark's plane wouldn't have landed yet. She envisioned him coming home to a silent, empty house. She saw him calling her name as he searched the rooms for her; imagined his growing rage as it dawned on him that she was gone. How long would it be before he realised she had left him?

She pulled her phone from her bag and typed him a quick message. She had to make it clear that she was leaving of her own accord. She didn't want to give him any excuse to instigate a search for her. She kept it short and to the point:

I'm leaving. It's over. I don't love you anymore. Don't try to find me.

It was blunt, cold, and more than he deserved. Grayson was another matter. There was so much she wanted to say to him, and no time for any of it. He would be home soon, and her heart twisted at the thought of him waiting for her, wondering why she hadn't come. She didn't want him to worry when she didn't show up, so she tapped out a message to him:

> Mark's coming home early. He'll be back soon, so I won't be able to see you tonight. I'm sorry. Goodbye and thank you for everything. Lisa x

She hit send, her lip trembling at the thought of him reading it. There was so much more that she wanted to say. *I'll never forget you. You'll never know how much you meant to me.* But there was no time. She still had the paintings. She would find a post office tomorrow and mail one to him. It would have to speak for her.

As they neared the station, she checked her handbag one more time for the essentials, and her fingers closed over the envelope full of cash that she had got from Grayson. Its thickness was comforting. Then she gasped as it struck her that she hadn't earned all of it yet. Grayson had paid her for tonight and she wouldn't be there. She chewed her lip, fingering the envelope fretfully. But there was nothing she could do about it now. She would try to find a way to pay it back to him once she was safe, when she was far away from Mark.

In the station, she bought a ticket to Manchester, where she would spend the night. In a day or two she would move on. A little village in Cornwall was her ultimate destination, but she planned to get there by a circuitous route, so that it would be harder for Mark to trace her movements if he was trying to find her. Before heading for the platform, she went into the toilets. Inside the cubicle, she took her phone apart and flushed the SIM card down the toilet. On her way out, she buried the rest of the pieces in a waste bin under a mound of sandwich wrappings and soda cans.

She didn't look back as she walked through the turnstile onto the platform and boarded the waiting train. All the tension of the last few hours caught up with her as they pulled out of the station, and she slumped wearily in her seat, overcome with exhaustion. The steady rocking of the train soothed her, and she smiled at her reflection in the window as darkness fell outside, the image blurring as her eyes swam with tears.

'Are you all right, dear?'

She looked across to find an elderly lady opposite looking at her concernedly.

'Yes, thank you,' she said, wiping the tears from her face. 'I'm fine.' She smiled. 'I'm going to be fine.'

EPILOGUE

'I'M NOT WRONG, AM I?' Grayson said to Isabel the following Monday as they stood side by side looking at Lisa's painting hanging in the library. 'It's good, isn't it?' He turned to her.

To his astonishment, she shook her head. 'No, it's not good.' He was opening his mouth to protest when she added 'It's … stunning. She's very talented.'

There was no mistaking the genuine admiration in her voice as she gazed at the painting, and Grayson smiled, experiencing a strange burst of pride. 'Good enough to be a professional artist?'

'Definitely.' Isabel gave him a meaningful look, and he knew they were both thinking the same thing.

'So why would Mark tell her she wasn't?' He frowned. 'Could he have been mistaken, do you think?'

'No,' Isabel said flatly. 'Mark doesn't make mistakes like that – not about art. His judgement is flawless.'

Grayson sighed. 'So he just did a number on her.'

'For whatever reason, it seems he didn't want her to have a career.'

'Fucker!' Grayson balled his fists in frustration. If Mark were here right now, he'd rip his head off.

'I could sell it like that,' Isabel said, snapping her fingers. 'Hell, I'd buy it myself. Would you like me to make you an offer?' She turned to him, her eyebrows arched.

'No,' he said softly. 'It's not for sale.'

'Didn't think so,' she shrugged. 'But it was worth a try.' She moved to the door. 'I'm going to make us some cocktails, and then you can tell me all about what you've been up to this week. I feel like I haven't seen you in ages.'

It was exactly a week since he'd got the text from Lisa calling off their last night together. Even though he'd known it was coming, he'd been devastated. He couldn't understand why he was so blindsided by it. He'd always known Lisa wasn't going to stay with him. He knew he wouldn't see her again once Mark came home. What difference did a few hours make? But he'd spent the whole day in Edinburgh looking forward to seeing her. It had been an agonisingly long day, and he had felt like he was hardly present in his meetings, just going through the motions and counting the minutes until he could be with her. Then he had got her text saying goodbye, and it had completely floored him.

He should have been more prepared. She'd been clear from the start that it was just business for her. But in the last couple of days she'd been so relaxed and affectionate with him, and he'd begun to feel that it was more than just a mercenary transaction on her part. She'd seemed as sad as he was that they had so little time left, and he'd started to hope. Maybe it was just wishful thinking. He'd fallen in love with her, and he'd almost let himself believe that she felt the same way. And if that was true, then maybe he could persuade her to stay.

Then she'd ended it abruptly, ahead of schedule. All

his hopes were dashed, and he realised what an idiot he'd been. He was just a means to an end for Lisa; she'd never pretended otherwise. He didn't resent her for it. She'd been honest and upfront about it from the beginning. But he was dismayed by how much it hurt. He'd never felt so broken, so helpless. But then he'd never been in love before.

The only thing that consoled him was the suspicion that Lisa wasn't with Mark either. In the few days he'd spent with her, he'd got the feeling that maybe she was planning to leave, and that was why she wanted the money. He hoped she *was* leaving Mark. For her sake, he hoped she was going far, far away, somewhere that asshole would never find her.

It had been obvious from the first time she'd come here that Mark mistreated her. His constant mocking and belittling of her that night had sickened him. But since then he'd discovered that the abuse went a lot deeper. He'd seen the traces of bruises on her skin, the bite marks on her tender flesh. He had caught the tensing of her body the first time he went down on her, the way she had braced herself as if expecting pain. He had been about to stop, thinking she didn't like it. But instead he had continued relentlessly pleasuring her until he felt her relax and let go, and he had felt a glow of pride as she started to trust him.

At first, he had thought that Lisa put up with it all because she still loved Mark. Now he suspected she was simply afraid of him. And much as he wanted her to be with him, he wanted her to get away from Mark more. Even if it meant he would never see her again, part of him would be glad – as long as it meant Mark would never see her again either. He couldn't think of a better use for his money. He only wished she'd asked for more.

Isabel came back into the room with a glass in each hand. She gave him one and they moved to the sofa.

'Why would Lisa send this to you?' she asked, indicating the painting with her drink. 'Were you seeing her? Last week, when Mark was away … did something happen between the two of you?'

'I …' He shifted uncomfortably. 'Sorry. I can't tell you. I promised.'

To his relief, Isabel merely nodded acceptance. 'Mark was around today.' She frowned, looking troubled.

'Oh?'

'He came to the gallery. He seemed very tense … almost angry. He asked me if we'd seen Lisa while he was away.'

'Oh? Why would he think we'd have seen her?' He hoped Mark wasn't suspicious.

'I don't know. I said they should come over for dinner now that he's back, and he said she was away at the moment, staying with family. An aunt, I think he said.'

He smiled. 'Lisa doesn't have any family.'

Isabel looked at him questioningly.

'I think she's left him and he doesn't know where she is,' he explained.

'You think she ran away from him?'

'Yes, I do.' When the painting had been delivered a few days ago, he felt certain that she was gone.

'Good for her,' Isabel said softly.

'Yeah, good for her. Grayson smiled. He hoped she was safe wherever she was. He hoped she would be happy.

'You really liked her, didn't you?' Isabel asked. Her tone was flat. It was hardly even a question.

He turned and looked at her. She was so perceptive, he couldn't hide anything from her. 'I loved her,' he said. It was a relief to tell someone, to say the words out loud. He just wished he could have said them to Lisa; heard her saying them back to him.

'I'm so sorry, Grayson.' She rested her head on his shoulder, rubbing his arm sympathetically.

'I'm glad she got away. She deserves to be happy.'

'You deserve to be happy too.'

'Not at her expense.'

Isabel sighed. 'God, what a waste.' She lifted her head. 'Do you know where she is? When she sent you the painting, did she tell you she was going away?'

He shook his head. 'No. There was no note – just the painting.'

Somehow he had known what it was the moment he unwrapped it, even before he'd seen the signature in the bottom right-hand corner. He was incredibly touched that Lisa had given him something so personal. He had been suffering agonies in the days since she had cancelled their final night together, tormented by thoughts of her with Mark. Then the painting had arrived, and he felt sure that she was gone and that this was her parting gift to him. Even though he still longed for her, it made him happy to think she was free and safe somewhere.

There had been no note with it, but he didn't need one. The painting said it all. It told him that he had meant something to her after all. She had given him something to remember her by, and he hoped that wherever she was, she would think of him sometimes as he would always be thinking of her.

AUTHOR'S NOTE

Thank you for reading *The Endgame*. I really hope you enjoyed it. *Playing By Heart*, the second part of The Endgame Duet is now available.

Want to know when I release new books? Sign up at my website to join my mailing list, and as a bonus I'll send you a copy of *Dinner for Four*, a retelling of the night Grayson and Lisa first meet from Grayson's point of view.

Clearyjamesauthor.com

ALSO BY CLEARY JAMES

Playing By Heart (Endgame Book 2)

Do Not Disturb

The Boss's Daughter

www.ingramcontent.com/pod-product-compliance
Lightning Source LLC
Chambersburg PA
CBHW010552170726
48285CB00011B/2868